INFAMOUS

by Black Madam

A MEMOIR

INFAMOUS

Black Madam
Book I

A Reality Reading Memoir By Padge Victoria
Windslowe

Copyright 2017

Cover Illustration Copyright © 2018
by SureShot Books Publishing LLC
Cover design by SureShot Creative Books
Book design and production by Black Madam
Editing by Ose Solutions Inc.
Author photograph by WRATH ENTERTAINMENT

Published by:
SureShot Books Publishing LLC
P.O. Box 924
Nyack, New York 10960
www.sureshotbooks.com
ISBN: 9781947170025

DEDICATION

TO NIKOLAUS, for whom none of this would be possible with out your unwavering love, devotion, and support through these the darkest days of my life & our union. I owe my all to you & only you baby. You are the greatest man I've ever met. Sharing life with you has been the best thing to ever happen to me. My love for you surpass the ages and beyond, and I can't wait to get back home to you, in your loving arms to carry on the happiness God has given us. I love you "BABYCAKES"

IN LOVING MEMORY OF YOU DADDY, JESSE LEON ADAMS, July 14, 1953 - March 26, 2003.You were always the book writer in the family. Who'd ever knew I would be taking up the rings. Thank you Daddy for all of your guidance and tough love throughout my life. Ironically, it's because of you, I am the fighter I am today. Since childhood you've taught me to never give up my dreams, to never back down, and to never settle for less.

Rest in Peace daddy I'll forever love you for all you were to us. Love always. Your first born, your "lil Granger."

TO MY MOMMY DEAREST DENISE. The one, the everything in my life, I truly don't know what I'm going to do when the Lord should choose to take you away from me. You have been the eye candy forever to my eyes, so pleasing to my heart since my childhood. Your voice is the soothing music to my soul. I know I tend to be hard on you when it comes to your character, but it's only because I love you so much and only want the best for you and your eternal soul. Anything I've ever done or said was simply to bring the best out of you. The mistakes I've made in life, I've only made in my aims to do all in my power to help you retire in comfort as you grow old, for you're the hardest worker I know. I love you Mommy V

TO POPPA. You've given me a second chance to be a "Daddy's lil girl" in my adult life, and I love you for it. For I was not afforded that chance in my childhood born a little girl in a little boy's body. Thank you for all the happiness you've brought back into our family. And most of all, the happiness you've brought mother in her chance to live and love again since the death of the first love of her life, my father. That is until you . . . You have completed us all again immensely. However, that position does comes with great responsibility. Thus, it is your charge and responsibility to merge our family with that of yours, as a perfect union to create balance. Hence, we gain a father figure again for our family, and not lose a mother in this process, to your family. We understand mother's loyalty to her new union to you and your family. Thus, it is your job to bring balance between the two. Never the less, we love you Poppa.

TO TONYA YVETTE WHITE. You've been my childhood friend since we were 9 years old. Starting our singing career together with our first Recording Contract with Sun Shine Group Records in Philly. You, I and Sherrie were the "SPECIAL GUESS" attempting to entertain the world. But now you're entertaining The Greatest Audience in Existence, for you are now in the presence of Almighty GOD, as you sing with the angels. I wish I could have said my goodbyes to you as I laid in my jail cell the day they put you in your grave. You will always be in my heart and forever missed. I love you Tonya Yvette White. You will always be the very "Special Guess" of my heart V.

TO MY DEAREST SISTER SHERRIE, **for you**

have proven in all these years of my incarceration to be indeed your sister's keeper. I love you CHER and am forever grateful for all that you and your children, Neveah and Jadus have sacrificed through the years, for being there for me. I can't wait to finally have the honor to return the love. You have always been the one who's been there for me through thick and thin like a true sister should. Even when we were at odds, our bond of sisterhood was never broken, never faltering as our love always exceeds pride, jealousy, and selfishness. Yours is a love many others in our family should mimic, for although many time even you fall short, your love, intentions, and heart, are always on point. I love you sis . . . you are the true definition of what THE GOOD SISTER is . . . FOR YOU'VE BEEN YOUR SISTER'S KEEPER and for your loyalty and love, I love you so much More.

THANKS TO MS. MARISA JOHNSON VALENZUELA, My College Professor of English Literature 101 and Writing 108, of Philadelphia

Community College Out Reach Courses @ Riverside Correctional Facility, Class of 2015. "Perhaps my Flowery Writing is good for something". . . LOL, thank you for so much, and all that you've helped me and my classmates with during that time of so much uncertainty. You, Mrs. Brady, and Mrs. Joann Cuttingham of Acting 131 were the BEST. #CCP ROCK!

SPECIAL THANKS, TO DUTCH (AKA THE BIG MAN) for scooping a MADAM up when everyone else was kicking her down. I am forever indebted to you, for you are my mentor and my Big brother in this new world to me of the written word that is the literary arts. I can only endeavor to be as great as you see me and my brand becoming. For like you said, you would do and did it. You set the sky for me to shine in it, and thus MADAM will be as mesmerizing as A Super Nova. Thank you so much DUTCH! I won't let you down like others have. You're in the company of The Madam now! And God knows I ride for mine. I won't stop the noise till you are free with us all at SURESHOT BOOKS & PUBLISHING #FREE DUTCH!

MY VERY SPECIAL THANK YOU GOES OUT TO MY PUBLISHER, MR. DARREN HERRINGTON of SureShot Books Publishing LLC, whom without your belief In the Madam, none of this would be possible. I know I drive you crazy with my frantic pace phone calls to you about some new idea, pitch, or concept, and like a patient father tending to his child . . . you listen and put it all into motion. Like I've always said . . . "We are going to have an obscene amount of success with the Black Madam Brand", so get ready for a very long ride. I love the belief you have in me. Thus, I will live and breathe this brand in order to make you and

DUTCH proud of the MADAM.

Thank you, thank you, thank you! to the SureShot Books Publishing LLC, DIGITAL, MARKETING & PROMOTIONAL TEAM, for your tireless work and efforts you put in the getting the word out on my creation of INFAMOUS. The internet will never be the same since you started the promotional campaign for INFAMOUS. I hope to have just as much a Monmouth Marketing Machine as you guys for the second book NOTORIOUS 2019, and the Drama Continues . . .

ACKNOWLEGEMENTS

To the many victims with whom my aims were only to help. I send you all my sincerest apologies for any harm I might have exposed you to in my quest to service you via my Black-Market Beauty methods. I would like you to know that with all that I've become aware of now, with the dangers of free- flowing silicone injections for buttock and body enhancements, I feel terribly saddened of the massive amounts of lives with whom I 've carelessly played a game of Russian Roulette with, and for that I can never work hard enough for your forgiveness.

And with Greatest Thanks to The HONORABLE JUDGE ROSE MARIE DEFINO-NASTASI of Philadelphia's Common Pleas Court. Thank you for a second chance at life to Right my Wrongs. You spared me from that 35 to 70-year Sentence in which the Commonwealth requested on my Sentencing Day, for that I owe my humblest appreciation and my promise to you to serve the community for the good from here on. I hope you can appreciate my new STP stance on battling this crisis in our community which claims many lives in the pursuit of BLACK MARKET BEAUTY. I will work tirelessly to help other not have to face the horrible outcome and factors as my cases brought to you court room. God Bless You and Thank you.

TABLE OF CONTENTS

TABLE OF CONTENTS

TABLE OF CONTENTS

ABOUT THE AUTHOR

Padge Victoria Windslowe who's also known as the Black Madam, is currently serving time for the involuntary accidental death of her client, due to her illicit black market silicone buttock injections and body sculpting services to many stars.

She's housed at Pennsylvania State Institution - Cambridge Springs for women and is engaged to long time boyfriend, now fiance Nikloaus, with whom she plans to wed upon release.

In addition to her literary pursuits, at present, Madam is preparing to launch a new product line she's designed while incarcerated in order to save lives of women who persist on seeking buttock enhancement regardless of it's deadly consequences . . . with the Brand Name ASSsets . . . (The safe Non Surgical Female Body Enhancing Under-Garment)

For more Literary works by BLACK MADAM, look for her next book entitled NOTORIOUS, and the many self help books she has lined up for release . . . Madam's 99 LAWS of POWER, Madam's Little Black Book & La GRAND GRIMNOIR book of Magic Works.

To get daily updates on the Madam as she serves her time, subscribe to her MADAMNATION Blogs at https://blackmadamnation.blogspot.com.

Visit all Black Madam social media via ww.wmadamnation.com.

THE PROLOGUE

It's day 27 of my arrival here at SCI-Muncy State Correctional facility in upstate Pennsylvania. It's a beautiful campus and not anything like what one would be made to think of from the reports of all my fellow inmates that have come before me.

I find the staff very professional and genuinely caring about the overseeing of the inmate population entrusted to them. Which is, from the door, a relief coming from a place like my county jail, Riverside Correctional Facility . . . in which I spent the last three and a half years of my life fighting for my freedom from a case that could have locked me away forever.

Not to say that Riverside Correctional Facility otherwise known as RCF was a bad place to be if one had to be in jail. It has its upside of the coin just as well as its downside, along with the many other county correctional facilities throughout America. The staff at Riverside could be a doozy if tried. They're very hood to say the least . . . and from "around the way." So that whole aspect in and of its self, kind of gets into the way of professionalism if you know what I mean.

Sometimes at RCF I must say, and please excuse my candor . . . it felt like the monkeys in the zoo were in the upper position of the social spectrum of things, and the human population . . . i.e. the inmates, of the higher and advanced intellectual order of things were at the bottom of this society held in captivity.

But in the last three and a half years there, I've learned to manipulate my course around the punk asshole correctional officers here and there. But for the most part, once I got to know the staff and they all got to know and love me, it made for a good stay if one had to be there for the duration.

However, compared to what I have witnessed thus far at first glance here at SCI-Muncy . . . Riverside Corrections could take out a jumbo size ink pen and began to take the much needed notes on just how to bring their facility up to standards. It's not that there's a major difference in the two, but when you have spent so long eating the slop prepared by RCF's dietary staff, which, in most cases, was made by anything but love and care . . . then upon first arrival to SCI-Muncy, and receiving your first meal . . . one that they would call their worst lunch of the calendar week, despite it tasting much better than what you've gotten use to these past years . . . it's easy to become bias from then on . . . Hash tag SCI-Muncy camp Rocks.

Not to mention the fact that the SCI-Muncy campus sits on such a beautiful mountainous spread of lush green lands up in the Pennsylvania Appalachian country. It paints a picture to one at first arrival, that of a beautiful English boarding school for girls rather than the State prison camp it's meant to be.

But enough of the niceties, let us cut through the fluff and get on with the drama and hearty meat of the matter of just why you ran out to purchase this book of mine.

This here is a book with a story of an ambitious young transgender girl who grew up with all the odds stacked against her. As you will read on, you shall see just how her story unfolds in a chapter of her life in which she could have done without. But it was God's will that placed her in the destiny to be caught up in the red hot center of an international scandal by way of a murder charge via illegal black market silicone buttock injections gone wrong.

It was a back ally cosmetic procedure she has performed time and time again on that of her very close friends, herself and many celebrity clients to boot, with two of them being romantically linked to hip hop star Mr. Craze.

This is also a story about a trial that takes place in Philadelphia with a blood thirsty district attorney that will stop at nothing, while doing all in his power to land this girl in prison for the rest of her life with his twisted recollection of just what happened that fateful day on February 7, 2011 in room 425 at the Hampton Inn hotel, out by the Philadelphia Airport which would claim Carmon London's life.

In addition to the international murder charge that's laid before her, this book will also tell a story of an ex-lover to the Madam who's now become a prominent mainline Jewish physician, who, for well over 20 plus years wore an insatiable lust for his once young and naive courtesan turned Society Hill's Madame, while as his wife stayed under the thought that he ended this love affair back in 1993 when she first found out about the affair, only to find out during the murder trial of Carmen London in 2011, that not only was her mainline husband and doctor still involved with his old flame, but now he would be playing the role of coconspirator in this silicone buttock injection scandal if he would not claim that he was only a mere pawn in the Madam's social and financial climb to the top of the world.

With his claims of never supplying her the medial knowledge of injecting, nor his involvement with supplying her with tools of the trade to successfully operate her illicit black market cosmetic procedures . . . by way of syringes, needles, lidocaine and the gallons and gallons of that "crystal clear candy" that's got the whole world going crazy in which to gain a bigger ass. It's the new oil business and Madam's got the game on lock.

So of course he's going to lie under oath on the witness stand in order to save his own ass. Thus, read on to hear how he doesn't think twice about tossing poor ol Madam into the tsunami that's headed at her by way of the Philadelphia DA's office in the means of a murder charge, conspiracy to murder, aggravated assault, possession of an instrument of crime and the illegal practice of medicine without a license. A total of 70 years in prison if they win their case against her.

This is also a story of a true and decent decade old love affair of a doting and devoted fiance to the Madam who later learns of her true identity of being a transgender woman when news of the scandal hits the world's media front pages of the news via CNN's Nancy Grace.

Although he has many questions, he is so enraptured

with her that even against his parent's wishes, he chooses to stand by Madam and ride the storm out with her to the end, as he supports her through it all.

In this story you will hear about the many fair- weather friends who flew south for the harsh storm of Madam's life. Those very friends and family members who never even lifted up a pen to paper to check on her through a letter of support. "Just twisting in the wind they left her to dry" . . . These were the very same people . . . family and friends, who were first in line on the receiving end when the times were good and the money was flowing in. "Oh how we tend to find out who are our true friends when the shit hits the fan."

In these pages, through it all, you the reader will laugh, cry and even want to throw in the kitchen sink as you will relive the struggles of the Madam in these pages that will leave you the reader in a better understanding of just what truly happened, and why all the lies were so needed in the attempts to bury a woman who just wanted to be loved, successful and famous as the transgender recording artist the Black Madam.

Enjoy her triumphs at trial, although she was indeed found guilty of murder in the 3rd degree at trial's end. Understand also why she entitles this time in her life, her Joseph's story . . . Genesis chapter 50 verse 20 . . . "What Satan intended for my bad, God has turned it around for my good . . . and for all that is being accomplished here now.

As Madam dares to take the rubble and destruction of the most darkest days of her life and make it all work for her greater good in book sales, a booming product line she calls ASSsets [the safe non-surgical buttock enhancement garment], a reality show . . . dubbed . . . Building ASSsets [based on her building her brand after her release from prison, documenting the building of her new product, her music and the rekindling of romance with longtime fiance.

All to rebuild a life she's always dreamt of . . . to be on top of the world as the Black Madam. Thus, read on and share in her triumphs in turning around an impossible situation and watch on as it all comes together for a once little boy named Forrest-Leone' from the Martin Luther King Plaza Projects of south Philadelphia, who grows up to become a beautiful woman who dared to climb to the top of the world on a situation everyone counted her out on . . . She is INFAMOUS.

INTRODUCTION

It was 2008, Obama was about to become the first black president of the United States of America. Every would-be video vixen was seeking out a body that would insure success on the music and video scene. Business was booming with reality starlets, exotic dancers and everyone all in between seeking out one woman who could change their lives for the better with a few sessions of silicone for buttock and body enhancement.

Madam had the game on lock, in simply living her life she became infamously known worldwide through the accidental death of an English exotic dancer who flew to her from Great Britain seeking these very same black market injections. Her name was Carmen London . . . It would be this acquaintance that would solidify Madam's name to become synonymous with black market buttock injections gone wrong through five years of international media coverage, a murder charge, trial and conviction that mixed with the world's fascination with her occult laced music videos and what many claim . . . ties to the Illuminus Sancti Illitus.

INTRODUCTION

Padge Victoria Windslowe paints a picture of her life in this book like the true artist that she is. Making you feel as if you are there with her through her journey of pain, sorrow, love, resiliency, and victory. Once you open this masterpiece, you are taken to the moment of her life as if you are going every step of the way in her present moments. This book is a definite page turner. Not only will you feel compelled to live the page with her, but you will be left with wanting more. Padge Victoria was born to make a living and a lasting impression on our lives.

by Erica Ivelisse Lungaro ...
Reiki Master/ Motivational Speaker.

INFAMOUS is "Black's" comeback answer to regain the title position of whether "Orange is TRULY the New Black!" Usurpers beware . . . BLACK MADAM's INFAMOUS Memoir is Raw, Relatable, Real, and Reigns Supreme in its own lane and genre. Once you pick up the reading, you'll find it hard to put down. Padge Victoria's story telling is a gift from the Story Telling Gods.

by Sarita Miller / Fight for Lifers Women's
Prison Activist.

I've been pulled into the Blackness! Black Madam's INFAMOUS is intriguing, educational and Insightfully provocative. It will give you a true understanding of the young Transgender's struggle to make something out of nothing, while keeping true to one's calling.

by Laura Persons/ Philadelphia Stylist Inc.

A young Madam reminds me of The Carry Bradshaw of a Trans Urban, True to Life... "Sex in the City". INFAMOUS RULES! #The_New_Abfab!

by Margarita Coria / Philly Urban Life.

THE PROLOGUE

THE OPEN LETTER

To My Dearest Sugar Daddy John
A/K/A
Dr. John Mancuso, M.D.
"When The Sugar Aint Sweet No Mo"

Dear Dr. Mancuso,

John, I can just imagine what you might have been feeling on the eve of the Infamous book release date. Wondering what will Padge say and reveal, and expose to the readers of your true nakedness and shame that could turn your world upside down.

The fact that you love to suck tranny penises as a pastime to unwind from a long day at your medical practice? No, that's way too easy. No matter what lies you've told to your wife Pamela, I'm sure she really knows the truth. You would dare get up on that witness stand to testify against me in order to save your own ass with a list of pathetic lies on me?

On us . . . and our history was mind blowing.

Well . . . sweet lil sugar daddy, your secrets are safe with me still. Never would I sell you out by revealing all the many times you've stole medical supplies from your workplace at Chestnut Hill Hospital to help me when I was in need of lidocaine, syringes, needles and so forth for my new thriving buttock injection business.

However, I can imagine even further your deep prayers to the Gods that the medical board never find out about all the fake prescriptions you've written to me and all my tranny friends through these last 20 years which are most likely still on file over at the Monument Road Pathmark Pharmacy back there in Wynnefield Heights, Philadelphia.

No, I won't tell a single soul of how you never cut off our relationship back in 1993 once your wife found out about me, and I was brought into the wicked light of your lies to find that you were a married man already. Yes indeed, it broke my heart deeply to say the least. But tell me John . . . Does Karen know that no sooner than she'd leave the room, you were back on the phone calling me trying to patch things up with me?

After fronting with me on the phone in front of her as if you really wanted me gone and out of your life completely?

Yes . . . those phone calls were so nerve-wracking back then when I was still so in love with you. Or should I say ... more in love with the idea of me being involved with such a powerful and influential up and coming physician as you.

I would think this book would have you living on pins and needles right about now . . . huh? Huh, John? Does Karen even know about the many years during Christmas Eve, you were in a frenzy booking our romantic rendezvous at the Chestnut Hill hotel just a few miles up the road from your office, year in and year out? While she and the children were out at her sister's house for the holidays?

I sure won't tell if you didn't. Madam wont' sell you out to save my own ass like you did to me, now would I doc?

Moreover, does your wife know about the many brand new luxury cars you would woe me with as gifts each top of the year? And I'm sure she would be delighted to find out all the hundreds of thousands of dollars you would lavish me with for hanging in there until just the right time, according to you . . . to leave her.

I'm betting you're probably swarming in your office chair right now this very moment loathing the day you took the witness stand as the prosecution's star character witness in order to lie to the world about us in order to attempt to shut me up forever in a state prison cell. However, what you have done was nothing short of sending me into a whirlwind of retaliation for the lies you spit. "Who dare contest the wrath of Black Madam," baby? They say not even hell has no fury like a woman scored. Lol . . . oh how they forgot to factor in the intense fury of a transsexual woman scored, which is tenfold.

*You would dare let your wife think that I was stalking you . . .
you pathetic rat. As if I would stalk you for 20 years, when it was
you indeed who could never live without me . . . your sweet lil
Madam. Supplier of all things exotic via my escort business in
which you were so addicted to.*

*Well John . . . your worst nightmare has just come true.
Run . . . run, to your shrink and confess all about it. You brought
this on yourself. All you had to do was tell the God forsaken truth
doctor love . . . but instead you couldn't do that. So now I'm
gonna do it for you and let the world see you in your naked shame.
As I dedicate this book to your wife Karen Mancuso and your
precious little children . . . Bryce, Taylor and John Jr. Let them
truly see who daddy dearest really is .. . Now you can call me
crazy ... Good Bye!*

*Sincerely yours,
XOXOXO
The MADAM*

PART I

CHAPTER 1

JUST THINKING OUT LOUD

It all culminated to a very surreal head as I halfheartedly watched the movie screen in the theater with Nik while thinking on one side of my mind at whether or not to send the blackmail letter I had just prepared for John. And just as good triumphed over evil in my mind, as I took a resolution to not send the post after the movie let out, my settled mind swayed back full throttle into the scene on the movie screen of a devil possessed woman in an elevator who stared straight into the camera at me sitting in the audience, and viciously proclaiming . . . "And I wanted you so bad" . . . It was a serendipitous moment where the elements and stars aligned for just that moment . . . that one purpose in time, of Nik and I going out on a date to see the movie DEVIL, directed by M. Night Shyamalan, so that Satan himself could use that screen in order to speak to me.

It was oh so terrifying to think that I was contemplating

such an evil deed. But yet deciding not to do it and making the Devil angry with me terrified me more. I left the movie theater and needless to say, I didn't drop the blackmail letter in the mail but ran home to tell Eve all that had just transpired at the movie. The battle was waging and good was somehow prevailing at this point in the fight for my soul.

Thus, I got a call from John anyway, stating that he would indeed give me the $50,000.00 bucks I so needed for a business venture. God was good, I told myself. My hands were kept clean, and I got the funding I needed to start my project, leaving me still room to complete the current music video I was working on . . . Phenomena without worry.

It made me very happy for the moment, the fact that I did not have to work like a maniac that week to procure the 50 gees by my own hands. Thus, I am free to stay in my zone and focus on the artistic side of the creation for my latest masterpiece. But oh how I truly felt like some pawn in a divine chess game of some sort for my eternal soul.

This would not be my only encounter by 3 degrees of separation, of some secret mysterious power controlling my destiny during the filming of the Phenomena music video.

It was just about three months earlier while filming the first half of the music video at the Philadelphia Sound Stage. The owner of the studio took me for a simple pretty face starlet he could take money from and not deliver up on his part of the deal on his side. The actual night before filming was to begin on the set. The owner did not have the sound stage freshly painted as our deal of $40,000 dollars agreed on. Which began a chain of many broken promises on his part. But this one in particular was his attributing the breach on his part was due to the fact that he was ill-prepared because

M. Night Shyamalan himself was waiting at the dinner table along with their wives at his home and he needed to rush home to join them for a dinner party. Promising me the paint job would be completed in the morning before I was to arrive on set with my staff and filming crew.

However, I and my staff of stagehands and crew techs were there at the moment to begin the lengthy process of setting up the props and layout for the Madamic order set.

Thus, he and I had a very rough start to begin with. It all ended badly when he very underhandedly tried to overcharge me $22,000 dollars for extra studio lighting that was supposed to already be in my package deal of production. Thus bringing my production budget way out over the pocket of what I had planned on.

"Oh why oh why do people bring this shit out of me?" Now this studio executive is holding all my stage prop property and transportation tractor for everything he claims I owe him. The asshole is holding my shit hostage till I . . . (who is now suffering from a couple of fractured knees from a mishap dance routine during taping the night before) come up with the extra cash.

"Oh baby . . . I will give him just what he wanted." I had Nik go to purchase me some crutches from the Rite Aid store so that I could become mobile enough in order to drive myself down to the sound stage in one of the crew's transport vans from my home, to north Philly . . . with Poppa already on the scene waiting for me in the executive's office . . . faces were cracked upon my arrival, when I bombastically hopped into the building obviously hurt and angry as all hell when I ordered Poppa to get my damn truck started, as I pointed to the slick executive with one of my crutches, while hopping on one leg for him to get into his office to receive the tongue lashing of his life, due to his subtle accusation that he would need to hold hostage my property for payment.

I don't know why some people always assume a trans woman to be such a pushover and demure for fear of someone finding out about her tee. I've been to the rodeo a few times, as Joan Crawford once told the big boys at a Pepsi company board meeting. And so, I meant business just as she did back then.

I pulled out my pen, as I would hope he didn't think I would be hauling the money over to his office location in the "badlands" of north Philly in cash. I wrote him a check for the outrageous amount he requested . . . with a soft smile and professional calm for the $22,000 dollars plus another $50 dollar tip I claimed to have promised one of his workers the night before for helping on the set (that was the overlay for the underlay) well, I did honor the $50 tip, for the boy helper was quite helpful. And . . . it was not his fault that he was working for such a shady boss.

As I pulled out of the loading docks of the studio, I watched patiently as Poppa pulled my tractor trailer truck out off of the sound stage property, and I was on the phone with the Bank of America that very next moment to request a stop payment on check #1625, as I ordered the telephone operator of the bank branch . . . "He's robbing me." I yelled like an old white woman.
She cancelled the check on the spot. I have thus yet to hear from him. I think he did send some of his hounds after me in the form of credit collectors by way of phone calls. But it was bad business on his part, he tried with me first, thus, I don't feel bad about turning his ass over like a "cheapskate-John" on the hoe stroll. Thus, he learned very fast . . . fuck with the Madam and you get fucked hard.

It was a really good laugh as I got to have the last laugh.

But, anyway . . . where were we? Oh yeah, no-way-whoesay did I actually carry out with the blackmail plans of Dr. Mancuso. I just didn't have too . . . he was a willing subject just as he always was. Even dating back 20 plus years ago. A $100,000 dollars for a fuck gift for New Years Eve, for the startup funds to my iMusicWeb casting network back in 1999. A venture I would have to abandon due to the sudden death of my father 4 years later. It would have been a great deal of success hadn't the restauranteur Steven Star hadn't been cruising like a vulture for the building iMusicWeb was occupying in downtown Philly.

Swooping in just as I was in mourning with my family, he caught me at my most vulnerable time and took the property right from under me when I became a few weeks late on the lease payment. As I drive by there now . . . all my renovation work has become the continental restaurant at 18 th and Chestnut Street.

It was indeed a very bad time for me, but business is business. I faltered on my side of the deal with the realtors. Thus, he was able to reap the benefits of my bad luck. I wish Steven much luck and success. That damn Steven Star. However, that is a whole lot better than what I use to have to say about the whole situation with him. But, it was no flim flam involved. He got the lot fair and square. But I did put a hex on the location on my last day of occupancy, picking up all of my things from my office there. Just a little something special before surrendering my keys. I know I was a stinker back then, but I's a saved woman now . . . delivered far from that once witch of a bitch I use to be, praise God.

There was once a time when the whole witchcraft and Dark Arts vibe of occultism once comforted me in my youth as an outcaste trans child. But now I can see everything so much clearer as a Godly woman. That's why the whole thing with John accusing me of blackmail on the witness stand bothered me so much. For once in life I did the "right thing" by not going through with the plot after seeing the movie Devil, only to later find in court that providence would have it that I would be punished for the mere thought of it anyway.

My life seemed to be eager to imitate art as I remember specific sequences from the movie Devil, where that scene in the elevator of the movie was actually filmed in an office building in downtown Philly. The very same building where I use to go make payment at Philadelphia magazine's marketplace section for my escort services. That whole scene in the elevators was as if it was made to send me some sort of message. Even down to the details of how the characters were trapped inside the elevator and all confronted with some wrongdoing in their own lives. One woman who was having an affair with a married man, another who killed a family in a hit and run on Bethlehem Pike . . . hum . . . I thought, John's practice is located on Bethlehem Pike. John's a doctor just as the one the woman is planning to blackmail in the film. This was definitely a message for me, I'm sure. Even down to the director of the movie, who is M. Night Shyamalan . . . freaky business to say the least.

Remembering all this now in retrospect leads me to now wonder with all that's taken place with the tragic death of Carmen London, could this all just be some twist of fate collaborating with some dark forces on some secret esoteric principality, in some realm making her death some symbolic blood sacrifice involuntary at my hands for my initiation into the New World's Order secret society of the illuminati? It's been said by many, that for one to obtain the success ones seeking in the sphere sanctioned by such secreted orders such as the entertainment business, one had to make a blood sacrifice. My heart hurts, my thought convict me. Could there be some real sinister workings that's brought me to this dark place in life?

Dealing in the dark arts can be a very dangerous thing as I can remember the feelings of being thrust into some sort of vortex of another dimension as I dabbled in it . . . It was the time when I was recording my track ROCK. Something so sinister in the track pulled at my soul, darkness from another worldly place far far away from planet earth called on me.

It seems ever since I recorded that song, life's taken on a different texture. Like I've opened up some door that can't be closed. Legendary occultist Sir Aleister Crowley couldn't have done it better himself. After recording that song . . . I took on the name ("The Beast"). I even had photoshoots and publi- city and propaganda actually displaying me in a prison of some sort. With my all seeing eye looking out of the prison door, with the word captioning . . . unleash the beast. Just as I am now locked in a cage, here as I sit now waiting to be released from my jail cell for the murder of an innocent.

Wicca, Satanism, The Black Arts, Voodoo and all in between the occult spectrum has been my life. However, I am now safe in my lord's presence forever more. I remember when I first took on the spirit of Black Madam. I was living alone in Society Hill and working in the recording studio with the rapper Styles. It was 666 Panama Street where she first took over me.

I was standing in my living room alone contemplating a stage name I would call myself . . . Black Madam, was literally whispered in my ear clear as day. I always said from then on it was not I who named myself, but indeed the name who chose me. Some spirit or entity chose the moniker for me. Jokingly, now I say that it was Madame

Helena Patrovna Blavaski, an old occultist . . . that did it to me. I don't know . . . just thinking out loud again.

If there is some supernatural force at large in my life, guiding me to some demonic destiny, what for and why me I ask myself over and over again. Have I pushed the limits one too many times in my search for the ultimate power? As if life's not complicated enough without all the hocus pocus? Could it be that my early curiosity with the Ouija board at such a young age and time in my life left me wide open for some sort of possession of myself? Why do I do this shit to myself? Why don't I just live and be happy like regular folk? I'm so not normal by a longshot. I'm so alien to this time and space I occupy.

CHAPTER 2

LET IT ALL BEGIN

Many have asked how did I get to this point I'm currently in . . . a state jail cell, awaiting appealment for an unintended homicide due to a silicone buttock injection gone wrong.

Well . . . Session after successful session, one of my good clients Schefee came and approached me after her fifth or sixth meet with me. She told me that she was getting really noticed because of all the great bodywork I was doing with her body. I mean . . . if you saw her, you would know just what I mean. You know . . . amazing stuff this silicone is. She was very proud of her new look, that it radiated from her pores. She had just landed a job at Viacom's MTV and VH1 standing in as a body double for the rapper Nikki Manaj. She pulled out pictures to show me just how MTV transported Nikki's head to her body. I was packing up and ready to exit the Microtell Hotel out by the

Philadelphia International Airport. She seemed very excited about asking me if I could also service a few of her friends and family members that asked about my work.

I explained to her straight from the door that that would be oaky, just as long as it was only family and friends. I love doing business by word of mouth for the simple reason . . . that when a person saw my work, there was no questions or doubt about what I could do for them. Apposed to meeting clients on a blind humbug and feeling as though I needed to go out of my way to sell my services. I just loathed the feeling of my having to persuade an individual to allow me the pleasure to make them beautiful. Go figure that one.

And furthermore, I was just so over the whole thing of getting clients from the internet. Thus, she and I agreed that I would see personal clients through her and our business together took shape. My first set of clients through Schefee were two family members of hers. A mother and daughter duo she said were her aunt and cousin. They were both gorgeous as Schefee was, so there was no reason at all for me to think otherwise. They'd come with a French poodle which I thought was weird because I like the room I'm about to perform a medical procedure to be as clean and germ free as possible with prepping the room with alcohol surgical wipe downs and so froth I would do before our session would begin.

We began talking about products—cheap vs. the more expensive brands. And what would be the body's reactions to a light product as the Adatosil 5000 vs. the heaviness of Silicon 1000 or its street counterpart . . . DC2X, a mixture of Dow Corning product and sterile saline solution. I like to give a selection being that everyone had a different budget, and not everyone could afford the top of the line products available being that my aim was to provide a service to even the lowest income level women who would otherwise never be able to afford this procedure by mainstream methods.

However, this duo was from an upper echelon of would-be buttock injectees. The mother worked in Manhattan real estate and the daughter worked for Deff Jam Records and was somewhat connected to the team of Jayz on an assistant and personal level. Thus we settled on the Adatosil 5000 hybrid mixture with an under layer of the Dow Corning DC2X for their foundations. I suggested the DC2X although it was non-medical grade, because it however was non-toxic and had a beautiful balance to give the buttock a natural weight than just going with the outright expensive Adatosil 5000 which gives volume, but feels so unnaturally light opposed to what one would expect an ass of such magnitude to be. Basically, I explained that in a compromising position with your lover . . . the buttock injections would be undetectable if administered the way I advised them to do.

Not to mention, that moreover . . . although the Adatosil 5000 was more expensive than DC2X, the more expensive brand was not as durable and much too temperamental in extreme cold and hot weather. The session went off with great success and I saw them about 3 or 4 times. I seemed to have made such a great impression on the pair that the daughter and I began to talk more about personal stuff and what exactly she did for Deff Jam and JayZ. Oh my God . . . God bless Beyonce, poor sweetheart . . . I am not going to be the one to leak the tapes but damn . . . smh. I guess one must take the bad with the good when you're dealing with a life such as theirs in the limelight. I guess he's still a good provide regardless.

The next few clients Schefee brought me were not so glamorous as the first. She sent me a god sister who was hearing impaired. Or did she say she was a niece of the African software developer she was engaged to? I can't quite remember. Anyway . . . yeah I believe it was the niece of the man she was to marry because I can literally remember her describing the deaf girl's uncle as "the stable money."

I also worked on her cousins who were hair salon owners and a second cousin who was a registered nurse in the Bronx. I dealt with them a few more times so that they could gain their desired results they were aiming for, and finally during the last session with these cousins of hers who owned the hair salon, we all got to talking after the session as I packed my bags to leave. We talked of the music industry and the affair that Schefee was currently having with rapper Jim Jones and her acting career.

I felt so very comfortable with Schefee by this point now in our transactions and told her that I too was also involved in the industry and was currently in production on my latest music video and were casting models such as herself for my Phenomena production. She seemed genuinely excited about our similar aspirations and I asked her if she'd like a role in the video. She obliged and I began to take out my personal smart phone in order to show her a prior music video of mine entitled "Come On In My Kitchen" that was currently being featured on FUSE TV that I completed about 9 months prior. I told her about all the possibilities in que with this next production and advised her to check it out on the big screen once she's home. She and her cousin Mandy, loved the video and thought it was very edgy with all the voodoo undertones. I forget now the actual Jamaican term they used for witchcraft. But it was in regards to the West Indies lango for Black Magic. At the end of the video, Schefee saw the closing credits and shouted to the top of her lungs, Black Madam? . . . that name is hot to death baby!

By this time Schefee and I's exchange was on a far more personal level than what we had prior to this meet with just silicone dealings. She seemed to now be becoming a friend. All felt so genuine, so real, so I never thought twice about it. A rule of thumb for me, was to never mix business with pleasure. And to always give clients my street name of Lillian, which was a name I loved as a child after seeing the made for TV movie Lace, back in the 80's.

My choice to always go by my street name with dealings of the black market silicone world was for no particular reasoning of ill workings. It just seemed to be a means in which I could keep my life compartmentalized. I mean . . . I can be so anal about that kind of thing. To the point whereas, at home . . . only Nikolaus can call me Vik, Vikki, or Victoria . . . that's just me and the way I operate. That's just a name I reserve for my man . . . and/or a serious suitor. And when I hear someone call me Lillian, before even looking at them, I already know they're acquainted with me on some street dealing level. So hint hint fellas. If you've ever met the Madam . . . and you've called her anything other than a variation of Victoria . . . I knew from the start . . . you were just gonna be a boy toy. Something to play with for the moment and to serve some ultimate goal of mine and nothing more. A name is everything to me. Thus, in laymen's terms . . . you were not anything more than a glorified booty call. And it was not my botty accepting any calls . . . you figure it out. CTFU!

Not for nothing . . . I believe names are the controllers of ones destiny. Names strike up patterns in the field of vibration, so how could they be only a calling card as many in the known reality believe. God used sound to form infinity, thus he said we are made in his image. Thus, one should guard their tongues wisely and understand that there is power in the word. My name Page is reserved for my family and other informal settings. While my formal name of Padge Victoria represents the epitome of high society and upper class associates. In the music industry I am known by Madam amongst studio musicians, record producers and so forth. My Christian name in which I was baptized under the authority of the Cardinal Archbishop

Anthony Bevalogua at the Cathedral Basilica of St. Peter St. Paul in Philadelphia was Gene'vieve G'ordon— French pronunciation. And last, when I was deep into the world of secret social orders under the OTO chapter—The Madamic Order. My mystical names are Padgevic and Damma, it was a real magical ordained sanction. Never am I to be called by my birth name of Forrest-Leone—two words blended into one. I do not answer to it, not because of some shameful reason or another of my past, but it's a name I hold sacred, a name bestowed upon me at birth by my maternal grandmother after a star, the lady Selena Threats G'ordon Bagley of the Philadelphia Black Hebrew church of the seven day advantage. May she rest in peace.

CHAPTER 3

MY FIRST ENCOUNTER WITH CARMEN LONDON

Anyway ... let us with no more delay of the infinitive theories of my multi-personality disorder and so forth, let us get back on to the story at hand. The final clients that Schefee brought to me were three young ladies from London. I was told that they were her family from England she had not seen for ages, who were also seeking to do some enhancement in order to pursue modeling and music video work as their cousin Schefee was currently doing.

Betty, Carmen and Theresa ... They were a cheerful bunch with all the excitement of being abroad and all the possibilities that life and this adventure would bring with them all obtaining "bigger bums" as they would put it.

Betty, of them all seemed very reserved and seemed to just be looking for some modest and simple body enhancement. She was married and had no entertainment goals in which she was unreasonably trying to achieve. Just simply wanting to look better for her husband.

However, Carmen was full of fire in her eyes. She knew exactly what she wanted and just how she wanted it. She had high ambitions to become the next video vixen to top the scene in the Euro music industry. She was looking to take the world by storm with a huge bum as some of the already established divas that came before her had done. She was extremely enamored by such women in American pop culture as Mrs. Dubai, Jennifer Lopez and the many reality girls on TV.

The last of the threesome was Theresa Gamfi who also went by the name of Rochette. She was a very pleasant and passive type of girl. Very agreeable and seemed to be onboard for whatever Carmen wanted to do. Their first session with me was to be the teardrop shape which consisted of the deposit of more weight in the cuff of the butt as opposed to a bubble butt which is more of an athletic shape like a Serena Williams the tennis player type. They all came with pictures of other models they would like to look like and we decided on products and would go from there. They all came to the same conclusion of the Dow Corning mixture I call DC2X because it was more in tune to their budget and that they could get so much more of it as opposed to using all the funds they had for just a modest amount of the more expensive stuff, and not really seeing the results they came so far for.

Not only did they choose the DC2X for economy reasons, they also loved the fact that I used it too, on myself and thought it would be a good selection being that they all came so far to the States to get this procedures done. It would allow them to get their money's worth and return home with good results to show for their journey to see me.

It turned out to be a successful session and went on without a hitch. Everyone at first seemed happy with their results. However, as I was packing my bags and cleaning up behind myself as I always do at completion of my work, I gave all the post operative care instructions to them . . . they should stay off their buttocks for eight to twelve hours. I also advised them to drink plenty of fluids as to flush out any of the product that the body was rejecting by way of urine. That is if the body should choose to reject some of the product which was normal.

It seemed that Carmen was a little unhappy however, as I proceeded to give my farewells. I asked her what was the matter, and she pulled me to the side for privacy, and we went into the bathroom to talk. She confided in me that she was looking to go much bigger than what we had accomplished and that she was interested in an additional product. A whole new session and round of injections to top off what we had just done. I explained to her that with this procedure you should take it slow and build up on top of prior sessions in a series of multiple visits. She told me that she was under the assumption that it was a one time thing and didn't really like the fact that she would have to fly all the way across the Atlantic from the United Kingdom several more times in order to obtain the massive results she was seeking.

She also went on to explain to me of a booking for a music video job she was auditioning for back home in London which she landed the lead girl role. But was later kicked off the job because the producers had later discovered that she was not as bootylicious as the producers of the video first thought, as she was sporting a pair of butt pads during auditions. Therefore, it was the utmost urgency that she obtain the results that her prosthetic buttock enhancement pad gave her on the shoot. She needed to look just as great out of her clothes in the more skimpy and sexy dance wear the video directors had in wardrobe.

I understood exactly where Carmen was coming from and assured her that she came to the best person in the business to obtain those outstanding results. But that it would indeed take time as did my own body. Schefee's body and the many other Mrs. Dubaiesque butts she's heard of that obtained them through me and this black market procedure. She seemed reluctant to take my advice, but shrugged her shoulders and said okay. We exited the bathroom as I gave all the girls a hug and left the hotel headed back to Power House soundstage in Old City Philadelphia to meet up with the cast and crew for an overnight shooting session of the crucifixion scene for the Phenomena video.

I got into my makeup chair after I ate from the craft table and prepared my mind to let the spirit of Black Madam emerge while my personal assistant and stylist Remika began to style my hair. Jessica, my niece, was working on my nails, but first opted to give me a limb massage to loosen me up, stating that I seemed tense and attributing it to my nerves of the long midnight shoot that was to take place in a few hours.

The Directors, Rob and Brian were doing all the light and camera blockings as Eve was directing the stage crew how to lay out the green screen for the gigantic cross in which it was to be crucified on with me on it suspended in midair. Just as I came out of hair and makeup, Kante . . . an old family friend of mine from childhood who was working as an intern on the production set, had brought me a glass of Absents . . . some green mysterious looking drink that Eve sent him off rushing to the wine and spirits shop to get for her design of the set which was to be a post-shoot interview for MTV, VH1 and FUSE TV. It was to be added to the Phenomena music video promotion package which included station identifications and stuff like that.

While I was getting into my bathing suit to be glittered down, Ramika came to me holding my purse and looking irritated. "What girl." I looked over to her trying to not catch a big whiff of glitter in my mouth as Eve spayed so erratically. "Gurl . . . one of your cell phones in your bag keeps blowing up." . . . I had her dig into my bag and hit the answer key as she held the phone to my ear so that my fingernails could continue to dry undamaged as I took the phone call. "Hello, what's up?" I shouted into the phone.

A voice yelled back, "Hey Lil, it's me Schefee," she said on the other line.

I said, "Hey what's up, what cha need?" That's when she told me that all was well with the girls at the hotel recuperating, but that Carmen had wanted her to call me so she could speak to me about something.

I explained to her that I was right in the middle of prepping to shoot, but Carmen told her that it wouldn't take but a moment. I told her to put Carmen on the phone. "Hello Lilian, listen . . ." Carmen's voice poured through the phone sounding upset. "I have a few more thousand pounds sterling left on me still for the duration of my trip." She proceeded to beg if I could please come back and give her more product. I explained once more to her that it was never about the money. But that she shouldn't get it done and she needed to heal from what she just had done. As stern as I could, I tried explaining to her that I didn't think it was a good look to go back into the injection site during the healing process so soon.

I told her that if she, Betty and Theresa felt up to it tomorrow, that they should use the extra cash to go sightseeing in the city and enjoy Philadelphia and have fun. I also explained to her that even if I could do the second procedure on her so soon, that right now I couldn't do it anyhow, as I was drenched in glamour from head to toe and on a video set about to start shooting a scene.

She seemed to be bothered by her failed attempts to lure me back to the hotel for another session. And without even a goodbye the phone clicked abruptly and I let Ramika put the phone away in my purse. We began to walk to the soundstage from my dressing area. I heard the loud and wicked thumps of the bass drum as the guitars began to pierce through my soul . . . I feel her coming to the surface I whispered to myself as the music started to cue up for Phenomena. The spirit of the dam one was rising to full blown possession as Black Madam took over me as we walked through the dark corridors onto the set.

CHAPTER 4

THE FAMILY BUSINESS OF ESCORTING AND TRANS LIFE

Strangely all throughout the shoot I could not seem to get Carmen off of my mind. I like to pride myself on satisfaction and a happy clientele base. For, injections was not just something I did for money, but an art like my music that I very much enjoyed the act of creation. It was a great side business that allowed me to pursue my music ambitions full steam ahead, as the precious trade that allowed me to maintain my free schedule while also allowing me the financial means to deal with the big wigs of the music industry on my own terms.

Furthermore, it allowed me to finally let go of the "family business" which was Lace Escorts and Entertainment. An escort service that I and my old friend Nikki James had started up back in 1993 out of shear desire to make a way for ourselves as young trans girls, when life did not seem so bright for girls like us in a world where two young black transsexual girls would have otherwise been eaten alive.

I can remember back then. I had just announced to my mother as I approached my 21st birthday in the autumn cold of the fall, all my plans to become a full fledge woman. Yes indeed mother I was finally ready to pursue a life as a transgender woman. The one that I felt in me since I could long ago remember. She (my mom) had asked me while we were visiting my sister Sherrie's house on Pierce Street just around the corner from our family home. What was it that I wanted for my birthday?

I remember boldly showing mom a picture of a very beautiful woman with very long silky jet black hair that fell all the way down to her buttocks with china doll bangs, an oval face, and almond shaped eyes with gorgeous full lips. Mom looked at me and asked . . . "What . . . you want a hooker for your 21st birthday?"

I laughed and said no . . . and began to explain to her that the woman in the picture was a transsexual girl. And I think I would like to get a sex change for my 21st rite of passage into the world of adulthood. My mother clutched her pearls and in her always sounding- exasperated black/Italian, South Philly, over the top gesture of brushing me off whenever a topic was too heavy for her, and way too much for her heart to bear . . . she said . . . "Oh . . . you'll have to talk to your father about that!" And just like that, mom let such great news go as she went back to discussing draperies and some other stuff like the coming fall fashions in the kitchen with my sister Sherrie as then my eight-year-old niece Jessica looked at me with utter confusion.

Jessica, not giving up on some curious questions thus

proceeding to bombard me with her curiosity as her mother and my mother stayed in the kitchen cooking our dinner . . . "Can a boy really change into a girl?" Jessica asked as if asking for a piece of candy.

"Yes," I answered her as I rolled my eyes settling back into the sofa, all curled up and cuntie reading the story of Renee Richards in her first book she had written about her transgender experience titled *Second Serve*. She was a pro tennis player who later went on to also get a sex change in the 70's. But anyway . . . to zoom onto it, I had a talk with my father later that day. He was not so indifferent as my mother was earlier that day at Sherrie's house.

With my nails all polished up blood red and all. "Yes I did". . . I marched right up those steps to my parent's bedroom the moment I got back home and told daddy (that mommy thought I should tell you something). He was busy at his typewriter working on a manuscript and asked what was it that I wanted to talk to him about. I sat down in his easy chair just a few feet from arms reach of his desk just in case my announcement was not received well. And as I had my father's full and undivided attention—["See I was a very shy kid . . . so daddy was definitely not used to me being so assertive and poised to address a situation I had at hand." I was usually the type of kid to just write all I had to say on a note if I wanted to express any grievances I was feeling, as I would then wait for the perfect time to give my parents my complaints which was most likely on the weekend after they had been drinking and partying with friends over visiting our home. Just as I did when I gave my opinion on important family matters as my sister Sherrie getting an abortion, or the whole matter that she was having sex at all at such a young age.

I was an old school kind of kid to say the least. So one could just imagine the thoughts racing through my father's head now that I was there before him expressing myself in the flesh and face to face. As I'm sure it at first tickled him to think he was finally about to have his first man to man discussion with his first born son . . . little did daddy know. . . it was indeed a father to daughter talk with his freshly new bold and blazing trans kid . . . poor father . . . smh . . .]

Well . . . here I go . . . "Daddy I want to get a sex change!" There, just like that once again I said it. Flat out and right to the point. No song and dance like I use to. I had serious business to undertake. There was definitely no tiptoeing through the tulips with my future as a woman on the line.

My dad always brought his children up to think and live outside the box. Whatever that meant. He always made us feel like we were able to express ourselves freely if we had something to say or a problem we were having that needed an adult's advice. However this was not one of those open door "come-by-yah" moments as I sat nervously waiting in my chair just an arm's throw from his right arm.

I guess I must have thought it would go over well with dad as he raised me up to be an individual to think for myself. To go with my gut instinct and to be true to my heart. Well . . . my darling . . . so not today honey! I just looked over at my daddy as he had just the most disappointing expression written all over his red boiling hot face. Just about the most disappointed look a father could ever give his child. As if he could have been okay with anything other than the words from my lips . . . "A sex change?" he softly repeated to me. "Where the hell

did you go get some crazy ass thought as that in your head Granger?" [Granger, being a name of affection he called me as a young boy.] I guess my birth name Forrest-Leone made him think of a forest "Granger" or something. As that name always reminded me of some old ("Smokey the Bear") PSA to stop forest fires TV commercial. And at this very moment my father was trying to save his very own personal forest from going up into flames from what he somehow imagined I was asking to be—some flaming tranny from the most unsavory side of town . . . 13th and Locust Street which was always considered the "Gayborhood."

"Well daddy," I said as I proceeded to speak, peeling my lips apart to utter a simple sentence. My mouth always get so damn dry when I have something so important to say. It's not like I've been so far off the mark anyway with my 85 percent feminine looking features and natural ways and gestures . . . I really wanted to say. As if I came to him like some strapping buck bursting with manhood written all over my face. As if I was some ol tractor trailer mack truck driving nigga catching him so off guard.

All my life, I've been painfully mistaken as a girl in the most inappropriate moments. Many more times than anyone had ever taken for granted that I was a boy. And now daddy's acting like I'm this super masculine of a jock here just defiling his plans of grandchildren by way of my family jewels. As if I'm just gonna race straight to the old neighborhood where he grew up in south Philly while wearing a great big old sign for all his gang-warring buddies to see just what became of Big Jes's son . . . smh . . . knowing all along the news would not have raised a single eyebrow in the pretty

lil pink dress I'm imaging him shaming to see me in.

"Well son . . ." as he reiterated the harsh reality of that

pronoun sounding resoundingly from his lip, "I'll tell you one thing," he said as he lit up his Newport cigarette. "This is the plan. You can be one of those gay homosexual dudes like your cousin over there on your mother's side of the family. . . Milton, or whatever the hell his name is. A homosexual's not one of the best things to be in this world, but it sure ain't the worst thing if you've got to choose between being a laughing stock or someone respectable . . . it's your choice here and I think we'll choose this path for you son. You go ahead and do that, and keep on the boy clothes like you been doing these past 20 plus years, and me and your mother can deal with that better. But that whole 'I wanna be a woman' thing is just stark raven mad talk son. You've just been around your mother too long. . . till now you wanna be just like her. But I'll tell you this . . . you're free to stay here at home under our roof and become a homo and all. Your mother and I can deal with that. We'll continue to help you through college and feed you and so forth. But if you think you're going to start changing up around her and putting on skirts and all with those fishnet panty hose your mother be wearing around here, just plain out becoming a spectacle of the neighborhood for all the neighbors to see you make a fool of your mother's and my raising you wrong or something, I'd rather see you dead. You ain't no goddamn girl and I won't hear nothing more of this crazy talk son."

Hmm . . . I thought . . . with defiance, I only ever had once before in my life when dealing with my father. Defiance I had to muster up in order to stand between my drunken father's fist about to hit my mother a few years prior to this day. It was a day I finally stood up to my father's then domestic abusive behavior towards my mom, for many years before he finally decided to put down the fire water for good and become saved in the Lord.

I told him that I was indeed still going to have a sex change, and I'm going to wear the prettiest dresses I could find, and he could keep all his plans of accepting me as a homosexual, like my cousin, Milton, on my mother's side of the family was. Because I was not a homosexual. I was born a transsexual woman and from there on I was gonna live like one at all cost. Even if it cost me my own family's support so help me God. . . I vowed from that day forth to be the best and most successful transsexual woman to ever transition. I walked out the door. I came back a few days later for all my worldly possession and didn't speak to my father for ten long years.

CHAPTER 5

HOT CAKES AND SAUSAGES

Meanwhile, that first year away from the security of my family home from which I grew up in the protection of my parents, I found to be quite difficult to keep my defiant promise to my father.

Boy oh boy . . . how keeping that promise was not going to be easy.

For a whole year straight, all I could afford to eat were cans of beans and half rotten potatoes while living in a studio efficiency apartment in downtown center city at 22nd and Spruce Street. Although I was living below the poverty line, I was living in the prime real estate of downtown Philadelphia, just a block up from Rittenhouse Square.

Luck must had been on my side with foresight when I landed that apartment back then with Katz Realty. I paid only $165.00 per month for my little piece of home in which

I was to blossom into this famous beautiful transsexual woman I dreamt of being. Times were indeed hard for me. I had to pawn a lot of my music equipment I had accumulated during my teenage years in order to keep up with my bills. I even tried to get on public welfare at the suggestion of my homosexual cousin, Milton from my mother's side of the family. But couldn't swallow the fact that I was well and able to work for my living and couldn't take the handouts.

I did receive one welfare check which was my first and last as pride took over the rumbling hunger pains in my stomach. I felt so embarrassed to be standing in a line where it seemed like all standing were giving up on the hope of a brighter future. As I signed the signature line to receive my $80 in food stamps and $120 in cash, I made a promise to the woman that was growing up fast within me, to never come back to this place.

From there on I had to come up with a hustle. See what I did was . . . while seeing this doctor named Philex Spector who was a doctor about 80 years of age, that specialized in transforming boys into girls by way of Premarin 2.5 hormone pills and estrogen injections at his office on the now Temple University college campus in the north Philadelphia section off of Broad and Cecil B More Avenue. The man was old as dirt itself, but knew just the right goods to give in order to get the job done. His shots were $80 each, which include a whole month supply of pills. But I struck up a deal with him to let me pay half of his service fee, and since I had medical coverage still pending from my failed attempts to collect welfare.

I had the doctor draft me up a prescription for the medications . . . (pills and injectables), and with that one prescription slip, I was about to begin cultivating a life of making a way out of no way. I took that prescription script to Kinkos copy store and Xeroxed copied me 4 copies. I kept the original to get my meds filled as the doctor originally gave it to me for. But the four copies I took home and used two to make blanks for the purpose of crafting up a whole new blank prescription sheet pad, 50 in all by way of the simple use of a little whiteout and about 5 dollars . . . jackpot!!!

In high school I was a great art student prior to my move from home with my family. So I knew just all the tricks to the trade with how to perfect the perfect fake. It took about three times, but three was definitely the charm, as I stood there in amazement of the new possibilities of life as a woman without the harsh struggles I was facing since being out on my own. I was now in the medical business.

I wrote up my first prescription and passed it off quite easily at the local CVS pharmacy just up the street from Kinkos copy store. It was so easy to do with a medical card I had obtained from my initial interview at the welfare office when I had first applied for public assistance. I guess because a prescription for female hormone pills and injectables weren't on any type of controlled drug list, that would warrant any suspicion that the prescription could be fake.

Bam!!! Just like that, I now had double of hormones with one set to sell from what would have only been one if not for my new magical means . . . Thus, I went home and called all my transgender girlfriends and announced to them all that I was now in the female hormone business. And boy did business boom for a while. That is how I was able to start acquiring all my new female clothing, makeup and partying money for the times of my innocent little life out on the Philadelphia trans social scene.

And partying it up I did at the hot "Studio 54" type club named the Nile on 13th and Locust Street in the heart of the city. It really was a great time had by all. With me having all this new found freedom and financial stability and for once in what seemed like an eternity . . . I could just be a carefree spirit. Life was getting good and I began to truly enjoy the nightlife on the social scene of this new exciting life I was embarking on (in "The LIFE.")

One night during my club escapades throughout the gay circuit of clubs on 13th Street, while coming out of another alternative nightclub called Starz, which was owned by a very rich homosexual philanthropist named Joey Vannoutty . . . guess who I ran into? No one other than my homosexual cousin, Milton from my mother's side of the family. Up until this time I had always shunned his company, as prior to my revelation just before my 21st birthday back at home in my parent's bedroom with my father about my wanting to have a sex change, I was too afraid to be in Milton's company, for others would ("OUT") me prematurely as a member of ("The LIFE") by guilt by association with cousin Milton. You know . . . the whole birds of a feather flock together type of thing. But now it was on. He and I talked all about my transition and he introduced me to many of his friends that had already been through the process. Milton and I became the best of friends at this time and even closer cousins in the family. He helped me meet all the right people on the scene which gave me an automatic status with all the city's prominent movers and shakers of the alternative life. And I began my social climb on the Philadelphia gay elite social and party scene.

Milton and I would go on to spend countless hours at each others apartments. And he would always take me out to splurge his paycheck from his advertising firm ob me. I was indeed a little princess when it came to my dear and beloved cousin "Milly" as I would affectionately call him. In the hottest fashions of designer female clothing, I was officially his fashion doll.

Things went on this way for a while until Milton met his lover Rob, who was the brother of his then roommate Charles. Charles later went on to die from AIDS complications, which left Milton in ownership of their massive bachelor home. This was the beginning of my seeing Milton less and less as he devoted most of his time catering to Robert.

I began to spend more of my time back at my own apartment entertaining many of my new found friends I had acquired hanging out with Milton at the clubs.

There was Angelique, one friend that I had met through a mutual boyfriend in which we both unwittingly found out we were both being played. His name was Lionell . . . a very handsome football player looking kinda of guy, who then put me in the mind of the Eagles football star Randal Cunningham. At first he seemed like quite a catch as he was a man's man kinda man.

I met Lionell at the club Nile and thought he was really hot. As he danced across the dance floor, his eyes watching my every move that night. Finally at about the end of his last dance, he walked over to me to ask my name. We got to talking throughout the night and thought it would be cool to hang out sometime. In the

next few weeks he and I started to date one another.

One night Lionell and I were hanging over one of

Milton's friend's apartment just off City Avenue. It was Lionell and my first real date together other than meets here and there as he walked me to and from the nightclubs in the wee hours of the morning. While hanging out at this friend's apartment, as it began to get really late, Milton and his friend suggested that we all stay overnight, which sounded okay since we were so far from either one of our apartments back down in the city.

The thought of Lionell and I spending the night together didn't really ring any alarms, being that it was nothing too romantic. Just a convenience being that we were so far out so late. We had just met and I was pretty sure Milton would be playing the respectable chaperone. Lionell and I arranged things so we could both sleep on the floor on an airbed in one of the extra rooms in this enormous old world, turn-of-the-century apartment. It was the summertime and the air was thick with so much testosterone. I guess Milton and his boy toy fling was in the other room getting it in which I wouldn't lie . . . had Lionell and I feeling very frisky.

Before you know it, it happened. It was really happening but just not as I would have imagined it. Lionell was taking all ten inches of the only thing manly on me in his mouth deep down in his throat. His mouth was so warm and wet as I felt the throbbing thick head of my penis explore the depths of his esophagus. Uncontrollably jolting each time his gag reflex collapsed around my shaft.

It was the most erotic thing I ever saw in my life thus far. This hard strapping of a man, down on his knees suckin me off as I stood there up against the ornately decorated antique wallpaper, with gold leafing in my beautiful pretty pink floral Versace couture silk dress.

Although I was very much enjoying what was happening, I must admit that it was rather daunting to imagine myself truly enjoying this kind of taboo sexual encounter with me in the dominant role. It was weird since before then, I only saw myself in a feminine light.

Confusion began to set in . . . I couldn't for the life of me understand just why this strong seemingly guy, the epitome of man, wanted to do something like this with me so ass backwards. "Literally!" As half of me enjoyed the pleasure of his falaciotic talents, the other half of me wonders why the hell does he want to stick my dick in his mouth with such a feverish frenzy. And that was not all. Things seemed to elevate to the next level fast. An ascension to yet another place I never thought I'd ever venture off into with a man.

"For crying out loud," this was messing up my whole damn psychosis of just what a Trans woman's serene life was and to what a new verging respectable woman was to be. In his frenzy of the moment, he reached into his back pocket where he seemed to have a glow in the dark Trojan. My mind went on to an animalistic ferociousness as he slipped on the condom to my penis and proceeded to lay down on his stomach. What the fuck, I thought to myself. This was becoming the ultimate turn off for me. For I was a lady at all times and to do what I think he's wanting me to do, could go against everything that I told my father I was not . . . a homosexual man.

As I looked at his super masculine body swarming and gyrating as he reached back to part his buttocks, some other primal feeling was taking over me. I began to throb even harder than when he sucked me off. And, before you knew it, it was happening again. But this time I was fucking this moncho of a man up the ass and he was loving it. It was an extreme animalistic act to say the least. But he seemed to enjoy it more, more and more as he begged me in a sort of little boyish kinda moan. It was all good for him and something so terrible to my ego. For now when it was all over, I laid there questioning was my father really right? Was I really just a homosexual male who could so easily enjoy screwing a man versus being screwed by one as a woman? And not at all this Transsexual woman I had so defiantly proclaimed to him?

After a few minutes Lionell asked me was I okay. "Was the fuck I okay??" I thought to myself . . . does this man realize that it was he who had just taken a huge penis into himself and not I. I looked at him in such disgust and said, "Shouldn't I be asked you that question?" Rolling my eyes at him in the glimmer of the full moonlight out the bedroom's bay window overlooking the suburban railroad tracks just outside the apartment building. I fell off to sleep.

A few hours later I awoke to the emptiness of the vacant spot next to me on the airbed where Lionell had last been lying just moments earlier. I got up to explore the huge luxurious grand apartment in the early morning sunlight, wondering where the hell he'd gone off to.

Oops . . . not in there . . . as I backed out of the room where Milton and his fling were lying there asleep in the nude with condoms still gripping onto limp dicks. As I softly closed the door back, being super careful not to wake the sleeping lovebirds. Out of my right ear I heard someone whispering from the direction of the kitchen. I didn't quite hear much before Lionell noticed me and abruptly hung up the phone. But there was enough that I heard to alert me that whoever was on that other line was someone of a romantic nature.

"Good morning," he said to me and asked me if I was hungry.

"Yes," I replied to him, and he began to get dressed, pulling up his fresh Calvin Klein jeans over his crotch hugging blackish/blue boxer briefs he had earlier worn at his ankles as he invited me into him just hours ago.

Looking like the total picture of an "around-the- way" thug boy, he threw on his black hoody over his ripped up chest and six-pack to die for, and headed out the door, and down the street to McDonalds to get breakfast for us.

While he was out, the suspense was beginning to crawl up my skin to find out just who the hell he was talking to in such a romantic tone over the phone. So masculine . . . so bruit and contrary to the freak bull (boy) I just slayed last night in the back room on the floor. So yes, I did . . . I had no problem picking up the phone and pressing redial. The phone range a few times before a voice answered through . . . "Hello you've reached the Fort Washington Holiday Inn, how may I help you?"

Now if my mind serves me correctly, I can remember Lionell telling me that he use to date this "fem-queen" named Angel who lived out in Ambler, Pennsylvania and worked over in the next town of Fort Washington at a hotel or something. So here we go now . . .

"Hi, good morning," I said. "Is there an Angel that works there?" Without a thought the voice on the line tells me to hold the line as she transfers me to another department. I waited approximately 30 seconds on the line before a tiny little voice spoke through the phone, that I can remotely remember sounding like Tinker Bell from the cartoon Peter Pan.

So here I go again asking the million dollar question of the hour after introducing myself. "Did you just get off the phone with Lionell?"

She gags and says reluctantly, "Yes . . . he's my boyfriend," she adds, now asking me just who might I be.

Once again I introduced myself as Page, and proceeded to tell her that Lionell told me all about you, but failed to add that you two were still in communication. I also went on to explain to her that he told me that you no longer were dealing with each other, thus, he's been dating me for the past few weeks. There is an uncomfortable quietness on the line as she collected her thoughts and revealed that he just made plans with her to meet up for drinks later that night in town once she got off work.

I told her that she had nothing to worry about with me, as after the shenanigans that transpired last night, I was no longer interested in him. He's totally not the type of guy I'm looking for and we said our goodbyes. A few minutes later Lionell comes in with some "hot cakes and sausages" and two very cold styro cups of milk to wash it all down. While eating our breakfast, I asked him to tell me more about his ex-girlfriend Angel. As he assured me that it's all over and she's no more to him than a free haircut as her family owned a barbershop in his neighborhood. I then went on to explain to him that I had just talked to her and she thinks quite differently. I guess he's thinking now, that old phrase of "a bird in the hand beats two in the bush," because he's now trying to assure me that whatever we spoke about, was all lies on her part, because she just can't seem to get over him. Now I'm thinking that it somehow must be the other way around in truth. Because it was he that was stalking her at work during the wee hours of the morning, but being that this was truly just a one time thing on my part and I really had no intentions of ever taking the "in-the-closet, down- low dude" seriously, because I was certainly not into fucking my dude no matter how hard he made me cum. I let the conversation on the issue at hand die down.

We later went our separate ways once on the avenue, leaving Milton and company still sleeping the morning away up in the apartment where I lost all my innocence the night before. "I'll see you tomorrow perhaps?" was the question that hesitantly fell from his lips. "Not even honey!" was what I was thinking to myself. But I just smiled and played coy with the boy, and said "Sure, I'll give you a call in a day or so." After heading home I called my friend Eve to find out if we were still meeting later on at the Nile Dance Club tonight.

"Yes . . . biotch, of course . . . it's so on tonight," she said on the line, and we went on to speak of other things.

It was a bright summer day as I searched through my wardrobe for the perfect shimmery number that would have all eyes on me tonight at the club. I felt like being a vision in white as I pulled out my new white sequin wrap dress I had just bought a few days ago from Ellenton Boutique on the square while out with Milton. "I think I'll rock this with my new stiletto heels I got from down South Street." My hair was already done, as I got it done for the get-together over at Milton's friend's place last night. So I was all good to go and rock out for a girl's night out on the town with just me and Eve.

I just love hanging out with Eve. I had just met her a few weeks ago while hanging out at the Nile dancing the night away with Milton. I saw her in the crowd as she stood about six foot three with flat shoes on, and looked like a strikingly beautiful Naomi Campbell dead ringer. She had this lovely Caribbean glow to her skin like she came from the jungle of the West Indies or something and could have very well given the hottest chick of that time (Pamela Anderson), a run for the money in the body department. Her breasts were everything to say the least, and because of not only her height, but more so because where we were at, I took a shot that she was a transsexual also.

"Milton," I yelled across the crowded dance floor while eyes still locked on her. "Look at her Milly," I shouted.

"She's pretty," he said back. "I wonder if those are her real breasts, and if so, how'd she get them so big like that?" As he danced closer to me with a Cosmopolitan cocktail in his hand, his pinky finger glistened under the light with the new ostentatiously flamboyant diamond ring that his new boy-toy had bought him to solidify their union. He told me to go over to her and ask. So I did just that. Being the best looking trans woman meant everything to me, so I mustered up the nerves and did just that.

Once I got up closer to her, she was like a towering Goddess looking down at me with adoringly big sisterly eyes. She pulled me off the dance floor and we went into the bathroom where a few of the older girls were at, sniffing some white powdery stuff up their noses with 20 dollar bills rolled up like straws, as they giggled while looking at themselves in the huge mirrors at the vanity tables and sink. It was there she formally introduced herself and proceeded to share all the inside scoop on the who's who doctors that can work magic on the cosmetic surgery table in order to transform the hottest trans babes on the scene. And that is how I met Eve. It was the early 90's and we were all just a couple of young Trans girls finding our way.

CHAPTER 6

HOT CHILD IN THE CITY

So we were on for tonight and I found the prettiest and daintiest number I had in my closet that screamed "cunt-tuna" after all the sexual exploits with Lionell the night before. I had to reclaim my body as a sacred temple for the future man of my dreams whoever he might be. The night is set just after I put on the finishing touches of my makeup, and tuck my lil peepee so that he doesn't find his way out uninvited. Once all done I gave myself a once over in the tall mirror at the door of my apartment. "Damn I look good," I thought as I closed the door behind me and headed to hail a taxi.

I got to the club a few minutes later. There was a long line out in front with all the B and C listers of the city's alternative wannabes waiting for the chance to get invited in. Eve is pretty popular, so I scoped out the line to see if I could see if she was waiting in it for me so we could use her

VIP status to get past the velvet ropes so diligently being manned by the security guards that everyone is trying to flirt with in hopes to win favor at the door. There she is . . . I yell "EVAH!" I yell again as everyone in the line looks my way. "YES!" I'm thinking to myself. "Darling" . . . as I was ready to turn it all the way up tonight under those incredible strobe lights that always make me feel like a movie star being chased by the paparazzi.

Eve finally sees me and waves her hand to me to let me know that we're cleared to bypass the line and head on inside. "Hey Eve, what's going down?" I asked in my usual rhetorical way just to bust it up with her as we began to ascend up those lengthy stairs to tonight's haven on the second floor from the entrance of the club. She began to tell me that there may be some drama tonight. She tells me that a girlfriend of hers is meeting her there at the club later that night. She then explains that she is traveling to the city from the suburbs on the R7 train and should arrive in an hour or so.

We then headed over to the bar to get our first of many many cocktails of the night and while nursing our drinks and searching the vast room for what will become our table and headquarter central for the night, Eve goes on to explain that her friend just found out that her boyfriend was cheating on her with some chick in the city, and she was coming to town to let the bitch know it was not going to go down like that.

With that in mind, I began to tell Eve more about the drama I got into the other night, with some guy I met a few weeks ago . . . and just as I go to get into the scenario, Eve's friend calls her from the other side of the dance floor . . . "Hey biotch what's good?" a short lil petite girl yelled as she headed over towards us.

Eve grabbed me by the arm to meet her halfway, to introduce me to her friend. With all that was happening so fast, in all the excitement of everyone dancing and all, I never even got the chance to get to tell her any part of what I had just gone through just the night before.

"Girl" . . . Eve started the introduction with just that single word. Eve swayed her hands toward me as if I was her newest creation and said to Angelique, "This is my friend Victoria." At that time in my life I had not had my name compartmentalized just yet, so everyone was calling me Victoria . . . as Eve then went on to introduce her friend to me as Angelique. Now at the moment I'm not putting anything together in light of all going on around us in the middle of the dance floor. Angelique and I smile at each other as Eve grabs our hands to joins her in a threesome dance set to the thumping drive of the house music banging in our ears. The night was feeling like a scene in some Queen of the damn movie or something as many of those on the dance floor were very gothly dressed in their vamp and blackish attire. Just as we got more and more into having a great girls time out on the dance floor, I looked over to the sidelines of the crowd watching on, and you would never believe, low and behold who walks through the parted crowd pulling on Angelique's hand, looking the epitome of utter distress. No one other than Lionell. He doesn't even notice that it is me on the other side of Eve, dancing as part of the threesome that's got all eyes on us on the dance floor. He's whispering something in Angelique's ear as he's pulling her off the dance floor.

Just as I try to reference to Eve, who's now dancing in a wicked frenzy . . . that her friend is being carried off the dance floor by the creep freak- bull, she looks over to me and shouts that "Ange" will be alright. And that the guy talking to her is her boyfriend. That's when she also chimes in to finish her story to me that we started just before she introduced me to her friend. "I'm so over him right now," she then shouted over the Madonna song now playing. "They're probably gone off to talk about the situation with him cheating on her with that chick." Just then I grasped the whole situation at hand now.

"SHIT," I'm thinking. "I'M THE GIRL." I signal over to Eve while she's still voguing to the song "Like a Prayer."

"What" Eve yells over to me as if she didn't understand what I just said the first time. "I am the girl that Angelique . . . AKA Angel's boyfriend was cheating on her with. "I am the girl she came down to confront." There's dead silence as the music comes to an end.

"Fuck! Victoria, what the hell are you talking about?" Eve pulls me off the dance floor.

Just barley off the dance floor I repeat, "Girl that's the guy that I was just going to tell you about," I said to her.

She said with fright in her face like I've never seen before on her, "Who LIONELL!"

"Yes bitch!" she quickly interrupted me and said, "Please tell me you did not get caught up in one of his sticky webs girl?" I looked at her across the table with the most pitiful expression I could muster up and told her that not only was I caught up in his nasty web, but also that we did the dirty deed.

"Oh MY GOD! Tell me you did not let that boy have you?" Eve asked, as if she already knew the answer. I looked around to make sure not to become a spectacle and went on to explain that it was something even worse. "What in the world could possibly be worse than that child?" she said.

"I did it to him," I squeamishly replied.

And with a sigh of relief in her eyes she said, "THAT's it?"

And I said, "Well yeah. Isn't that just the worst?" That is when she let me in on all the dirt about her dear friend Angel's boyfriend Lionell.

It seems that that was Lionell's M-O. His little thing he did seemingly all of the time. To have a girlfriend who lived so far out of the city limits, so he could have just the right amount of space to play. He loves to prey on the new Trannies on the scene in order to get them to slay him in bed. "What," I shouted out.

"Yeah gurl," Eve said and went on to explain that as much as Lionell looked so masculine and like a woman's dream guy, he was a straight up butch- queen. I really don't know what Angelique sees in him. Eve ended the story and looked back over to me as she ordered another cocktail at the bar. "And you miss thang'," she then said smirking as she lifted her drink up to take a nip. "Miss I'm so sweet and innocent. What in the world were you thinking being his new 'top model'?" I was tongue tied as she pointed to the entrance of the club where they were headed straight for us. "OMG!" I'm thinking as they get closer and closer and the disco light seemed to pulsate harder and harder upon their every step closer.

And as soon as Lionell got close enough to realize that I am with Eve and Angel, and I must have been there all along before pulling Angel off the floor to talk, he darts to the men's room. And that's when Eve lets Angel in on the whole thing. A few moments later, all I can see is Angel's face full of disgust as she storms towards me shouting, "He cheated on me with this thing?"

"Oh boy, it's about to go down," I'm now thinking. She's now going off on a tangent about how a decent girl can't have a good looking dude in the city without some wanna be thirsty transvestite thing trying to get him to fuck them behind his girl's back.

Signifying to me on the sidelines. "Well" . . . I told her that whatever she was thinking . . . it didn't go down like the way she had just explained. I further more assured her that it was not I, who was the dick hungry one in the brief encounter that her boyfriend and I had.

She stopped in all her antics and inquisitively, but reluctantly asked me what was I trying to imply about her boyfriend. That's when all eyes were on me as the crowd began to draw near when I told her that she needed to speak with her man and take whatever happened between us up with him. I then went on to advise her that if she was really concerned about just who fucked who last night, she should find Lionell and get the matter straight.

Gasping for air and obviously not getting enough of it, she headed straight for the men's room where Lionell was still hiding out. Within a flash of a beat it seems like they were back on the floor in front of Eve and I as if to confirm what all I just told her was a bold face lie.

"What!" he shouted towards me as she finished whispering in his ear. Lionell shouts . . . how he didn't fuck me last night. She interrupts his rampage as Eve and I look on, to hear Anel correct him by letting him know of my claims to have fucked him and not the other way around . . . as she shouted out, "She said she fucked you!"

And there right on the spot I witnessed the most award

winning Oscar performance of my life. There, as he threatened and stomped in a failed attempt to intimidate me. [To tell the truth I really believe he would have even laid hands on me if it was not for the fact that I'm sure he was afraid of what my cousin Milton would have done to him had word got back to him of all his shenanigans.] He was shouting and putting on a show for all as if he didn't even know who I was . . . only punching me outright there where I stood could have only made his sentiments more believable.

However, through all the chaos, I looked over to Angel and told her that I did not have to lie on my dick like that. That all that was needed for her to detect just who was speaking the truth, was to take him home tonight and examine the merchandise and she would truly find that I had been there.

Three hours later, back at my apartment, the telephone rang. It was Eve and Angel on a three- way call. With Angel crying and apologizing for the mayhem that transpired at the club earlier that night. It seemed that she had in fact took Lionell home to his place, stripped him down and yes, she, upon close inspection of his sore rear end, could clearly see that her lil hood dude was not what he put on to be. The nigga was a true bottom boy. And with all her "realness," he could not bring himself to tell her in all their 2 years together, just what it was that he loved so much about having a transsexual girlfriend . . . which was DICK!

And that was my introduction to my lifelong friend Angelique for now more than 23 years and counting.

CHAPTER 7

MAKING NIKKI JAMES

Now, to add on yet another complication to my story, my reminiscing could not be complete without the mention of 3 names to help you journey completely with me to this point in my life. And those names are Billi Necole Summers who, because I thought her last name Summers reminded me so much of the seventies television show . . . "The Bionic Woman" with the lead character's name being Jamie Summers, I affectionately dubbed Billie Necole as "Nikki James Summers."

About 21 years ago, when Nikki was just a budding lil transsexual tiny bopper from Topeka, Kansas, Angel had introduced us together that summer. Nikki James, being the friend that I mentioned earlier who started in the escort business with me accidentally.

This was about six months since the day Angel introduced me to her friend Nikki who was then named

Billi who came to Philadelphia from Topeka in order to attend a ball. I, at that time was just starting to blossom out more into the mainstream straight social scene when Angel approached me and said that she wanted to move into the city, and was in need of a place to live.

Although I had only a studio efficiency apartment, I opened up my doors to her if she could reach one condition. That was to pay half of the

$165 a month for rent. She obliged, giving me three months rent in advance payment as we moved her right in later that same day. Hence, when Nikki James came to Philly to visit Angel for the ball, her visit would be to our apartment in the city.

It must have been a recession that my hormone prescription business was shielding me from. Or just everyone I knew was looking to move in with me. Thus, my cousin Javont had also called me just a few days after Angel moved in, to ask if he too could stay with me in my small cramped one room studio apartment. I gave him the same conditions I had just given to Angel, and he was now living with us too, in a "threes-company" television show type of way. Which all worked out for me great, being that he was never really home because of his night job, and came home to sleep only three days a week. The other days of the week he would be out at one of the three girlfriends he was juggling around.

By this time I was always out of the apartment also, being entertained by all the businessmen and men of means who I would meet out on my day-to- day business of my prescription hormone racket. With both Javont's schedule and mine, the apartment was left to Angel most of the time . . . where she could entertain a host of her homosexual friends she had met on the gay ballroom scene.

However, little did I know it then, we all were being watched under the watchful eye of the building's somewhat, self-appointed watch dog . . . Ms. Catherine who lives on the top floor of our walkup brownstone apartment building. It seems that upon my first moving into the apartment just after I had left my parents home, there was a bit of a discrepancy when the telephone company came by one day when I wasn't all moved in yet and asked her if this was going to be the location to install the "Banggie Boy Productions" phone.

The phrase "Banggie Boy" then being a derogatory hood phrase for urban thug boys . . . However, Ms. Catherine took the word Banggie Boy . . . for BANGING BOY . . . which left much room in her mind to wonder just what her new neighbors had in mind for her respectable building in which she lived for over 20 years.

I think personally that if Ms. Catherine wasn't so damn nosy, and she wasn't so into trying to figure out what a Banggie Boy production was, and had just came right out and asked me and not jumping to conclusions that it had some sexual connotation of a boy-toy sex service, as I later came to find out she assumed. I could have had more fonder memories of our acquaintances to record in my memories of her back then.

I guess it was the fact that Angel had so many of her butch-queen homosexual friends running in and out of our place, with all the flaming antics that they gave amongst each other's company and all whenever I was out. Coupled with my cousin Javont's quest for the title of world's lover by way of using our center city apartment as his very own love lair in which to bed every woman he came across at his job. All made for a very interesting sound combination continuously resonating from our one room efficiency, in order to fuel Ms. Catherine's already warped imagination of just what my apartment was being used for. And with that being said, I could just imagine why my own string of rich white men who were then courting me for my affection became the last straw. With white men being my cup of tea, and me being theirs also . . . my dance card was full every night with all the love interest who flooded my door.

It would be because of this colorful array of characters parading in and out of my studio apartment, to leave a very bad taste in Ms. Catherine's mouth as she gladly reported all that she suspected to our landlord Mr. Katz. And no sooner than that, our free spirited nest all seemed to be fraying apart.

Angel and Lionell later got back together, with the deciding factor on their reattachment being that she move into his apartment with him, so she could better monitor his activity . . . not to mention . . . now that she was in the know of what he truly wanted . . . she could give him everything he desired at home without finding it elsewhere. My cousin Javont, actually found someone who could keep up to his sexual appetite and they moved in together in a new place they found, not too far from me.

Finally, there is peace. I have my apartment back to myself, so I thought. Although having two previous roommates contributing to the rent left me carefree to live in center city scot free, the peace of mind now that I felt by having the apartment back to myself again was priceless.

____

CHAPTER 8

FALSE ACCUSATIONS AND LIES

My new peace of mind was very short-lived after about 3 weeks of quiet time in the studio apartment alone, which was lovely to say the least.

However, just as I was beginning to gain full appreciation of my quiet space, one evening while I was sewing a new outfit together, the doorbell rang late one Thursday night. I'm wondering who could it be, as I was expecting no one at all at such a late hour.

After throwing on my robe and running barefoot through the hall and down the steps of my building, I pressed the intercom. "Hello." A familiar voice comes through the other side. "Hi, it's me, Nikki James," she says as I just remembered that a few days ago I received a letter in the mail from her telling me that she was planning to move here to Philadelphia. She seemed to have taken me up on my invitation of me helping her out if times ever got bad for her out there in the country. I guess she really bought into my whole motherly persona I tend to use with my hormone prescription pill side hustle. As I had helped her begin her transition without having to go through the whole therapy route of seeing a doctor and getting cleared for hormone medication, as I sent it to her through the mail in order to bypass her need to find a doctor for transitioning all the way out in a no man's land like Topeka, Kansas.

Whatever the case, my newly found space and private times were now coming to an abrupt ending, as our conversation ensued of her needing to stay with me until she found a place of her own. Although I now was back to having zero privacy, it wasn't in an unpleasant kind of way. Nikki James and I clicked well together. Both of us were educated and were very upwardly mobile and seeking out a better side of life than what living home with our parents offered. There was only one thing that bothered me about my new kin-mate. She smoked like a steamship spewing smoke on its last leg. To say that she smoked like a trucker would not have done my recollection justice. Thus, we agreed that she was to do all her smoking out on the fire escape of the building, just off to the side of my apartment. And with that, a perfect union was forged. Nikki James and I made a wonderful home together. We talked about our ambitions to go back to college. And even our hopes and dreams of marriage sometime after we had both had our sex changes. We seemed to compliment each other so well, I never even realized that my clientele for my hormone business had just about dwindled down to nothing, as a new doctor in town offered a great deal of service with castration which took just about all of my paying customers, and left me and Nikki James just about destitute.

Although I was really loving my new found friendship in Nikki James, I couldn't help but wonder from day to day what we were going to have to do in order to pay the rent and eat. To even make matters worse, in the middle of the afternoon one Sunday as Nikki James and I were just relaxing around the apartment, the phone began to ring. "Hello," I said at the same time hearing a voice come through the phone saying, "I know what you're up to."

I said hello again perhaps thinking that the person on the other end must have misdialed the number and had not realized it yet. But still, as I said, "Hello" again . . . still the same words came through the receiver as if my second address did not set him straight.

The man's voice persisted once more, this time adding more to his verbal assault. "I know just what you're up to and the cops are on to you. In the next few days you'll be hauled off to jail."

"Excuse me," I yelled through the phone, asking "who the hell is this?"

The voice said, "I'm your landlord, Mr. Katz and I know just what you're doing. It's a disgrace!"

Now in my own mind I'm trying to figure this shit out. I'm thinking . . . Then it comes to me . . . "Oh shit," I'm thinking. They must be on to my pill mill and all my counterfeit prescriptions that I've been passing off at the pharmacy up the street. "But how and what the hell does Mr. Katz care anything about that?" I asked myself.

Meanwhile, Nikki James is now right up under me trying to listen in on this mysterious call. I'm not selling narcotics. What the hell is it to the landlord?

As the many possibilities run through my mind as to

what Mr. Katz could possibly care of my selling hormones . . . He continued to rant and rage on about some atrocities of life and the degradation of society by filthy people such as myself. "Whoa . . . whoa," I yelled back into the phone. I'm thinking what the hell is this crazy man talking about? Still trying to keep my cool in order to see if we are on the same page with my assumptions that he's got to be talking about my counterfeit prescription script racket I had going on . . . I mean I was barely ever selling out of the building. I would usually go to meet all my clients in town or at the club.

How in the world did he get wind of what I was doing? Or perhaps the FBI had cued him in and one of my clients was a confidential informant or something. But who the hell would go through the extreme to go under cover as a tranny and grow breasts in order to bust a small time racket as the one I had going on? That in the past few weeks had dwindled down to nothing? Then it all came into focus as I listened in more at just what Mr. Katz was saying. "A PROSTITUTION RING!!!" I yelled as Nikki James looked on.

"And you've got five days to vacate the apartment or the police are coming in there to get you."

"PROSTITUTION," I yelled again, for that was the furthest from our minds. Although I dated alot, and we use to have more than our share of the building's visitors, prostitution never was a part of any of me or my visiting friends mind. Katz went on to let me know that he knew all about my sex services under the name of "Banggie Boy" productions. Which in his mind, by what has been reported by nosy Ms. Catherine upstairs, I had to have been running some type of whore house—sex for sale situation in his apartment building . . . OMFG!!! I'm thinking . . .

Then he tells me that I have 5 days to vacate the premises or I would be expelled by force by the Philadelphia Sheriff's office and taken into jail for running a prostitution ring. My being young and naive to landlord tenet laws, I took him at his word and hung up the phone in shock as to explain to Nikki James what Katz had just said to me. Immediately I stopped what little prescription business I had left, trying hard to not add fuel to the fire already brewing in whoever might know of my illegal activities and pass word on to the Feds, who were on my track with my black market activity.

It would be a long week as Nikki James and I tried to figure out just what in the hell we were going to do. She had spent all she had in relocating to Philadelphia and I was certainly not about to abandon ship and go crying home to my parents. Thus, saying goodbye to the beautiful new life I started as Padge-Victoria.

Finally it hit me. I had remembered back when I first announced to my mother about wanting to get a sex change for my 21st birthday and the beautiful girl in the picture I had shown her. That beautiful long-haired girl with the full lips and almond- shaped eyes was the ad for an escort service in downtown Philly. She had been featured in the Philadelphia City paper's back page section for adult entertainment and escorting . . . the bells and whistles began to chime in. If I am going to be blamed for an activity, or something I was not doing, or ever thought to have an involvement in . . . If it could make me a quick dollar and help us out of this quagmire . . . then why not live up to everything I've been so wrongfully accused of?

Thus, Nikki James and I being then down to our last

few bucks with the now halt of my hormone business, decided to pawn our last valuable possessions, which was a few gold rings Nikki had and a pair of earrings I had just received from one of my suitors. In all, we go about 85 dollars, just enough to place our own ad in the Philadelphia City paper for escort and adult entertainment and a couple of cans of baked beans for that evening's dinner.

We then went on with the planning of not necessarily a full fledged sexual adult service, but perhaps more like a private dancer service of some sort, as one of my favorite songs at that time was Private Dancer by Tina Turner.

Nikki James and I were very innocent to the world of the sex industry at the time. However, we knew of a few girls who were friends of ours that were anything but innocent to the concept of sex for sale. As they dubbed turning a "trick" to the more respectable term of "Dating" as the many of them would make light of the whole concept.

Whatever the case, Nikki James and I was sitting on prime real estate in our Center City location, almost a stone's throw from the thriving Philadelphia business district. Despite our place being a small studio unit, it was in the perfect location where a person could leave his office for his lunch hour, come over and be back at his office without missing a beat. All we needed to do was find our willing and able product for demand if it should pop off. Thus, we began our recruitment of girls to keep on call if business should take off.

It would be a few desolate days as we waited for the ad to be published and the publication to hit the streets. It was Sunday when I first got the call from Mr. Katz and it would take until that Thursday for us to see if the ad would generate any interest. Nikki James and I barely had anything to eat, as we put our all on the line in a longshot in order to get out of our looming situation. We were truly trusting in fate and were the first children of destiny as we went out on that limb with blind faith in our new mother.

We had gotten to the point of being so hungry that we had to muster up the strength to make tracks over to Milton's place to see if he would feed us as Mr. Katz's warning of eviction came so close. Prior to hearing from Mr. Katz, it seemed that Nikki James and I had worn out our welcome with my once most trusted cousin Milton . . . as now fate would have it, this very day, more hungry than ever. Nikki James and I would show up at his apartment unannounced. Milton had been planning a romantic dinner for yet another boy-toy he had met while out on South Street the night before and didn't take kindly to the two of us showing up without calling. It was a very hard hi . . . for the fried chicken that smelled so good frying up in the kitchen permeating through the door that had Nikki's and my mouth just salivating like two starved stray cats on the prowl. We would have sold our souls that night to sit at his table for dinner, but my one track mind cousin was not having any of it. We were interrupting his quest for some fresh ass.

Finally, Milton gave in to our pleas at the door for something, anything to eat in order to soothe our rumbling stomachs. He ordered us to wait at the door as he went to grab us two chicken wings for Nikki James and myself to eat on our way back home to our apartment far far away from any threat of our interference with the piece of hot ass he was having for dessert at the end of his dinner.

As we both took hold of our piece of chicken wings, Milton had no problem with scurrying us off so he could get back in the apartment with his friend. I was so hurt and pissed off at the fact that my "blood" was putting some dick and ass or whatever way the cookie crumbled in his corner before family in need. My last words to him before he shut the door in my face was a somber tone of "Milton, I ain't gonna be this broke forever. You mark my words and remember this day, for I will never forget it either, cousin."

And with those chicken wings we walked the nine city blocks back to our place. Nikki James and I made those pieces of chicken last like they were the last thing we would ever have to eat on earth.

Walking up the stairs to the apartment, with hunger pains still in our stomachs, loud moans and groans of emptiness in the pits of our bellies crying out, I turned the key to that lonely, empty apartment that we would soon have to say goodbye to by weeks' end. Thinking nothing more than how good that one damn piece of chicken wing tasted, with Nikki James thinking the same thing. Defeated and not knowing what tomorrow would bring, my resolve to call my father was looking like our only hope.

With all that we were facing, we were feeling more and more hopeless as the minutes transpired. We were hungry, and a hungry stomach could change even the strongest of resolve.

I knew I didn't want to hear it. My father's lecture on coming back home on his terms. Taking off my women's clothing I had grown so comfortable in. The dreadful haircut I'm sure he would demand and above all, my dreams for a sex change all going up in smoke. For me those things seemed so trivial when thinking about Nikki James' situation. It wasn't like I could take her home with me. What was I gonna do? I was becoming an almost mother figure to her. She was only 17-years- old and in my care for better or for worse, and it made me so sad to think of sending her back to Topeka, Kansas where no one understood her trans struggle to succeed in life.

The mood in the room was dark and gloomy. It was as if our very own Titanic ship was sinking and there was absolutely nothing we could do about it. I new just what I was going to have to do, although I couldn't dare speak the words to Nikki James. I had to place my pride aside and do what was good for not only myself, but for her wellbeing too.

As my body grew numb and the tears whelped in my eyes, I reached for the phone to dial home to my parents, but something was different in the dial tone. It was the dribbling tone to alert me that I had a voicemail waiting to be listened to. I put in my pass code in order to retrieve my message, hoping perhaps it was Milton who had somehow came to his senses and decided to tell me and Nikki James to come back over to his place for dinner. But to my utter surprise the telephone voicemail prompt alerted me that I had fifty-three messages waiting for me to listen to.

I'm thinking it must be some sort of glitch in the system, because why otherwise would I all of a sudden have so many unheard messages waiting for me in such a short timespan away from the phone? Nikki James looked over to me to ask what was I looking so puzzled about. And that's when I told her that the answering machine says I had so many messages.

Message one: "Hey Lalnoi, my name is Bill. I'm a professional businessman in town on business and I saw your ad in the paper.I've finished up business early today and had a few ours to spare for the evening, and could use a little company. Please call me back at the Four Seasons Hotel on the parkway. I'm in the penthouse, Suite 1530. Money is no object.

I sat there stuck for a moment as I went through each message in my voicemail bank. Each caller offering money for companionship. I was no more good to say the least. As I became frantic, Nikki James came back into the apartment from smoking her last cigarette out on the fire escape, she had desperately retrieved some of her old cigarette butts from the fire escape to combine together to make a whole new cigarette in order to smoke in her attempt to curb her hunger pains.

And that's when I told her of the news and all the messages of all the potential clients waiting for our response in order to book 'em. The only thing was, it was too short of notice to get any of our friends to meet up with the callers because we thought the ad would be coming out the next day, Thursday. However, because of the coming holiday, the publication put out the ad a day earlier, which seems to be no more perfect timing for us, but we had no workers available to work.

Finally frustrated that I couldn't get any one of the girls already accustomed to the escort business as of yet, Nikki James volunteered herself to do the job. Once again hunger trumped all, as we're not in our right frame of mind. Now Nikki James only being seventeen-years-old, technically still a minor in the state of Pennsylvania. Again my protective motherly instinct stepped in and advised against it. However, with eviction on the forefront anytime after tomorrow and the hunger pains in our stomachs now, we were in dire straights.

The cash above all else was calling our names and we

were ready to answer it with a resounding YES! We desperately needed the money for us to find a new place to live and get something for us to eat.

"I'll do it," I told Nikki James in a terrified and reluctant tone. "You're under age and it wouldn't be the right thing for me to allow you to do something like this. For one, if we got busted" I went on to explain, "not only a pandering charge could come of this, but I could go down for corrupting the morals of a minor too, along with any other gamut of charges we could get if this should go bad."

I was the adult in the situation. Not to mention that I was also the one who was a fully and well developed transsexual. A big ass, titts and a ten- inch fully functioning penis which seemed to be what all the calls were for. Thus, I took on the burden, and became The Madam's first worker.

CHAPTER 9

LOSING MY INNOCENCE

As we returned a few of the phone calls and booked about five out call engagements, we had no time to wonder or fear. Destiny was giving us a chance to prove just how bad we wanted to succeed in our mission to keep on our road to not only getting our sex changes, but also finding immediate relief from the most currently pressing issue. And that was to find a new home for us to continue on our journey. I dressed in this cheap black lace bell bottom number and wide sleeve cat suit and heels. I did my makeup heavy, almost as if I was trying to hide the frightened girl deep down inside of me, struggling so desperately to keep the promise I made to my father of succeeding no mater what. Nikki James and I set out the door on foot the eight blocks to the Four Seasons Hotel.

Walking the eight blocks in the dust of the early evening light, I felt on display for all to know just what I was about to do. It felt like I was selling my soul as I walked on hoping that no one knew that I was about to throw my goods up to the highest bidders. That walk to the hotel was the most terrifying thing to date that I ever had to do, for I was going against everything in me in order to do what I was prepared to do. Embarrassment was an understatement. However, I was determined to get the job done at whatever cost. The brilliant light of self preservation led the way like only she could, for I was no longer going to be that once innocent girl just searching in the dark for my way. After tonight I would be damaged goods. A woman with a price tag to be bought like an object.

I felt that every street corner I approached, the cars driving by, knew my intentions. The people on foot . . . faces all seemed in the know of all that my mind contained and the sacrifice I would be making tonight for some strange man whom I've never met, but only knew his voice. This indeed was the most humiliating thing I could ever do. And not because it was a situation of sex for sale, but mostly because up until that day I never had any thought of doing something that I absolutely didn't want to do . . . for a dollar.

We entered the grand hotel lobby which seemed like an infinity. I scurried straight for the elevators, hoping the concierge wouldn't stop me to ask any questions. "Come on elevator," I whispered underneath my breath as I looked over at Nikki James who was so calm and cool. Finally the elevator came and we were the only two to board. Up . . . Up . . . Up to the floor I was to give it all away.

Before we knew it the elevator came to a halt. We were now on the penthouse floor of the plush five star hotel. As we walked down the hall searching each shiny brass door tag for penthouse room 1530, my heart began to ferociously bang out of my chest.

Room 1510 . . . next room . . . 1520 . . . and just as we were quickly approaching room 1530, I turned to Nikki James and told her to wait further down the hall from the room in case we were walking into a police sting operation like the ones I use to see on the TV show COPS. I told her that if it was a sting operation I was walking into and were to get arrested, she should act as if she didn't know me if I was hauled off out of the room in handcuffs. Otherwise, she should stay close enough to the room so that once I was in, she could hear me scream if this Bill had turned out to be some sort of maniac looking to kill whoring trannies.

I knocked on the door, and by the time I went to knock again for the second time, the door opened up to a beautiful palatial suite with a very handsome well dressed businessman who seemed very relieved to see that I was indeed all that I described myself to be as this mystery woman named Laloni. He introduced himself to me as Michael and said that he had only used the name Bill because he wasn't even sure if he would really go through with such a meet and was 75% ready to not answer the door. That is, until he looked through the peep-hole and saw my face. He seemed to be a very refined gentleman of wealth and good breeding. My mind began to relax more and more as he went out of his way to make me feel as comfortable as he could. It was such a relief to me that Michael turned out to be nothing like my thoughts of a man who would call an escort service to find companionship in a call girl.

We talked for a few more moments as he offered me a

cold glass of orange juice and asked if I would like to have some of the shrimp cocktail he had just ordered from room service. As hungry as I was, I had to fight the ravenous reaction in me to eat all that was there on the nicely set table with a very crisp white linen tablecloth and the beautiful flower arrangement of fresh cut assorted of pastel roses. He then walked over to the table as I was gorging on the shrimp to hand me a banking envelope from Capital bank. I looked into the envelope, trying hard to act as if the money it contained did not mean a fraction of the importance to life or death for the woman I had become.

Little did I know, the envelope I was holding in my hands had enough money to fill Nikki James' and my stomachs for months if needed. The money was in crisp fifty dollar increments. Brand new bills that he must had just gotten from the bank just for his rendezvous with me. He seemed just as new to this sort of thing as I was, as he very bashfully advised me that he would be very fast, and not come close to using up my hourly rate. I assure him that the rate was not my concern, for if it was, I thought to myself, I would be here for hours with what he just paid me. In a relieved tone I told him that he need not rush and that I would do whatever he liked except for penetration. I figured in my head that a blow job with a condom couldn't have been so bad. After all I would be technically sucking on a rubber, and who wouldn't do that for a quick come up if one was in my shoes. Not to mention, Michael looked and seemed like a man I would have loved to had met on a much more personal level.

As he came closer he held me in such a warm embrace. It felt as if we were longtime lovers meeting back up again after a long separation. His holding me surprisingly aroused me much more than I ever thought some scenario like this could ever do. I pulled out a condom and began to lower myself down to my knees. As he began to undress, taking off his suit jacket and unbuttoning down his shirt, I unzipped his pans to softly grab into his underwear that was holding in it the smallest penis I had ever seen. With his pants puddled down at his ankles and his half unbuttoned shirt exposing his very sexy hairy chest . . . in that very moment I understood why such a handsome rich man as Michael would ever consider to call on a service like the one we were offering. Having such a small penis led him to have such high anxiety that he felt as though he could never fulfill a woman's desire in a normal relationship. Thus, why ever even try. He was the type of man to submerge himself into work and business to amass millions of dollars and would call escort services every now and then in order to release some sexual tension whenever the time presented itself. I did not know him and nor did he know or care about me on a personal level, so who cared if he had the smallest dick in the world. He'd walk away from this room once our encounter was over, with his pride still in tact to take on another business venture with no one in his world to ever know his BIG little secret between his sexy hairy thighs but some call girl. And who cares what a call girl thinks . . . right?

Well no sooner than I could put the condom on him, and try as hard as I might to grip on to such a small wonder with my hands all oiled up, I couldn't believe it. No sooner than we just began we were finished. Michael had came into the condom as I was attempting to roll and secure it around his ball in order to fill up the condom and anchor it to something. It was not only the quickest, but the first grand I had ever made in my life I was thinking as a knock came to the door. It was Nikki James making sure I was all right as Michael had screamed to the top of his lungs as he was ejaculating. As Michael went to look out the peephole, he led a dripping trail from his still wet penis. It's all right, I told him. It was only my friend at the door to make sure you were not killing me and we smiled.

I told her that everything was fine and that we were just finishing up, and to wait at the door and I would be with her in a moment, as I could see she was at a loss because it was only just moments since I had just entered the room and already we were finished. He asked why didn't I let him know that I had such another pretty girl with me, and how it was a poor shame to have left her waiting out in the corridor as we had all the fun inside. He then gave me another five hundred dollars for her as a tip for her time waiting in the hall as he jokingly added that it was so nice of her to act as our security detail in case anything was to go wrong. As I exited the suite, he assured me that he did truly enjoy my companionship and asked was it okay if he called on me again the next time he was in town. Michael, through the years, would become one of my number one clients as my escort business grew. I never saw him again personally, but throughout the years he and I . . . I would like to say became very good acquaintances.

I walked out the door to meet Nikki James at the elevator just itching to see my face in order to read it as a successful venture or failure, as she asked me in a defeated tone, "What? He didn't want to do it?"

I said to her with a big grin. "Actually, yes," and went on to explain to her during the ride down in the elevator, that we had finished within minutes of my arrival in the room. I showed her all the money that we had made and explained that he even gave her a five hundred dollar tip as we went screaming out of the hotel lobby to hail a cab into our destinies with a whole new world just ahead of us. That night we had a steak and lobster dinner and went back to the apartment to book several more overnight appointments. We had generated about six thousand dollars in all by the morning at sunrise. Our lives would be forever changed from then on. I went out that morning to find us a beautiful two bedroom apartment in Old City Philadelphia, and was all moved out of my studio apartment with still a day to spare. Thank you Mr. Katz for surely changing the trajectory of my life for the good.

And that is the story of how I became The Madam. By the next day I had rallied up all my staff of girls for that day we all planned to begin the whole enterprise anyway. And Nikki James and I were already secretly ahead of the game as I had been my initial first escort of my business. Nikki James joined me in the day- to-day running of the successful business, as we had more than enough girls to work, that I never had to put myself on the front line again.

I DO IT FOR MY BITCHES THAT BE BALLIN
DAM MADAM
THE SINGLE
MADAM
OLD SCHOOL MEET NEW
MADAM MUSTAFA

CHAPTER 10

TRANSITIONING FROM MADAM TO BLACK MARKET MEDICINE

Many years would pass with the success of the new business I called LACE Entertainment after that movie I saw as a kid many years ago about 4 rich schoolgirls away in boarding school. One of them had become pregnant, and all being such close friends, they chose to hide her pregnancy from the school masters and their families. When she delivered the child, they named her Lillian and placed her up for adoption. The child later grew up to become a very beautiful and sexy woman who became a call-girl if I'm not mistaken, who discovers the truth about her biological mother amongst the four now prominent society women, and began to reek havoc on their lives in order for them to reveal just which one of them was her true mother. It was a fascinating movie and the storyline was riveting. Hence, the movie resonated through me for so many years after seeing it. I later took on the street name of Lillian. So there you have it. No . . . Lillian was not some random name I just made up from thin air in order to avoid law enforcement while partaking in my black market activity as the prosecutors in my trial has implied.

The name Lillian was a name I had taken on long before I started pumping people with my silicone business. It was a name that was very sentimental and dear to me in which a huge pool of people knew me by. Therefore, Miss Assistant District Attorney Bridget Kirn and Mr. Carlos Vega, you were wrong about me sneaking and hiding under false names and personas to allude being discovered for the doing of any malicious deeds.

So, many many years after operating Lace Entertainment, I became finally happy to move on to a more, what I felt noble profession beyond facilitating an avenue for men to cheat on their wives and significant others. There were three main reasons that were ushering me out of the escort services and into the black market silicone business. One would be because of a woman named Diana. She was my advertising rap for the Trentonian Daily newspaper who handled my Princeton, New Jersey and surrounding south Jersey area advertising and throughout. Through the years of advertising, she and I became rather fond of one another. She would get me in on all my advertising sales the paper was about to run for a discounted rate due to all the years of patronage I gave her. She would even do me the much needed extra favor of keeping my ads running even when I had fallen far behind my deadlines due to being out of the country on vacations or business.

To say the very least she and I grew to enjoy the short

brief moments on the phone together and the days I was in the area picking up my daily cash payouts from my many services I had running, I would always find a moment to drop in to pay Diana a visit in her office.

This relationship with Diana and I grew as she went off to get married and expand her family as she would love to show me all the many pictures of her children as they grew. That is until a few years later, just after her seventh year wedding anniversary. Diana called me up on my service phone and not my private phone as she would usually do in order to check in on me.

During this phone call I could hear that she was hurting as she asked me in a heartfelt sorrowful voice the question that I wished I could have brushed off by just saying, "That she was being overly suspicious." But this was about a woman's husband that I looked at as a friend.

They now had three and a half children and I guess he was having a case of the 7 year itch. Diana, being my sales rep and all, practically knew all the service numbers I advertised by heart, as she was the one who had to renew the accounts daily. Thus, when one of those numbers came out on one of her husband's phone bill calling log records, Diana was devastated because she knew this could only mean one thing. Her husband had to be fucking around on her with an escort. And if not my services per se, yet . . . he sure was interested, as the same number kept showing up on his cellular phone bill until finally Diana gave me a picture of her husband to check against my surveillance camera footage of my Princeton service, as that was the closest one to where he worked in order to see if I recognized anyone who looked like him.

Dead on, there was no mistaking it. On camera 8,

filmed during a very late night work evening, I saw her husband on film giving a blow job to Tatianna while on the receiving end of an anal episode with another worker of mine named Alexus Ward. Who had become a favorite amongst the locals in the area because of her massive size penis countered with a beautiful face.

It seemed that Diana's husband had been visiting my service daily on his breaks and late evenings from the construction crew he was working with just outside of the Quaker Bridge Mall, just up the road from the Red Roof Inn on Route One.

It was a poor shame and I truly felt Diana's pain as I had to be the bearer of such bad news, as I watched the glassiness of her eyes just tearing up before me. It broke my heart to have to tell Diana, yes indeed her husband was seeing not only one, but two women of my service that were transsexual. Ironically, it would also be that these escorts were the very women that Diana had helped me craft very interesting ads for . . . SMH.

It really hurt me to know that because of me, she would forever more have a crack in her marriage's foundation. From that point on, my soul couldn't continue on with the business full throttle. After 11 years of making the quickest money on average of thirty thousand dollars a week, I wanted to be done with it. However, I didn't know how I would segway myself and lifestyle out of the adult business.

The other reason was the combination of my recent deceased father and my new love Nikolaus. As for my father's death, being involved in such activities that he would have deemed an abomination, tormented me to the core of my gut to think that he was now able to know the true origins of my wealth from some supernatural view in heaven or such. That he could witness the true scope of just what all my life contained in order to live this life I've grown into. It was just this feeling of disappointing him any further than what I had already did in life with my transitioning that ate at my conscious. The last thing I now wanted to do in his death was let him see my true self as no more than a panderer of whores and prostitutes as I'm sure he would have called it. I wanted out.

Now, where Nikolaus becomes involved with my decision to leave the "Family Business" was because I felt that the Lord had blessed me with something so pure and sacred in him and our fresh new relationship. Nik was something pure and clean compared to all that I had experienced and witnessed in my road through the adult industry.

Nikolaus, being untainted by the world, seemed to offer up a new chance for me to see the world through the innocence of his eyes again. His mother had gone out of her way all of his life, with home schooling and all in order to shelter him from what it seemed was the very person he would fall in love with and lose his virginity to, me. His mother's aim was to shelter her only child from the wickedness of the world and the wilderness of sin only described better in the biblical story of Sodom and Gomorrah. How oh how, could then Fate's twisted humor bring this innocent to cross paths one day in a supermarket as a sales boy . . . with such a heretic as the Black Madam.

He deserved better. He deserved someone just as innocent and pure as he was, but I just didn't know how to give him up, nor did he ever want to hear of it. So bit by bit service by service and girl by girl I began to downsize my life in the adult industry until all I had was a few girls running.

I can remember driving with Nik to his new job at the flower shop in our town of Narberth, Pennsylvania. It was a very beautiful sunny Saturday morning to be exact. I can still remember it like it was yesterday. The smell of the freshly mowed lawns with the fresh cut grass in the air. A total picture of pure innocence in the suburbs. That is until that goddamn phone rang as we were just a few blocks away from his job. All would have been well if that fucking phone had not rang until he was dropped off. Then I could have easily answered the phone and resume business as usual. The phone range and rang as the caller wanted to give me his perverted request I'm sure.

I knew it was "him." With that particular ringtone it was always going to be him. It couldn't have been anyone else but some disgusting client on such a wonderful day as that day looking to spoil my pure serenity that Nik and I were enjoying as we listened to the soft sounds of classical music filtering through the car's radio speakers.

Damn it, I need the money and it would be unfair to not catch every dollar in the air, if not for me, but for the few girls I had still on call who were depending on me for their survival.

I answered the phone. "Yeah." It was him alright. Some sex-feen hungry guy just waiting to suck some tranny dick for breakfast. I spilled out the description of the girls on call and proceeded to answer his perverted questions. Like what size was her penis, and if it could get hard or not. And finally whether or not she could ejaculate if she was still on hormone therapy.

I quickly whisked him off the phone with a bar- raid of

all the answers I've learned to give through the years that would insure his arrival.

I kissed Nik goodbye as I jumped into the driver's seat of the car to take over. I would now have the car to myself until he got off from work. With the phone still in my hand, damn . . . I spoiled a beautiful serene morning with the antics of some horny man's delight. I was finally through with it, come what may I thought to myself.

As I drove home, frustrated with tears in my eyes, I prayed to God to please deliver me from this mess. I wanted out of the "Family Business," but with a way to still survive. Just to still afford to pay my rent for the apartment and keep the note up on my car. I was sure that Nik and I could make ends meet. God just make a way.

CHAPTER 11

THE TRANSITION OF A MADAM

Although Nikolaus and I were deeply in love, I couldn't help but realize the looming fact that we could not live on love alone. As I drove up the country road just a few blocks down towards our apartment, my personal phone began to ring. It had to be either my sister Nicole or one of my close friends like Angel. They were the only two people who would call me at such an early hour on a Saturday morning.

Ring . . . Ring . . . Ring . . . Ring. It's Angel. "Hey girl, what's up cunt," she said through the phone in her 'I'm so happy kind of tinker bell voice."

"Oh nothing," I said back to her. Just dropping Nik off at his new job.

"What . . . was y'all arguing or something?" She could definitely tell I was already agitated at such an early hour of the day.

"No," I replied. "Why you say that?"

"Just something in your voice," she replied back.

And that is when I finally unleashed all of the frustration that I had pent up inside of me over the phone to her.

She must have been the "angel" that I had just asked God to send me. I expressed all that I was feeling about the life I was living and that I was to the point of realizing all that I was blessed to be able to accomplish surgery wise with my transformation throughout the years of dealing in the "Family Business."

I had accomplished all my goals and now had no true valid reason in just why I should continue on my life with the perversion of having to deal with the men that would call such a service as the one I had been running for all these years. I explained to her that I could very well go on to living a good life with Nik as a full woman and be truly happy for once. Angel had never heard me complain about making a dollar in all our years of knowing each other, so her ears were all mine as I proceeded to explain to her of my feelings for Nikolaus deserving so much more than a girlfriend who ran a whore house.

And that's when once again my destiny took on a new turn in life. She said, "Padgie, why don't you go back into body sculpting work with the silicone business that you tried to do back in the mid- nineties?"

Back then in 1995 Angel and a few other of my friends let me try out my hand on body sculpting in order to save them all from having to travel back and forth to New York City, where the prime sculptors were. At that time I had gotten under the wing of one of the best sculptors in the business, as she took on a liking to me from all the times I visited her to get my own body done. She taught me everything she knew and would sell me the silicone product at a nice discount. Angel and many of her friends became my willing guinea pigs. As I took Angel from a modest looking "around-the-way" kinda looking girl to the point of a car stopping bombshell with the new body I gave her. She was my walking billboard for all to see, and boy did they see her. She could never go anywhere without causing massive commotion with her beautiful hourglass shape figure and boodilicous ass.

If my memory serves me correctly, the woman who taught me how to do body sculpting and all its important tips . . . I remember her telling me that she wanted to teach me for just the reason I was now crying to Angel that very day. "For if ever the time came that I no longer wanted to run an escort service" . . . for she knew deep down in my heart, I was not a girl who cared to be involved in that type of work, but felt somewhat trapped in the underworld of flesh that I created. Angel, now began to pitch me in hard core. Reminding me that she's always getting complimented on her body everywhere she goes. She also went on to tell me of how just yesterday a few exotic dancers down at the Candy Shop on South Street, noticed her awesome bodywork while she was trying on some new dance outfits and ballroom attire. She assured me that if I was to get back into the business of body sculpting, I could really do well for myself if I was to be committed to it.

Thirteen years ago by this time, when I first learned the technique of sculpting, I was too afraid of blood and possibly contracting HIV via a needle accidentally pricking myself, if one of my clients should be sick. Being that most seeking silicone bodywork back then were in "The LIFE" and had a very risque lifestyle in the sex industry where HIV was then running rampant. But now, however, the demand for body sculpting has bled into the mainstream, with everyone wanting a bigger ass. Times were different and just about now, anything was a better step up from what I was doing with the "Family Business" and all.

I went home that day and pulled out a few old supplies that John once gave me on my first attempt to start up the silicone business. I'd called him up to see if he would be able to get me new stock. He more than obliged to helping me, as this meant there would now be reason for him to come by the apartment that he helped me acquire in order which to try to bed me, after mom met Poppa and we left our home in Wynnfield Heights to go our separate ways as Poppa courted mom for marriage. However, what John didn't know was that I was now madly in love with another, and just wanted him for one reason and one reason alone. That was for supplies and for him to reacquaint me with the technique of aspirating a needle for injection.

He set up to meet with me on a Thursday, as that was his only day off from his ambulatory clinic in Springfield, Pennsylvania. It use to be the day he would always want to meet me many years ago during our affair. Thursday came, and Nik was once again at his job.

Ding Dong. Just like clock work the doctor was on time for his house call. I'm sure John's wife, Toni would think he was running errands after dropping their youngest son, Brian off at softball practice. SMH . . . for some reason Jewish professional men love them a piece of Madam.

I had to once again straddle the thin line between drawing John in in order to do my bidding well, and not going too far to the point of betraying my heart with

Nikolaus. But that would be easy though, as I would always play the "depressed and lonely damsel in distress," keeping him off of me for feelings of guilt that he was being a "shmuck," an old Jewish phrase for a sexual creep of some sort. It was a term he would use in our on again off again extramarital affair we had been carrying on since I was 23 years old back in the nineties. It was a relationship that was very prosperous for me as John would give anything when he became inflamed with his passion to calm his loins. In our then 13 year friendship at this time, he had surly spent over a few million dollars on me in his endless courtship of my sexual favor. Finally, I explained to him what it was that I needed, and he had no problem giving it all to me. Lidocaine, needles, sedatives and silicone. Thus, I was now in business and away from the dreadful "Family Business" that I had now grown to loathe.

PART II

MEETING DR. JOHN MANCUSO A/K/A "JOHN"

It was about 7:58 p.m. on Halloween night, October 31, 1993. The apartment in Old City that Nikki James and I originally moved into in our haste to leave my previous landlord Mr. Katz's property was very short-lived. It lasted about a good month. The business of transsexual escorts had turned out to be a very lucrative cash cow and business was just too much for our quiet apartment looking over the historic district of Old City. Attracting a lot of attention due to high traffic of business and the buzzing of our doorbell at all hours of the day and night, as this apartment quickly became our first in call location.

Things in fact at this apartment had gotten so busy that it brought on some frustration between Nikki James and I as to who would be the one to keep the location in order to receive guests, and who would man the phone in order to do the booking of the girls between them seeing clients. Things were just so hectic from the instant success of the business that I had to opt to seek out yet another business apartment separate from our living space. 1329 Lumbard Street was a perfect fit for me, as money spoke volumes to the realtor considering that I had no credit history established just yet, but had all the on hand cash needed for my soon to be new landlord who was a cash hungry dealing type.

As a matter of fact, if my memory serves me correctly, he loved money so much that he would even go as far as to photocopy all my down payment cash as my deposit receipt for our new ultra modern luxury loft apartment. Which he said was my receipt for "sealing- the-deal." Move in day would be the next payment of the remaining $4,000 of the balance I owed. It was Halloween afternoon once everything was moved in from all the various deliveries by places I had been out shopping for furniture and home goods from. As the last delivery came in, our brand new antique French provincial living room set, I was drained, and had to take a moment in order to catch my breath. The phone had been ringing off the hook all day with all the deliveries and clients all wanting to know just where we were now located.

Once everything was all set up in place and I was just putting on some girly finishing touches to the layout, a call came in—transferred to our new business phone line. It turned out to be a professional man about 33-years-old wanting to try a falacio session with a well endowed beautiful transsexual woman that appeared to be as young looking as possible. As it turned out, I had the perfect girl for the job. It would be my distant cousin who was also transsexual, the Ms. Renee Karan, mother of the House of Karan on the gay ballroom scene.

Renee was a beautiful transsexual, and was known to be Philly's finest in "Fem-queen" status as she had a strong and striking resemblance to R&B singer Toni Braxton. Renee had a face like a babydoll and a body of a blossoming teenage girl with perky tits with nipples shaped like the perfect flat headed baby bottle nipple. The men loved her as she was what many would call unclockably passible (momma couldn't tell/poppa couldn't tell) that she had a dick hiding under her school girl cheerleader's outfits. I billed her to this new client as a fifteen year old school girl from Hawaii named Mikalah for $700 an hour which included his fantasy request. He wanted to give head and end his encounter with his receiving "Greek" which in layman's terms meant (anal) from who would—in reality be a young boy serving him the goods.

The appointment was set, and I went back to preparing my new business setup and contacting all my workforce in order to give them our new location of operations. It was a lengthy process that would take a few hours as the time seemed to pass in a flash of an eye, as the sun was setting quickly in the backdrop of the ceiling to floor and wall to wall gigantic windows overlooking the city. It was a Halloween night and I really wanted to get back home in order that I and Nikki James got dressed up for the big annual masked ball that our city held in the posh Grand Hotel, A-Top the Bellvue Stratford. I was to be the beautiful Marie Antoinette and Nikki James was to go as Cinderella. As I looked back at the setup, I could not help but notice just how swiftly life had made a turnaround for Nikki and I. For just a few months ago we were on the verge of becoming homeless. But we were now gonna be alright, as I shut off the light in order to leave. Just as I flicked the switch for the last lights on in the bar area setup, the business phone rang, and not wanting to miss a beat, I ran back to my office to answer it.

It was the door intercom system that was linked to our new phone system with a client down in the lobby for an appointment that he said he set up earlier with Mikalah. "Oh shit," I thought, as I had just remembered that I'd forgot to call Renee to set her up. As I buzzed the man in, I hurried in order to call Renee so that she could come right over for the "date," and I could get home in order to get ready. The knock was already at the door the moment I had hung up with Renee. I now had to stall him as she rushed over in a taxi as soon as possible.

Time was not being kind to me at the moment. It seemed that I was going to be late for the ball tonight if Renee had not come through the door in the next minute or two. However, after trying to do my best to stall the client, he and I got to talking as I wondered just what the hell was taking her so long. To relax the moment as we both sat there waiting for the intercom to ring, signaling that I would then have the client head up to his room, as Renee would need to get herself ready in the downstairs powder room, I served him a glass or two of wine at the bar setup. Still no ringing of the door. As he and I talked a little more, he introduced himself to me as John, as we chatted up in order to fill the emptiness of waiting. He began to talk about his profession, where I learned that he was a doctor and immediately my interest was peaked, and my own guard began to drop as I shared a glass of wine with him. I had always fantasized about being the wife of a doctor during my transition. I had heard of many girls having a "sugar-daddy" that was a physician and living happily ever after. Needless to say, from that moment on I would welcome all of the "Doctor's" advances towards me. Finally he asked if I was also a transsexual, and if so, how he would love to just hang out with me instead. I agreed with him as I told him that yes, I was indeed a transsexual also, and let's just say I paid Renee off when she finally arrived for her troubles and her taxi because this one was all mine.

We did much more talking than anything that night as I phoned home to let Nikki James know to go to the Masked Ball without me. John seemed extremely interested in me on a more personal level than the quick encounter he originally set up for. Before you knew it, it was time for him to leave and we exchanged personal contact info.

Two days later he phoned me and asked me out on our first of many many dates. Our first date was up in the Quaint district of the Chestnut Hill section of the city near the hospital where he was working as a resident surgeon for gastroenterology. It was a beautiful park where we walked, as he held my hand and told me how much he really enjoyed my company. We later went to dinner at a restaurant in Mannyunk Hills where he introduced me to the Mayor of Philadelphia at the time, and we later went by his apartment near the hospital, where he invited me in as he grabbed his lab coat for his shift overnight on call. There, in his living room and all the way into his bed we had our first sexual encounter, where he would ferociously suck on my penis like a seasoned pro. Here I was in yet another situation where as the dude wanted me to be this super dominant transwoman that I just was not. Just like Lionell, it turned me off. The thought of a man wanting to do these things, or should I say wanting me to do these things to him. But I took it as par for the course and gave him what he was looking for, as I had all plans of making this upwardly mobile doctor my husband. As I began to give him more and more of the thing he seemed to live for, he would take my dick so far down his throat that I could feel the inner working of his respiratory system just above the entrance to his upper chest cavity. "Damn, this doctor really knows what he's doing," I said to myself as I felt sensations I'd never had before.

The lining of his throat had felt so tight, as if I was inside the virgin pussy of a fresh little school girl trying her best to act grown. "Take that ... Take that," I would tell him, as I became *not* intoxicated by the actual act, but the thought of me becoming this Jewish man's black beauty of a wife. The Synagogue in which John belonged to would have to get ready, because it was indeed going to be a new sheriff in town that toted a very big gun. Things got to be so intense that there was even a few times that John had passed out as asphyxiation set in when his gag reflexes collapsed and locked on my dick. I got so scared that I would kill the poor man before I could get him to the altar the way he loved to take me so deep down into his tight pink esophagus, his fauces and pharynx juiced my overgrown clitoris like the sap getting sucked out of a tree by a suckubuss. The strong outer expanded part of his tubular corolla controlled me to my ultimate ejaculation, spewing like a slingshot, releasing its load straight down his neck. WOW . . . that doctor has a good head on his shoulders. Goddamn!

Our dating would last all the way through to my 23rd birthday where he brought me a beautiful diamond encrusted necklace he had saw me eyeing out on one of our dates (Harry Wiston). It was a forty-five thousand dollar piece with my topaz birthstone in the center of all those diamonds with matching earrings. He would also end the evening with us out on a yacht he had chartered with its private chef cooking up all the seafood I could ask for as we sipped on champagne floating along the shore of the Delaware River just off the pier of the Charter House restaurant.

John and I began to be inseparable as he would call me many times of the day and pick me up to take me on day trips all over the city. I was definitely falling for him for sure, as he had already fallen hard for me.

The questions about my running an escort service came up a time or two, as I assured him it was just something I was experimenting with, as he also assured me that I would forever be all he needed. As I told him I would be willing to pull the plug on the service the moment I received a little blue and white box from Tiffany's containing the diamond ring that would solidify our bond. We began to meet what seemed like every night for dinner and hot romantic sex between his busy work schedule at the hospital. I would travel up to Chestnut Hill by train to a room he would leave reserved for me at the Chestnut Hill Hotel just across the street from the hospital he worked at. It was a beautiful blossoming of a great love affair, so I innocently and naively thought. I figured I could forget how I met him through the connection of an escort service for transsexuals, if he could do the same. It was a great match as we complimented each other so well. We would spend many late night hours on the telephone like two adolescent school kids in love, as he would work throughout the night at the hospital and opened up more and more to me about his life and him finally feeling like he had found true love in me. Yes, I was in it too for the long haul, as true love began to take hold of me like I never knew. I had fallen head over heels for John as he made me feel so secure, safe, and loved, as it did not matter to him that I was transsexual. With him, my past did not matter. It was only what was standing there in front of him now as he would put it . . . and that was a beautiful love he had long desired. I loved every moment with John, and when we were not together, I loved every moment that the clock would tick closer to the moment when we would be back in each other's presence.

That is until one night before what would go down in history as my worse Christmas and holiday season to date, as he and I sat on the phone conversing about our future together and all our plans of being married. I suddenly heard a woman's voice in the background asking him who was he talking to, and if he was cheating on her, how she would kill him. As she said, "I swear to God I'll kill you John."

John told me he had to call me back, as I stood in suspense till the following morning when he called me from the hospital asking to meet with me, noticeably shaken up declaring his love for me and telling me that he had sure hoped I had meant all the things I told him of my loving him. Later that day, that's when he revealed to me that he was already indeed a married man. Toni was a girl that he had dated through medical school, but didn't really love her deeply like the love we had felt. She was a nurse that he was just wasting time with, who had trapped him by getting pregnant. So he did the right thing in order to honor his family and hers by marrying her. My heart was sinking fast as I could not contain my emotions that I was not his one and only. He went on to explain that he had two sons, Steven and Ryan. Thus, he was staying with her only for the boys sake, but now that he had finally found true love in what we had, he was ready to leave it all to be with me.

I was now in shock . . . I mean a Jewish doctor for a husband, as I would be the "Black-Jewish wife." . . . Yes, but little Jewish step children were not in my plans for a future. However, as I had truly grown to love John, I was willing to take him any way he came.

Toni was not having it. For surely not going to let John go that easy as she threatened to (OUT) John to all his associates and colleagues and high society friends that John had fallen in love with a transsexual and was planning to leave his wife and children for a chick with a dick.

John was scared out of his wits at the revelation of Toni's plans to (OUT) him and told me it would be the ruin of him if she did what she said, and that he could not follow through with our plans. Toni and the boys, he could live without in a life with me, but the hospital and his profession defined who he was as a man and he could not see himself surviving such a social and professional scandal.

We would play a tug of war for the next few months, leaving me emotionally devastated at the end with my picture of me as Mrs. Doctor John Mancuso . . . The doctor's wife burning down in flames hotter than that of the ferocious passion in which John loved to eat the gun. John would continue to try to see me as he placed Toni on a high prescription of valium, leaving her to sleep most of the days away, which would give him ample time in the rendezvous he would plan for us to get away. Now it was seeming as if John wanted his cake and to eat it too.

I began to purposely leave evidence of my being there for his wife to find. As of now she hadn't fully won the war. Lipstick on his collar, on top of his balding head, just where she could see it, but he could not. I even left a pair of saliva dripping soaked panties in the passenger side of his car from John's insatiable appetite for what he would call his midday "tongue- twizzlers." However, I just called it "giving me head in the passenger seat of his car" right in the parking lot of the hospital he was working. He would ask me to meet him there for his lunch break each day, and boy he sure did enjoy his lunch break of "Cock-Sandwiches," as he would exit the car, fixing his tie enraptured beyond belief after performing oral every day for lunch.

It was a situation however that couldn't go on much longer. I finally cut it off when Toni threatened to kill herself. And in the mix of what John had called "pathetic make-up sex with her . . . boring . . ." they conceived their third son Brian. I began to feel that John was just using me now to get his sexual kick off of "Cock-Sandwiches" without paying the bill. Game over!

We went our separate ways. However, I have to admit I was very hurt because of the way he handled himself and felt he was no more than a trick anyway. Toni deserved more, and I was glad to be free of him for I deserved more also.

A few years would pass of no contact between he and I. He and Toni would rise in his profession and become one of the top GI surgeons in the country, and I began my ascension in my own right of becoming the Society Hill Madam.

Building my escort services in Old City, Washington Square, Rittenhouse Square, Penn's Landing waterfront area, Society Hill and the Art Museum area sections of Philadelphia with central command station from my home in Society Hill. John was very much so, a memory in the distant past as I began to blossom into more and more of the woman I had always dreamt to become as no longer a pretty transsexual girl, but indeed a business savvy and beautiful woman of my own means. I had indeed transformed into a transwoman who could pass as a genetic female, thus, I was no longer dealing with men who only desired me for quick tranny encounters, but real men who were seeking me out as potential wife material.

After all, I had become a lovely, ambitious and successful woman as I cornered the market on the transsexual escort service business and now was beginning to cross over into the market of employing straight females and even men to work for me. I had six services running all simultaneously and reeling in the cash at all angles.

One of the places was a gorgeous high end 5 bedroom townhouse at the point of the prestigious Locust Square at 20th and Locust Street. At that time I had a transsexual working for me and managing that location by the name of Alexus Ward. One morning while I was there dropping by for my daily inspections of the place and to pick up the cash box from the overnight profit, I walked into one of the rooms in which Alexus was servicing a client, which was not unusual, as the whore business was never ending. As I walked into the room, I found no one other than good old Dr. Mancuso sprawled across the bed with Alexus' 11-inch dick in his mouth. OMG! As he stopped a moment for a breath of fresh air, he finally realized that they had company. With embarrassment registering over his pathetic face with her dick still in his mouth, he stopped . . . as I just looked at him shaking my head, thinking how he was still up to his same old ways. I truly wasn't surprised to see him as I knew no one who could suck dick that well could ever stop. All I could do then is what it seemed John could not. And that was to think of Toni and the boys.

By this time John had been at the top of his game in his profession and had developed partnerships which formed his private practice of CHMS (Chestnut Hill Medical Specialist). Springfield Ambulatory Center . . . An office at the Abbington Memorial Hospital and had moved to Chief of Staff at Chestnut Hill Hospital where it all started. He, his wife and children moved from their small apartment in which I had first met him, to a plush mansion in the prestigious Belmont Hills outside of the city. He seemed like the perfect picture of success and now wanted to make up for the way he last left things with me by offering the world to me.

Luxury cars, high end properties, hundred thousand dollar checks at a time just to say "I love you baby."

Startup monies for any new venture I wanted to invest in, all in his hopes to help me leave the escort business, such as my iMusicWeb corporation which was the webcasting network I was developing in 1998 to 2000, up until the death of my father.

They say that guilt can make a nigga tilt, and it seems that's the same case for its Jewish counterparts, because Dr. John Mancuso had now become my latest cash cow. With all this guilt he had pent up inside of him, of our once beautiful and true past, he was willing and able to do and give anything at my command. He knew I truly loved him back then and the guilt through the years must have eaten him alive, because after our second chance meeting in my Rittenhouse Square escort service, he was willing to give me the world to make it all up to me and have a second chance at the true love we once shared. However, by this time I was no longer the green young naive girl he had met back in '93. I was on a mission for world domination and I had no need for true love from a man who loved dick more than I did.

So yes, he was no more than a game that I would play—

a fiddle to fine tune to my every need. And I would play by my own tune with him all the way to the bank. That is until the death of Carmen and our 20 plus year affair hitting the front page of the world's news broadcasts. There he would be, his cowardly slithering back boneless excuse of a man. As he would back into the shadows and allow himself to be used by the Philadelphia's District Attorney's Office in their case against me in order to save his own ass from the conspiracy charge he would have been facing. What a fucking pussy . . . as he would dare lie on the witness stand against me.

"Well, the cat's out of the bag now Doc . . . ol Johnny Boy." Oh what would I give to see your face as you read these pages and gag off of that. The truth really does hurt doesn't it daddy? And that is the part that the Doctor plays in this whole situation.

He was willing to give me anything I asked for . . . and he did. Even all the medical supplies to help me in my silicone business. Anything that he could give, in order to have the chance at sucking my DICK. Only little did he know I had it removed back in '94 and would string him along for decades, lusting after what he loved about me most. My big boy toy that was no longer there . . . Now let's get back to our story.

ABUSE VICTIMS
RIP RIGALI
philly.com
FEAR FOR
FELINES
CATS TRAPPED IN FIRE
SIXERS
STOMP
SPURS
399
TWIN METAL
ADAM' & THE

CHAPTER 12

A NEW LEASE ON LIFE

Now getting started in the silicone buttock injection business happened fast once Angel put all the pieces into place, but it didn't happen overnight. Once I gave her the go ahead to tell the few girls she knew who wanted my service, right away I had a few clients to use as my calling card. I started out with two dancers from the Philadelphia exotic dancing and escort circuit of strip clubs. Toya who worked at club Onyx, a very well know Philly strip club that catered to a somewhat rowdy bunch and was far from the upper echelon of men that I was use to dealing with in my prior business of Lace Entertainment. The other girl was Nikki who was a pleasantly plump internet escort and sex worker who was very well versed on all the internet blogs such as Make-me-heal.com., Topix.com and the many others that catered to an underground fixation on cheap cosmetic procedures by way of the black market.

I met up with the two of them one day over at Angel's house up in the greater northeast part of Philadelphia for what was arranged as our first consultation and session in order to begin the transformation that would get the two of them to their desired look. I arrived about 7:00 p.m. on schedule and began the setup of sterilizing my massage table and the surrounding areas with alcohol. The massage table I was able to purchase with some of the remaining last bit of money I had left over, as my escort services dwindled down to nothing. It was my call out to the universe that I was willing to go out on a limb on trust, that all would work out just finein the new business it had blessed me with, thus I was happily willing to spend my last on the needed supplies to start up business with all intentions to win. Although I had performed this very procedure many, many times in the past on my willing friends, I couldn't help but feel nervous. It was my first bunch of paying customers who were paying for perfection and nothing but. Nerves and excitement all twisted up in one. I technically hadn't done these injections since 1995 when I lived back in Society Hill. A lot had changed since them days. Back then the pumping business revolved around only the transgender community predominantly. With service providers like the legendary Ms. Joann Lane of Harlem, New York, and the transsexual she took under her wing and taught the business. Ms. Kelly Harper who serviced icon Rap Lil 'Kim after she was released from the Feds, may she rest in peace. Anyway, I must not forget about Natasha who pumped the girls out of her apartment up in Washington Heights, New York. She would later be the one to teach me the technique of pumping a few years later after she had completed all of my own bodywork.

Yes, these times were indeed different than that of the nineties. However, a body's still a body, and whether it be a transsexual woman or a genetic female, the procedure was still fundamentally the same. Although now, the demand for buttock injections and body sculpting via silicone injections was now coming from the genetic females mostly in the entertainment or planning to get into the entertainment industry. There were few here and there that wanted enhancement just for their own personal reasons of self-esteem and whatnot. I love those clients the most. It gave me great pleasure having been the one on the receiving end of such gratitude and appreciation for helping them obtain the body that they had always longed for but felt nature forgot.

So the table was now set up. I did an alcohol wipe down of the buttocks, marked the area with a sharpie, and it was now the moment of truth. I gave a brief assessment of just what each girl was looking to attain. Toya went first. She was a full-figured woman with beautiful striking facial features. She would put me in the mind of a genetic female version of the late gorgeous Kelly Harper in her hay-day, which was a compliment in the highest regard, being that Ms. Kelly Harper was a true traffic stopper in the eighties when she first came on the local Philadelphia Tranny scene displaying all the work she had been getting done up in New York by Joann. Many, many people thought Kelly favored the Hollywood movie star Rachel Welch. At one time Kelly Harper was proclaimed by all to be the most beautiful transsexual woman Philadelphia and probably the world had ever seen.

A bubble butt is what Toya wanted. She had already been blessed with a great ass to start with. Massive at that, so I would suggest to her to get a little more bulk in her hip and thigh area in order to level everything out. Then we could build up more ass if she liked to. She obliged and decided to trust my eye on the matter and the work commenced. Four needles in each cheek on and around her boy pockets we began to build her hips out. I would pump about 2 quarts in her by the time I could really see any difference, for as I stated before, Toya's ass was massive and already naturally huge, thus her hips should be just as impressive. But I was on a mission and that mission was to please my client no matter what. If I were to be successful in this endeavor, I could build a name for myself in the underworld of body sculpting by having Toya become my walking billboard as she would no doubt be back on the dance scene flaunting and dancing at all the hottest spots and gentlemen's clubs advertising all the great work that was to become my signature style.

In about seven sessions in all. Each session about $1,000 dollars each, we accomplished our work mission. Once I started working on her and committing to myself to nothing short of perfection . . . I was almost ready to pay Toya for the work I was doing on her. It was like chiseling out a masterpiece once completed. And to tell the truth, I must have paid Toya in order to work on her body, for as much as the silicone I would use to complete her work, was worth much more than I was to receive from her in cash at the end as payment. But I was an artist by nature, and I would stop at nothing to build great bodies with the canvas that was set before me.

The other girl Nikki, who came to see me with Toya was a sweet and kind specimen. She was thick as hell, but had a pretty face also in a baby doll kinda way. She seemed more of an intellectual hustler than Toya was, who was a diva in the hood. Nikki was reserved and was just working her way through nursing school by way of a little bit of dancing and an ad she had running on Eros.com as a pleasantly plump escort. She wasn't looking to get as much work as Toya, but no doubt she wanted her fair share of the candy. With her, we worked on the heart-shaped type ass and her saddle bags and hips would end up taking four sessions throughout three months time, which transformed her body into living and oozing seduction.

Once we were completed with her body, her demand on the escort site went through the roof, as she also got gastric bypass surgery and slimmed down to a size eight from a previous size 32 plus, which made the work I did on her stand out crazy. Once her work was completed she gifted me a Hermes Burkin bag worth $20,000 dollars from all the work her new body had given her, as she said she owed it all to me. I was so honored with the gratitude I received from Toya and Nikki . . . words could never express, for little did they know they would be the specimens to enhance my life as well. Because of their seeking me out through my friend Angel, trusting my artistic judgement, my life would never be the same. And to not have to go back to the "Family Business" was all that mattered.

On my last session with Nikki, she asked me if it would be okay if she talked about me and my work online with the blogs she belonged to. . . The forums and wherever else she could post up her before and after pictures. I told her "sure" and thought nothing more of it, as I was more than okay with the money

I was bringing in already. So, if I could keep that up, I

was cool. She took down my prices and products available and we went our separate ways.

It would be no less than three days when Nikki would call me up to let me know that she had received many inquiries and interested parties from the internet post she had placed up about my work. I asked her just how many were there and what were they looking to spend.

I would never be ready for what Nikki had to say next. She had about ten girls lined up for the following week, for sessions totaling over five thousand dollars each for butt injections, hips and a few facial refinement sessions worth five hundred dollars each. That following week I used a few of the dollars I had made working on her and Toya to resupply up and got about 3 gallons of silicone from John. I would meet him at the parking lot of the Dunkin Donuts on Bethlehem Pike in Flourtown, just behind his medical practice at the Flourtown Commons. I was anxious as he pulled into the parking lot beside my new Jaguar that he had just given me the money to purchase that fall before.

He pulled up in his silver m3 BMW. Still in his lab coat and green scrubs as he jumped out of the car to come over to greet me. We hugged and by the poke from his crotch area through his scrubs, I could clearly see he wanted more for his generous delivery. He had told me how seductive and beguiling I looked in my thigh high leather punk rock boots, black tights and leather biker jacket, wondering if we could take a ride in his car down to Fort Washington's Best Western Inn, which was located—"hold your weaves people"—just right across the street from the very Holiday Inn in

Fort Washington that I'd met my now longtime friend Angel who was working there some 15 years prior to date.

I told him that I couldn't. I had to get to class which he had also given me the money for in a desperate attempt to keep me near him, around the time he bought me the Jag. However, I did tell him that I could hook up with him at a later date, because I was really in need of his advice on a few medical matters with the new business. He proceeded to go to his trunk as I popped mine open. And there he unloaded three gallons of what might as well had been liquid gold to me. He gave me 3 boxes of Sterno 16 gauge needles, with six boxes of syringes, two boxes of multiple personal vials of Lanacane in order to numb the skin, along with a few prescriptions for me to pick up some much needed hormones for my personal usage.

John was indeed so much more to me than what many would call a glorified "Sugar Daddy," sweeter than sweet and enough to give a girl a cavity, that nigga was Madam's new "Candy man." As a matter of fact and, quiet-as-kept . . . that would become his new name on my mobile phone list for discretion. So whenever my cellphone rang with ol' Sammy Davis, Jr.'s song playing "The Candy Man," as my ringtone for him in my purse, I knew it was Dr. Mancuso, aka, John calling with some more candy.

CHAPTER 13

BLACK MAGIC, WITCHCRAFT AND THE OCCULT

All was set. After today I'm thinking I would make a great come up. About fifty thousand dollars plus, for no more than about five hours of work. So . . . let's see . . . Five hours of work I'm thinking at just about ten thousand dollars an hour was the starting rate for many of the super models to get up out of bed and consider doing a job. "Shit," I'm thinking, "I'm behind the game," . . . lol . . . I gotta get on point." If this is the kind of money I could be generating on a regular, thus, I feel the peaking head of Madam's ambition ringing loud and clear.

It seemed that God had just answered my prayers . . . I thought . . . so that I never had to return back to the "Family Business" ever again. The sessions with the many clients that Nikki had brought in went very well. Nikki continued bringing me in clients by the truckloads, paying anywhere from three thousand to ten thousand a job, not to mention what free word of mouth advertising each of my very elated clients were generating.

The oil business was booming and it seemed that I was the new anointed official oil bareness climbing my way to the throne to be queen. Month after month had gone by . . . perhaps even years. Life was good. I could spend all the quality time I wanted home with Nikolaus and travel the world from Paris to London, to Thailand and Tokyo making newer and newer business alliances with suppliers and physicians abroad. I'd fly into Bangkok to meet up with a new friend named AP, a tutu driver Nik and I met one night just hanging out in the red-light district of the city. AP was very well known on the black market scene in Bangkok and had no problem introducing me to all the who's who of the city's thriving under belly of illicit activity. Hanging out with AP was nerve wracking and thrilling all in one, as Nik and I ventured out to see the famed ping pong shows and many other xxx rated sex shows in the seedy underground network of one of the most notorious sex scenes in the world. In many of the places AP would take Nik and I, it seemed as if fate was leading the way as we would run into all kinds of people whom I could connect with for many, many other business ventures beyond the silicone business I had established.

Thus, I started looking to expand my services in black market beauty. Skin was in and I had noticed while away in Thailand that so much Rx restricted products and supplies for beauty in the USA were freely being sold over the counter in pharmaceutical stores in the malls there. Skin lightening and clearing agents were a big deal there, and this is where I came up with my import/export business plan for a product line called "Light-Ning" . . . in a bottle. Which was an injectable skin whitening product that people like Sammy Sosa, the famous baseball player was using to lighten his skin. While in Thailand, I arranged for tons of the active ingredient agent which was L-Glutathione to be imported in from Bangladesh in India, and business expanded to a new successful annex, to what success I was already having in the silicone industry. Needless to say, body and skin was making a killing.

With most of the money I was making, I wanted to be very careful about it, and not squander it like I had done so many times before with my escort business capital. I was not the young and dumb girl I had use to be. Thus, it was time to make wiser decisions. A lot of my money from the "Family Business" went into transforming myself to the woman I am today from male to female with sex changes for me and any of my employees that wanted to fully cross over.

I wouldn't exactly say that I threw money away back then, because I was helping to make a lot of people happy and fulfilled with themselves. However, I had nothing to show for it all when I walked away from the old business. Thus, it was very important for me this time around, with the good Lord's blessing, to make it all count for something and build a good life for Nikolaus and I.

I used a little of my new found wealth via the Silicone Oil business to invest in my music career. I built a personal recording studio in Nik's and my new home we had just moved into just shortly up the road in Ardmore, a stones throw from our old apartment in Narberth.

After starting the silicone business and traveling so much, we acquired so much stuff in our global travels that our one bedroom apartment had gotten very cramped very fast. We were now citizens of the world and needed a more stately home to reflect that sentiment.

Our old apartment indeed had become much too small for the success Nickolaus and I were experiencing in my thriving business of pumping a clientele list that seemed to be growing as word spread of my talents literally around the world. The home we moved into was a five room townhouse with three levels. The top floor was where Nik and I had a beautiful Henry the Eighth style stately decorated bedroom full of beautiful Bergondi and gold accents. Our California king size bed had a canopy with four post mahogany points and curtains which gave our room a definite allure of old world money. The room was so beautifully decorated and furnished, the directors of my "Come On In My Kitchen" music video used it in the actual bedroom scenes of the video.

The second room on the same floor with our bedroom chambers was a beautiful dressing area that was like walking into heaven when you entered it with all the wall to wall white furnishings and carpets. That was where I housed all my beautiful clothes and footwear I had become so addicted to purchasing from my travels around the world. From jewels to my Red Bottom shoes, to the furs and bags, diamonds and bobbles . . . Madam definitely enjoyed her trappings of what it meant to be a success in her underworld, in which she reigned supreme at the top of her game.

On the ground floor of this palatial home was where I was to make magic. In the very literal sense of the word with The Wrath Entertainment recording studio . . . in this studio it was to mean business in the realm of the Dark

Arts. During this time, I was deep into the occult scene of magic and sacred geometry. With the many, many, many books in my collection and family's library on the study of altering ones reality to a divine design. With all this knowledge at my finger tips, I had now come up with a plan to incorporate this master science of real life magic into my design while building the recording studio in my new home.

First thing's first. The isolation chamber also known as the sound booth would be shaped into the powerful occult symbol of the pentagon. The reasoning for the pentagon shape for my iso booth was because a star fits perfectly in it. Thus, in the science of sacred geometry, a pentagon shape harnesses stars. Therefore, in music it's used to birth stars . . . hence, a "recording star." Yes, I was really going all out with this new recording studio of mine. As far as the layout and decor, it was to be black with silver hints from the carpet to the black charcoal colored walls. The mixing console was to be strategically set to align with the Eastern Star. North, south, east and west with all the elements of the planet stationed on every point of the ceiling and facing the rising sun. Stepping into my new personal recording studio felt like I was boarding a galactic vessel in which to take me to another world. utilizing this layout in my studio was a basic magical setting and format used for magical ceremonies for centuries in the Dark arts and I was ready to enchant and beguile the music in which I was to create there. Facing any type of alter towards the rising sun is said to invoke the God power. That is why all Catholic churches' altars face east. And lastly, this is the very format that is used in the Illuminati mystical groups such as the OTO and any of all the sects that want to truly harness real occult powers of the universe for their command.

I've performed many successful magical rituals in the past with just the use of this format. The four symbols of power here are the Earth, Fire, Water and Air . . . not necessarily in the order that I listed, but together these symbols communicate to the cosmic beings that guard our earthly realm, who are powerful enough to see into one's lifeline. Once these beings take notice that you are consciously aware of them, and are beckoning their service, thus you are welcoming them into your life of your own free will and choice . . ."Kinda like the old vampire movies where you must first welcome them into your home". . . and thus, they can forever connect and imprint on your life's essence. Thus, they are now there for the good or bad in order to reek havoc on your life or bless you with wealth untold.

So yes . . . It's these very powerful symbols of our realm that I placed on the right of my mixing console and left. One in the back of the command production seat of the Mixing console and iso booth and one in back, just like the following diagram . . .

WARNING: PLEASE DO NOT ATTEMPT TO USE WITHOUT BEING PROPERLY EDUCATED FIRST IN THE DARK ARTS . . .

Mystical Sacred Geometrical Layout for studio Occult Entertainment

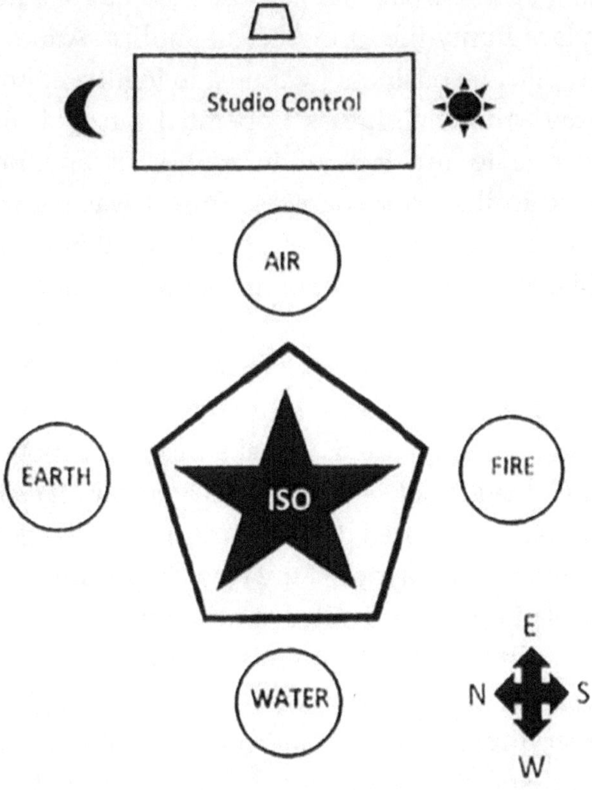

With this powerful design, given whatever planetary alignments are at play . . . the stars, the moon, the sun and the many other planets in our solar system are positioned, could cause a powerful combustible magic effect for the Magi. Now bear with me here . . . all this hocus pocus talk will all come together sooner than later in this book, so just follow with me during this time of starting my new silicone pumping business as I had just emerged out of a dormant, quiet place in my life of my occult studies. A life prior to the new silicone business I was just living the epitome of a bland and mundane life as I operated a half dead escort service due to my lack of interest in it anymore as I explained in the prior chapters. Thus, I was getting deep into anything that might offer up some excitement into my life while Nik would be out of the house working for many hours of the day.

However, once I moved into our new home, I was still at my tail end of interest in the occult and mysticism. Therefore, when I started to make this crazy money from pumping, the idea of sacred geometry was still fresh in my head, thus it manifested itself into the materialization of my design and master layout of my recording studio. After the design of the studio, I filled it with the best equipment money could buy. The Fantom keyboard, Pro-Tools, top of the line computer recording software, Niuma microphones and everything else I could manage to fit into that dedicated space. I had tons and tons of top notch record making equipment to use at any producer's delight. The new studio was a playground for anyone wanting to make a great record. And it was all right inside my home . . . how convenient.

"So one would think" . . . but in the hustle and bustle of

my thriving silicone pumping business, I had never really found the time to enjoy this new studio. I found myself, whenever wanting to be creative and record, to just call down to my longtime record producers Borris Franz Richard and Taj over at BMR Entertainment, thus going down to Philly to the city where they and the other producers, who did a lot of work with the Fugees and Wyclef Sean along with Lauryn Hill. Taj and Franz had been for years my go to team to make my signature urban goth sound. Needless to say, my own personal home studio had become no more than eye candy, and a status symbol of my new success in life as an oil baroness.

Years would pass before that night would come that me and Nikki James would head down to my studio half drunk and tipsy, to lay the vocals for a new track I had just got in which I called Ruckus. Thus, by the time I would finally get to use my personal studio in order to record Rucus, my fascination in the occult had long since past for a while, as it came and went like the wind with my mind preoccupied or not. I was living life in the fast lane once again and had forgotten all about what laid beneath the surface of my beautiful recording studio at home. Which was a powder keg of black magic via sacred geometry, patiently waiting to be activated.

With all that life had opened up to me, with all that money could buy, my magical High Tech Altar disguised as a recording studio sat quietly waiting as I paid out hundreds of thousands of dollars on music video productions and promotions for my next budding career as a recording artist. I had paid for music videos and photoshoots all around the globe, coupled with transportation for me and my staff, the many background models and film crew to document my every move of building my brand on the music scene.

The scene was set and I was finally going to get my shine in the light as The Black Madam, recording artist and producer in order to attract the attention of the super producer Mr. Craze. The juggle between businesses came very easy to me. Like I said, I am great at compartmentalizing my life. So that quality made life in the fast lane easy for Madam. Although . . . however fast life was traveling, I must admit times at home with Nikolaus was priceless. We would sit up in our bed watching movies on our huge plasma TV that he loved so much. To say the least, life was lovely. I now had a wonderful well-balanced life I had arranged down to the separate cellphones with one family plan for Nik and I to communicate with our family and friends and closest associates.

Phone two was the phone I would use for the music

business agents, or whatever else I had going on for the moment to funnel through it. And a third phone was for the business that cultivated my new life . . . the silicone pumping business. And still a fourth phone was devoted to my skin bleaching product and company . . . www.biobeautylabs.com, and lastly, a landline for the recording studio and a slew of ready to program throw-away phones, I kept in my dressing room drawer for any new ideas I came up with on the hum-bug and needed to establish a separate contact for. It was all about compartmentalizing.

It was maddening, but I even kept a "world phone" for when Nik and I were abroad on pleasure. Thus, all our other phones were forwarded into, as I kept no assistant to run any part of my life but music productions. I can even recall being with Nik on the Champs-Elysees strolling along one evening in Paris when I was phoned by my production personal assistant Ramika to inform me of the good news that my first project, which was a sinister occult style music video "Come On In My Kitchen" was airing at that very moment of FUSE MUSIC TV. As that combination of events ensued . . . I thought to myself . . . The Madam was now on her way to world domination if lady luck kept dealing me such good fortune.

fuse
where music lives
COME ON IN MY KITCHEN
fuse -this-month-
BLACK MADAM
The Urban Goth Queen
fuse > URBANMUSIC

CHAPTER 14

AMBER ALERT . . . SCULPTING ROSE BUD

Once back in the states and settling in back at home from a long and tedious European tour of meetings, sculpting, networking and partying like a rock star on the European social scene of the Parisian nightlife with Nikolaus, I got a call from Eve letting me know she had a new client for me and wanted to give me the "skinny-low-down" on the exotic dancer she had been photographing in her new hobby of photography and airbrushing in which she took a special interest.

She emailed me a few of her completed airbrushed shots of her new muse in order to let me see just what I had to work with. "She's a cutie pie," I thought to myself as I then conveyed to Eve my thoughts of her new find, as I clicked through her work. We booked a pumping session for her a few days later in a motel up in East Brunswick, New Jersey, a place I was very familiar with from back in my days of running the escort services. It was the Howard Johnson on Route 1. We were to meet there because of the three of us—Eve, myself and her new friend—I was the only one mobile. And Eve and she were staying there working ads from the back page of the New Jersey Star Ledger. Eve at this time was doing S&M work as a dominatrix, while Rose Bud was working an ad from the hotel and dancing at Sue's Rendezvous up in New York during the late evening hours to make ends meet. Sue's Rendezvous was a strip bar in which many of the music industry scouts would frequent for new video talents.

Rose Bud was a cute and petite bombshell from the start and not at all the diva that I assumed she would be from what I saw in her photos Eve had shown me of her in my e-mail inbox. She was very interested in my service because she said she had been hearing high praises of me from many on the Philadelphia gay scene and Eve, while she was then one of the face and body girls from the House of Karan.

I went over her desires for a bottom heart- shaped ass, some more thighs and fuller apples in her cheeks. Eve also took a keen interest in my markings with a sharpie pen for my injection sights, because Rose Bud was going to become her new project. As I directed her which ways she should position herself for optimal comfort during the procedure, a high since of fear seemed to engulf this girl as I was injecting her buttocks and thighs. I didn't hear a sound from her, which was a bit weird, being that I prefer to keep an ongoing dialog between me and my patient as to ask questions such as how are they feeling and so forth and whether they're feeling too much pressure than they could stand, with the brutal stretching of the skin that injections cause. But in all, I got one word answers, if any at all. I stopped to ask her again . . . was she doing okay . . . and that's when I noticed that she seemed truly terrified, crying in Eve's lap.

I felt as though I was doing something so wrong to her that I wasn't even too sure if she truly wanted to continue. Well, she sure did, and it just turned out that she was really sensitive and emotional about finally getting what she had been desiring most of her life—a bigger ass. She was currently working out of the adjoining hotel room linking to Eve's. And I won't speculate to say and put Rose Bud's business out there like that if she didn't say it herself. But the hotel we were at was notorious for classified escort prostitutes and so forth. And me, knowing Eve, if a chick with Rose Bud's looks was hanging around with Eve in that situation, and under her care as Eve was clearly looking out for her, I'm sure Rose Bud wasn't around for nothing. Either Eve was fucking her, or she was turning tricks for Eve on the low.

I had worked on Rose Bud through the course of three and a half years to help her attain the mega bombshell body she wanted. And once we were done, I recommended that she get some liposuction in her mid-section to get rid of her baby fat pudge, in order to really make her work outstanding. And outstanding she would be, because shortly after our work was completed, Rose Bud had called Eve and I to let us know that she had caught the eye of a talent executive from Deff Jam while stripping at Sue's Rendezvous one night, who was scouting for fresh faces to put in a new Ludacris music video. So Rose Bud wanted Eve and I to come get her from the motel she was now staying at close to New

York with her longtime lesbian lover Travon, in order to take her into Trenton, New Jersey to buy some fire red weave hair so she could have Eve weave it in before the video shoot. Eve was all gong hoe to do it and asked me what I thought. I had told Eve and Rose Bud to hold their horses for a moment and asked Rose Bud was she still rocking the crewcut she had the last time I had seen her. She said, "Yes." That's when I explained to her and Eve that with the way her body now looked, with the hot work we had just completed, she should be a bold bitch and stand alone as is. Do not do anything to your hair but bleach it, I told her. Wear the Bold blonde buzz cut and rock out like that. All the other would be video vixen starlets will be sporting long flowing hair weaves with zero personality. You Rose Bud, just need your beautiful face, that bad ass body of yours and that fucking bold, blonde bitch of a buzz cut to steal the show. It would not even be two months later when a new star would be born, and her name was ROSE BUD.

Rose Bud called me up so excited after the video shoot thanking me for my guiding her away from an otherwise bland performance on her debut video shoot. She said she did everything I told her to do, and all worked out just as The Madam had said. When I finally got to see the music video, I could do nothing but laugh, as there was baby girl "Rose" practically sitting on Ludacris' lap shining like a star as his main chick, while all the flowing haired chicks were just accessories and hating on Rose Bud because she tore the walls down on that set.

It would be this shoot with an aid of a friend to get another one of Eve's pictures of a pre-starlet Rose Bud e-mailed to an assistant of Mr. Craze for the spot in his

ROBO COP music video, and that was all she wrote. Fate had stepped in and taken Rose Bud to the top of the music industry without even having a record deal!!! As Mr. Craze's new girlfriend. Over the next few years Rose Bud would continue to call on me and my services as her and Eve's friendship faded. Rose Bud and I stayed strong as I was now the key source to her maintaining her knock out curves.

She and her management team would continue to bring me other high caliber celebrity clientele from all throughout the entertainment industry, along with many romantic female companions of some of the top male entertainers of the world. Many of whom I will honor our confidentiality clause, but I can never be the blame if my secret "Black Book" get's stolen or lost into the wrong hands now can I? Or even worse yet . . . to end up on some online auction site like eBay or something . . . "times tend to get really hard sometimes," one can never know. Then everyone's secrets will be told. Oops . . . And not to mention the men in the industry who found their way to me in hopes of having their penis' pumped because naturally it was not doing the job.

My encounter with then X Brown's girlfriend Nina, who's now on basketball wives and the great work I've done on her wonderful body. Then singer Winston's flame Dez from Philly who also was once Rose Bud's ace in a hold "play-sister" until drama happened between Rose Bud and then Dez's sugar daddy, son of Philadelphia Seventy Sixers Star. I can go on and on about all the celerity encounters and their dirty deeds on one another, I've learned via the Candy business I was in. With the top being a certain hot female rapper now who bares the title of the best female

MC. It gets scandalous with the candy. TRUST.

As far as this rap diva in question, when it came to dealing with her . . . it was a missed adventure never beyond a few phone calls orchestrated by Rose Bud for pricing, scheduling, and products. It seems that Ms. Wonderful had had the misfortune of getting her bodywork done by a person using a lessor superior product which gave her the bulk, but left her rear end hard and lumpy out of clothes. Hence, the reasoning the other client of mine I mentioned earlier named Schefee was hired by Viacom to do Ms. Wonderful's body double work in pictures and video.

Ms. Wonderful seeing the wonderful work that I had performed on her then BFF Rose Bud during the time she shot the Massive Attack music video, I became heavily sought after by Ms. Wonderful and her Young Money team with Lil Wayne in order to fix what another had did wrong to her body.

However, that deal fell through for me to do the corrections on Ms. Wonderful's body before I could get started due to some bad blood between Rose Bud and Ms. Wonderful, due to one BFF's boyfriend sexting the other BFF some nude pics and racy dialog. So basically in laymen's terms . . . it was pics of a dick that caused that job to slip away. Their BFF friendship, and everything including my services that came along with the friendship of Rose Bud's was lost.

Although it had hardly even mattered by now, for I was now planning my next exit out of the black market silicone business into a full fledged life as the recording artist Black Madam. Female recording act and producer extraordinaire by way of a friendship with Rose Bud solidified through silicone leading all the way to Mr.

Craze as my soon to be producer. The table had been set for my intro into the private inner circle of the STAR NATION camp as Mr. Craze's new hot controversial and beautiful transsexual recording prodigy. Rose Bud was to play an important part that she was more than willing to play. She wanted to get me in with Mr. Craze in order to add more stakes in the fire as she put it, as she loved the fame that came with Mr. Craze, but just could no longer stomach being in a relationship with him. I was now to play the pawn in Rose Bud's game. That is to get her security in the entertainment business without ever having to fuck a "butch-queen" like Mr. Craze anymore. Meanwhile, it was a game that I very much didn't mind playing pawn, as Madam had high ambitions of her own.

Rose Bud's infatuation with Mr. Craze was dwindling down to anything but blissful love because once he had filmed a scene in the "Keeping Up with the Money" reality show during his time in New York City, Ms. Dubai was already plotting her moves to become Mrs. Craze.

CHAPTER 15

THE END OF ROSEBUD & MR.CRAZE...
& HELLO MS. DUBI

This was the plan... Rosebud was to get me signed into Mr. Craze in order to solidify an invisible union of hers with Mr. Craze via The BLACK MADAM and thus, I would become her new link to the industry. As, she was afraid her star would fade out of the limelight without her current title of being Mr. Craze's girlfriend. Thus with This Plot She Would Have No More Need for Mr. Craze at all for sustainability to the life she's grown to love in the music business. As Mr. Craze would now become my problem or blessing as. that is just where new thriving artist as myself needed to be. by the side of one of the music industry's make a rap artist and producers. For Rosebud was never truly into him in the first place, as he was simply playing a means to an end, as Mr. Craze was Rosebud's then only means out of her life of poverty back home in Philly. Not to mention deep down in her heart of hearts, she truly still loved her ex-lesbian lover Trevon was still back in Philadelphia... struggling as Rosebud went on to leave her to be with Mr. Craze. but with the promise to later return back home to reunite with her when she'd found her own way, away from the egotistical clutches of such a controlling maniac as Mr. Craze was in their relationship.

Rosebud longed for the long time love she had left back home in Philly. For a guilt ridden heart would convict her daily, as she had confessed to me of how she wouldn't think twice to phone stocking Trevon in the late hours of the night just to hear her ex-lover's voice. Once she even told me of how she loathes this sleeping with Mr. Craze, because his hygiene wasn't up to par. Thus, Rosebud would equate having sex with him, to that of having sex with an ape. Which now brings me to understand just why he would make the statement once they were over, and he is now dating Ms. Dubai - of how Ms. Dubai had demanded that he take up to 20 showers after his leaving Rosebud, before she would dare consider being with him. Hence. it was only because Ms. Dubai cleverly equated his poor hygiene order to being with Rosebud, which helped to not have to embarrass the man for JUST PLAIN STANKING!

This was a perfect Psychological move on the part of Ms. Dubai, with getting what she wanted out of Mr. Craze, without sending him on his usual ego trip as he had grown accustomed to when he was with Rosebud, "good thinking Ms. Dubai". but after all, one would never expect anything less of a child of one of the most clever MOMMAGERS out there in the industry. who could parlay her child's SEX TAPE into a Multi-Billion- Dollar Family Empire.

An ape on top of her back to give words verbatim of

just what Rosebud expressed to me it felt like to be with Mr. Craze. At times when she was making love to him, all she ever wanted to to be, was OVER... as the stench from his on brushed teeth and bad breath would give her a stomachache every time he would touch her. I would ask her why she wouldn't just leave him she was someone happy, but it seems a girl would do anything to be on the arms of a Rap Star. And besides. No one could smell his breath through the television screen where she loved to be seen with him at all the major music industry events. It was the price she thought she had to pay for her time in the limelight.

Finally our plans fell through when coming home, back into the country from a trip to Paris, Rosebud along with Mr. Craze and his entourage disembarked their private jet in mayhem as Mr. Craze seemed to be having one of his bipolar episodes, due to being angry with the outfit choice Rosebud had wore to arrive home for the flashing lights of the paparazzi were waiting to capture their every move. Thus, he demanded that NO one help for Rosebud carry her luggage in order that she feel what it would feel like to be a nobody again back home in Philly, if she was to ever choose to leave him. Therefore, her having no resources for living, back to the deplorable life of turning tricks and dancing on a strip pole to survive, after being in the epitome of a life of success with him in the industry as his girl.

"THAT WAS IT!" she said, and I didn't blame her one bit, although her move in haste would ruin my plans and link to Mr. Craze for my own musical aspirations.

She called me up crying... telling me just how humiliated she had felt standing there in the middle of the airport with men all about her within Mr. Craze's crew of cronies, and not one of them would help her as she struggled with her heavy luggage, as Mr. Craze berated her. yelling for her to go back home to Philadelphia, and take off those $50,000 diamond earrings she was wearing that he had given her during their trip abroad, and ordered upon them for her new life without him.

Yes! Mr. Craze was a full DIVA to say the least when it came to his ego. Thus, I told Rosebud that I wouldn't wish that kind of disrespect on no one, just to get ahead. So, needless to say, from then on the relationship is going nowhere fast as she began to plot her exit off the scene. Now it was up to me to find a new path into the music industry as the Black Madam.

It was not the end of the world however. I got a call two months later from Rosebud asking me to meet her at the Doubletree Hotel at Broad and Locust street in Philly. She had just landed in the city at the Philadelphia International Airport with her new manager and personal assistant and needed me to come and deliver her some "Candy." I told her that I would be there once I was done with my clients for the day, thus she let me know that I should bring extra product for not only her, but her assistant too. in which she was treating for her birthday. It was Sunday, February 6, 2011.

I was running late that evening because I was stuck in my office still, after seeing over 10 patients, and still had to go online to book a massive 22 seat flight with my own personal assistant for an excursion trip to Thailand for many of my clients who are also interested in getting some major cosmetic work done as in Nose Jobs, Breast Implants, Lipo Suction and more. For in my many travels back and forth to Asia during my own mission of Sexual Reassignment surgeries, I had forged some very fruitful and lucrative relationships with many many great Plastic & Cosmetic Surgeons.

And, with these friendships, I struck up very good business transactions with them in myself as their "MIDDLEMAN" who would book and bring them several clients at a time from America, Canada, the UK, Europe, and wherever else my many clients flew in to see me for buttock injections from, but wanted more than what I was able to do with more serious cosmetic work. I would dub this enterprise... "Secrets of the Orient," and I would stand to earn 20% of every surgical procedure performed. Thus, I was to book the foreign hotel accommodations and medical procedures for the women I was to bring in, and basically serve as a nurse, personal tour guide, personal caregiver and more, as they convalesced and recuperated on the tropical resort island of Koh Samui in the South China Sea just off the Gulf of Thailand where the Bandon International Hospital was located in managed by my Physician friend Dr. Chimchoke, whom I now served as his assistant in brokering him new international patients globally. Although Dr. Chimchoke worked on the island of Koh Samui, he lived on the mainland of Surat Thaini but commuted daily to the hospital on the local ferry boat. Chimchoke and I would become friends quickly, as our partnership expanded as we combined our talents to generate quite a nice revenue stream.

Dr. Chimchoke was a wonderful and gifted surgeon on staff at Bandon International Hospital and in the arrangement we would have, I would be the source to bring him many clients that would never have considered traveling to him for their work. There were many bookings for our venture, as I had my hand on the pulse of all who were seeking cheap and economical cosmetic work, but could not afford the Rock Star rates of the overpriced physicians in America & Europe. Traveling with the many women seeking services through my "Secrets of the Orient" excursion was a pure blast that brought me much enjoyment, as I would be introducing many women traveling with me to a different way of life and part of the world in which they would have never otherwise experienced.

With my "Secrets of the Orient" enterprise, I got to do all of my traveling for free. While staying in many unique and exotic resorts and hotels throughout the world while making a boatload of money. I had the same arrangement with the cosmetic surgeon team in Montreal Canada, in Paris France, not to mention my beloved Dr. Marales in Quito Ecuador, and was working on solidifying a deal with a Plastic Surgeon in London England... that is until an International Scandal was soon to come my way. But we'll talk about that in due time.

So, after booking these flights in setting up the hotel stays for my next Thailand Tour, I was all about done. With the clock just hitting the 6:45 PM mark when I left my home office to head from the Mainline onto the expressway. down into the city to meet up with Rosebud at the Doubletree Hotel, unload my supplies and headed straight to her room, I had just arrived on time at 7:30 PM sharp.

I knocked on the door and I was greeted by a California tanned rosebud. She was looking great as usual, as I settled in for more sore from the visit, although we all knew the highlight would be my delivery of "The Candy." We talked about all we have been doing in accomplishing since the last time we were together and she seemed really excited to introduce me to her new personal assistant Maria. We also shared laughs about the time I had told her I fell out in hysteria when I saw her on an award show with Mr. Craze... Tripping over the whole Taylor Swift thing, and how I was still in disbelief at the fact that she finally let him go, and how it was finally over for real this time.

Rosebud blushed as she then went on to tell me about this new up-and-coming rapper from Pittsburgh Pennsylvania who just had the scene with a track called Yellow and Black. She showed me a picture of him on her iPhone, and for a moment I thought she was now downgrading just in order to try her best at staying in the limelight. I was glad for her that she no longer had to suffer at the hand of Mr. Craze's disrespect, but I felt this latest attempt at yet another rapper was Rosebud's desperate attempt to clutch onto her prior lifestyle for dear life, as it was unknown to her as to what her future held, and a life without Mr. Craze's Crazy Ass.

Furthermore, I had never heard of this new rapper and thought that perhaps she would get over the infatuation fast, and thus move on to someone more befitting such a beautiful girl as she was. Nevertheless, she truly seemed genuinely happy proceeded to tell me how they had bet. Who would've ever thought that Twitter would be the new matchmaker service to the stars?

It seemed this new rapper... Wizard Keefa had been stalking Rosebud when she was out jogging in the year early hours of the morning on the beach on California. She said that each morning he said he had watched her for about two weeks straight, and then on Twitter he finally left her an inbox message to alert her of what he had been up to. "CREEPY STUFF!" Rosebud thought it was cute, I thought it was crazy, but with our mind when it comes to finding love in the industry. For I love the simplicity of a low keyed man, just as the love that I'd found in Nik.

She then said she would later invite the mysterious Wizard Keefa to meet up with her in order to keep her company jogging each morning. And that was the start of their love affair. Although I had great qualms about the whole shenanigans of his creepy ways, I then remembered how things seemed very weird with my first acquaintance with Nik, but we had turned out all right, thus I figured perhaps it was a good thing for Rosebud, especially after Mr. Craze. And once I got to see a picture of her new love, and studied his whole persona a little more, I saw exactly what it was that she saw in him. He was the spitting image of her ex-boy/ girl lesbian lover Trevon back in Philly, that she had left for Mr. Craze those few years back.

The one she would forever regret dumping for what looked like from the outside looking in, a great life of glitz and glamour was such a rap star like Mr. Craze. After we talked a little while longer about the possible budding relationship with this new guy in her life, she started to dish all the dirt to me on her into the R & B singer "Gey Songz" little flying, and showing pictures of his very small penis on her iPhone. As a matter of fact, it seemed a little Rosebud had been pretty busy out there on the West Coast these last few months getting over Mr. Craze. As, she went on to show me a host in a wide assortment of many male celebrity Dick pics, where she then went on to explain to me that for some strange reason, one she and Craze broke off... she started to get date offers and text messages from celebrities sending her pictures of their penises.

Listen... I don't quite get into all of that right now... as I's be in love and all, But Guuuuurl in the boys. I see why Ms. ReeRee had such a hard time getting over R & B singer X - Brown. Damn! "Dis Nigga'z Packin." and ladies. and any boys that are interested, the pic of his penis looked heavy and greasy wet as if he had just pulled out of some wet ass or pussy. What is an understatement. Hi there X - Brown (DEUCES!!!)

"ROSEBUD!!!". I screamed. laughing my ass off. where the hell did you get this picture from, as I could clearly see she was now looking at me sideways. "Ooool. you nasty little bitch," was all I could say as I smiled and continued to thumb through her little cell phone "Dick-tionary."

As she smiled back at me, she just said "Guuuurl. You have no idea," the industry as a whole sloppy mess of everybody "Having E'rybody," just like in the Philly and New York Ballroom scene. And with that, we had started our (what would be) final session. It was nothing major. She just wanted to touch up some spots of Cellulite she was beginning to see, as baby girl was getting old. Hence, the reason why she would always wear leggings well participating on "Dancing with the Starz". as her star would rise in the next few years to come.

She also thought she could stand to use a little ass lifting injections I specialized in, as she thought her ass might be getting flatter due to all the back and sex she used to have with Mr. Craze, as the heavy impact of his ramming her anally from the rear in which she too compared to her days of fucking a wild ape. "I digress."

After finishing my session with Rosebud, I did a starter obsession on her assistant Maria. She was some chick from

Canada Rosebud had met while she was filming her scenes in the Russell Simmon's Reality Show, hoping to land her own show she was currently pitching around to the "Love and Hip-Hop" TV producer, Mona Scotts which she named "SHADES of MADNESS." Maria also had a jewelry line in which she wanted Rosebud to serve as the face of.

Before leaving the hotel room to head home once I was all completed, Rosebud said she didn't want me to leave just yet and wanted us to just kick back in order for room service, we all just kicked off her shoes and it's very expensive cheeseburgers. However, I could only stay no more than an hour to busted up with her, as I soon had to say my goodbyes, as Rosebud pulled $15,000 in cash out of her luggage to pay me for my time and services to her and her assistant, which she said the cash was part of a large lump sum she had earned for making a celebrity guest appearance at Club TAO in Vegas hosting a string of parties all week long.

It's pretty late now, and I'm headed home to my car. But no sooner than I'm about to hit Walnut Street in order to reach the highway without getting caught up in traffic, as the Philadelphia Eagles game is about to let out of the stadium, whereas all the traffic from South Philly will soon be filling up the streets of Center

City with a sea of fans and the team's trademark colors of green, white and black, fight to get home to their neighborhoods. And then like clockwork, I get a call my cell phone from Nikki James wanting me to drop by her place and pick her up in order to come to my place for a few days.

(It's going to be a long night in traffic.)

But it's something I have to do, as I am well aware that Nikki James just loves being out at my place and spending time with me like the old days. She loves to use the expression "The Country House" when referring to my home out on the Mainline and how tranquil the suburbs makes her feel fond memories of her childhood back in Topeka Kansas, as opposed to the Center City life I had left along with the "Family Business." So I swung by her home in order to pick her up and attempt to beat the massive traffic headed our way, but surprisingly... The traffic throughout the city seemed to have dissipated while I was going the opposite direction to pick up Nikki James, which made our commute as smooth as butter. Thus, headed on out to the expressway, and back out to the Mainline.

CHAPTER 16

MADAM AND NIKKI JAMES CREATING RUCKUS

Nikki James and I chatted up in the car on the ride home as I called Nikolaus to let him know I would be running late for picking up Nikki James. He asked if I could stop by one of his favorite Japanese restaurants, Tampopo to pick him up his favorite spicy eel over a bed of rice.

Once back in the car, Nikki James and I are listening to a music track I had just gotten from the studio downtown sent in from this production team out in Boston called Poor Sammy. It was a hot track that had a reggae tone beat to it. Nikki James must have already been tipsy as she could never go too long without a cocktail in her clutches. Because, once that music hit them speakers, she went ballistic as if she'd been tied away for years and finally was released on the world in a raging storm of ballroom blitz. She loved the beat and was bouncing all over my car practically.

I mean this girl was really in some sort of transient groove as the track seemed to unleash a primal need to move while sitting there in her seat as I drove up the highway to the mainline exit.

She stopped only to ask me who was the music by . . . what recording act . . . what singer . . . and I told her it was a beat produced for me to lay some vocals over for a production team just getting started in the business. I also went on to tell her that if she liked the damn track that much, she could help me record tonight by engineering the session for me in my home studio late overnight.

She was so excited to volunteer her services to assist me in the producing of my vocals tonight, just as long as we could stop by the wine and spirits shop in order to get her a re-up on her alcoholic beverage before we headed in for the night. It closed at midnight and we had just made it in the nick of time as the last customer was still getting totaled up at the register.

About 45 minutes in the house, Nikolaus is up in the bedroom watching his favorite movie with Chris Tucker and Jacki Chan . . . "Rush Hour III." This is about the 60th time he's watched the damn film, but it's Cool . . . I love how the simplest things keep him content.

Now Nikki James and I are headed down to the studio when the doorbell rings. It is a delivery for Eve who is down in her room still at work on her airbrushing program she had just bought in order to start up a new full time business with airbrushing for major magazines and photographers.

As I stopped to see what goodies Eve's just ordered late night, we all hung out in the kitchen to talk about this and that. My meet with Rose Bud and the many nasty pictures she showed me. We now began to all make our way down the stairs as Eve's bedroom/ office is just off the side of the recording studio on the ground floor.

I began to set up the track on the pro-tools software as I am asking Nikki James to help me with the microphone setup. Everything is now set up to go and I pour myself a delicious strawberry margarita Nikki James just made us as we began what looks to be a late night of recording vocal tracks. I noticed that she must had gone heavy with the Joseh Quervo Tequila as it went straight to my head in no time. A cocktail always tends to mellow me out from all the world's stress as I began to let Padge go and Black Madam emerge from the depths of my inner soul. I had been in medical mode for the past few weeks as I was generating the few hundred thousand dollars I needed for the promotion of an up and coming new video production and promotion.

With all the technical side of recording practically set up to run itself, I let Nikki James know just where and how she needed to punch me in and out on the track to capture my vocal performance. By this time now, Nikki James had a job working in recording studios up in New York doing voiceovers for major television commercials. So without a hitch, she got the feel of engineering down pack and we began.

The beat of the track began to bang out of my headphone speakers as I began to get even more acclimated with the mix of the track so much closer to my ears than what I had heard in the car as we drove home earlier. The track was indeed hot like fire and I was about to perform in the sound booth as if I was performing in front of millions. As I felt the top of the verse leading me into the groove, I borrowed a verse from Snoop Dogg as I could hear Nikki James punching me into the track . . . "Murder was the case that they gave me . . . now Madam's half crazy . . . they're coming for that ass injection lady." I go on and on rapping as if I had done this shit all my life. The lyrics just came to me effortlessly and as Nikki James punched me in and out of the track, it all seemed to sound so seamless as my voice in the mix of my headphones sounded muthafucking hot as blazin' fire. I do a few vox over dubs and the whole things pops as if it was meant to be.

Nikki James was loving it and I was loving it even more as I overlaid an accompaniment vocal with my lead. I repeated the first verse again . . . "MURDER WAS THE CASE THAT GAVE ME, MADAM'S HALF CRAZY, THEY'RE COMING FOR THAT ASS INJECTION LADY" . . . as I repeated those words I could feel a tingling sensation go down my back as something inside me warned me of saying such words as I have always been a strong believer in the power of the tongue. The words were beckoning me . . . I know for God I should change these lyrics and take the song at a different angle as I've dealt in the dark arts enough to know that words can carve one's destiny.

As the track began to build up with so much character from my gut, it was the things that made a hit song, what seemed to churn in my psyche. While listening back to the track on replay . . . the field speaker rumbled in playback mode with a voice that was not my own anymore, but that of the channeling of Grace Jones with a wicked slap Jamaican accent. It was as if the song was forging itself, and I was just a vessel in which it was to manifest itself into this world. It was beginning to also sound like one of those hot Riannah songs with the darkness of an island ritual.

Just as I was beginning to feel the smoldering vibrations in the sound booth telling me that I was not alone, Nikki James stopped the track, telling me how we needed to celebrate with another drink. "NIKKI JAMES" I screamed . . . "don't ever stop me in mid motion like that on a track." We stopped to take a break for a few minutes as Nikki James ran straight for the liquor. In a short period of time, drunk as all hell, we headed back down to the studio to indeed finish raising hell as we were overly excited for the creation we were producing. I began to lay another track, then another overlay. Then I went on to begin shooting shade at Ms. Wonderful, whom I hadn't yet got over the fact that she blew me off because of whatever her and Rose Bud was going through. Now the shit is getting stankin. Reeking with high shade, I'm deep into my zone as I start prophesizing on the track . . . rapping about Ms. Wonderful's head on, a silver platter, being carried down a creepy dark hallway of a creepy house by triplets as if they were in the Jack Nichols movie "The Shining." As I get sucked into the track, I go even deeper into my occult knowledge mixed with my grandmom's old school Baptist rants to the altar in church as I began to speak in tongues as I start to recite some Charlie Manson shit I had just saw on a documentary. As crazy as it was all sounding from the outside listening in, Nikki James and I was in rapture with a truly spiritual creation. "A pocket full of poesy's, casket full of dead roses." I challenged the cosmos for all they were worth.

Either we were just plain out drunk by now, or this track sounded like a hit waiting to be released immediately!!! It's now time that we act a little on the song with voiceovers of theatre and drama to the track and I tell

Nikki James to rewind so I can punch in some "Breaking News Stories on the television and radio . . . of The BLACK MADAM on the run from the law on some mass murder type shit." The track was almost complete by this time, but it ain't quite done yet. I start really digging into the astro plane of the 4th dimension. Cause now I'm beginning to chant as if I was casting a spell on the shit. Drunken like no other, Nikki James and I were fucked up and the track sounded like we were calling out to the dark side of death. They say that mind altering intoxication can really bring out one's creativity . . . and now, I know just how true that saying is. By this time I'm so deep into the zone of creativity, stoned out of my mind . . . all I can now see is Eve entering into the studio shaking her head in utter disgust. "What the fuck are you doing Page!" she shouts over the music playing through my earphones. Nikki James hit the stop button on the track, as I'm still hearing Eve full throttle screaming as the music comes to an abrupt halt.

"THIS SOUNDS LIKE SOME EXORSIM SHIT PADGE!!!" Eve yelled, as I came walking out of the iso booth, expecting great praise from her for the masterpiece we were in the midst of producing. "What the hell are you doing?" she said. "What were you just saying?" Now, I'm not really getting just where she's coming from with her non-support of such a great creation, cause like I said, the track was sounding hot to Nikki James and I. However, Eve said it sounded like I was possessed and calling up Satan from the depths of hell.

Nikki James, While drinking yet another cocktail, started in on Eve about art. What it was . . . and how we were in the artistic zone and that Eve should get out if she can't understand the process of artists such as us, creating the next big thing—a hitsingle.

Eve, shaking her head again, just exited the studio back to her bedroom, claiming that I was never going to learn until Satan comes up from hell to drag both of us back down with him. All I could say was the track was fire.

Now don't get me wrong. I did feel very weird when I recorded that first opening line of the track about murder and injections and all that. I did feel that I was hitting too close to home with me still being involved in the injection business, and challenging fate with such strong language. Looking back at it all now, I was definitely being reckless with all I knew about words and just how they can attract its sentiments to the speaker, for good or bad.

But I was also an artist who loved the act of creation. It is one of my greatest joys in life. The night Nikki James and I recorded the track RUCKUS, we were definitely making the perfect recording. The lyrics seemed to marry the music with such utter perfection that it had to be. However, perhaps it was a track that I should not have recorded right then and there, being that I was still in the injection business strong and still had many clients booked that coming week for services. That track seemed to truly become a hit recording right out of the gate, although it never saw the light of day due to what was to happen in my life next . . . It was indeed a hit in its own right as it hit straight home . . . unleashing RUCKUS in my life.

If only I knew then what I know now, I would have never challenged fate with those words falling from my lips and the careless whispers in my head beckoning me to unleash chaos in my life in the guise of the possibility of a hot new sound recording. My ego was on high, and it would soon be grounded as my future was to soon reveal itself to me. Because that moment in time, during the recording of RUCKUS, all my guardian angels assigned to watch over me from the heavenly realm must have all been sleeping. Because all of the fallen ones from the depths of purgatory was about to breathe life into those words I had just recorded in that isolation booth, making my life a living hell. For the Holy Bible tells us all . . . be mindful of the words from your lips . . . For life and death lies in the Power of the Tongue.

It's late at night now, the recording went well. I had just recorded one of the hottest songs in all my years of recording, and I did it all right in my home. I felt good as I powered down all the equipment after saving to memory the work Nikki James and I had just created. As I headed up to bed to get some much needed sleep before a busy day in the morning tending to a few international clients of mine who were flying in from London for their second round of silicone injection sessions, life felt good and for once in my life, yet again, I felt like things were going to go just as I wanted them to. As I walked through the living room headed to the stairwell leading up to my bedroom, I see Nikki James is now listening to some of my Nina Simone collection on the stereo, while nursing yet another cocktail. "What am I going to do with this lil surrogate child of mine," I think as I watch her deep in thought.

"Good night . . . Nikki James" . . . "Alright Bitch," she affectionately says, signifying a great time had with our many antics in the studio that night. "I'll see you in the morning," I say as I went up the stairs to bed.

I opened the bedroom door to the menu screen of "Rush Hour III" on repeat. Nikolaus is out like a light and naked on the bed. I kiss him on his penis and then on his forehead and cover his body up with the comforter. I cut off the lights, get undressed and shut down the DVD player and TV and get in bed.

162

Paris in the Fall

After hearing Nikki James listening to Nina Simone's song as she sings so deeply about love in Paris, I couldn't help but drift off to sleep thinking of Nikolaus and my last romantic getaway to Paris in the fall of 2008. I'm sure many of you've probably heard of the tune "April in Paris." Well, a few years back I wanted to rewrite it to "Paris in the Fall" literally.

One day as Nikolaus was out of the house at work, I got to thinking about just how much of a hard worker he was. No matter how much crazy money I would make, he would just have to do his part at all times. I would bring probably a thousand dollars to every dollar he brought into our household, but it never would bother him at all, as he would treat me like he was my only means of support. With his small menial paycheck he would still lavish me with gifts as if he was the one with the major bankroll in the relationship. He was the proud type of man to never want from me what he wasn't or able to give me himself. A "salt of the earth" type with good home values. But then there was me. The over the top Madam who needed to be in the limelight at all cost.

I remember one particular time I just had to get some plastic surgery just because I missed the feeling and the high that I would always get the night before I was scheduled for work. I wanted to get some work on my eyelids as I felt they were looking rather aged. I wanted liposuction also to rid myself from some stubborn fatty deposits I had on one side of my waistline. Oh, and not to mention the mini-facelift to maintain my youth that I thought was fading fast.

Thus, it came the choice between getting my surgery and Nikolaus quitting his job in order to tend to me as I convalesced. As much as he hated to, he would dare let go his job in order that I could do what I wanted at all cost. Thus, this one day after healing all up, I was on the internet looking around for a great gift in order to show him my appreciation and also to shut him up from never letting me live my superficial choices down. Thus, I had to do something so nice to show him I cared.

And there on the internet it hit me . . . Being that he loved the movie "Rush Hour III" so much, I opted to take him on a romantic getaway to the hotel in which Chris Tucker and Jacki Chan stayed at in the movie which Nikolaus wanted to visit someday so bad. So while life was good to us, that day I surprised him while picking him up from work and whisking him off to Paris right from work as he was even still dressed in his CVS Pharmacy stock boy uniform as we boarded our first class Air France flight to love. We were off to a magical adventure just the two of us. We arrived in Paris where, however, upon first arrival we had a slight complication in the room choices as we checked into The Hotel Plaza Athenee.

I had originally booked our room with the full traditional Louis the 16th furnishings in order to let us enjoy the full feeling of submergence in the past. However, the room we received upon check-in was a super modern room that I could have easily gotten in our homeland at the Waldorf Astoria or something. I wanted my Nikolaus to feel as though he was the king of France. But the whole thing was off, down to the view of the Eifel Tower and all. Everything was all wrong and the hotel management could clearly read the disappointment all over my face as he and his staff scurried around to rectify the problem.

"Excuse-moi Madam," he would say, hoping that I would not want to take my business over to the RITZ. I explained to him that we were looking for an authentically decorated room of a certain period. And without another gesture he had whisked us off to one of the top rooms in the building. It was a palace to say the least. Nik and I had been transported back through time as we entered the room that was obviously fit for Queen Marie Antoinette herself. The walls were all gilded and adorned with gold leafing and all sorts of French motifs that screamed magnificent, with chandeliers sparkling. With five rooms in our new suite for the three weeks we were to be in Paris, there was more than enough room to live like royalty. The room value was six thousand Euros a night. However, because of the hotel's error, we received it for the set price of our first room of one thousand Euros per night. I had been to Paris plenty of times alone in business or with other friends and all, but nothing felt as good as seeing Paris through the innocent first time eyes of Nikolaus. Within moments as he changed out of his CVS uniform to get showered and dressed in one of his many suits I had purchased for him, he was transcended into his own Rush Hour III movie, as I would film him all throughout our visit with my cellphone camera.

Our nights together were filled with horse drawn carriages throughout the night in order to get us from one location to the next. I had the best Caviar I had ever eaten, as I watched Nikolaus enjoy his first illusive Cuban cigar. We would rendezvous with friends we would meet all throughout town, as we would live like the transatlantic couple we were.

Late morning brunches on the terrace of our hotel room overlooking the streets, we would bask in the hustle and bustle of the Europeans making their way through life far, far away from the world we new back home. We hung out with the art scene and danced the nights away with the bourgeoisies that would be so attracted to our air of Americana flair. I loved seeing Nikolaus become so acclimated with the culture all about him. All the great spots we hit with precision as we truly enjoyed the French life. However, despite being in the most romantic city of the world, Nik and I were so busy that we never had time to make love in the city of love. With Euro Star train rides across the countryside of France, we traveled to London on the weekends as time seemed fleeing and we had all our lives to make love whenever we wanted. But for now we enjoyed the innocence like two kids lost in love.

CHAPTER 17

FEBRUARY 7, 2011

7:00 a.m. I wake up and check my business voicemail. Schefee has left me several messages . . . "Good morning Lillian. It's Schefee. My cousins are here from London and at the hotel already. I'm in traffic, but I'll be there to meet you ina bit. Chow."

8:00 a.m. Still in bed . . . so tired from the night before. My back is killing me . . . Got to get a more firmer bed . . . Nikolaus still asleep.

9:00 a.m. Nikolaus is up and getting ready for his morning jog. I can smell coffee brewing which means that Eve must also be up and in the kitchen cooking breakfast. Nikki James is in the shower as if she wasn't the drunkard just a few hours ago. God, can this girl hold her booze.

10:00 a.m. I am up now and head to the bathroom for a shower to get my day started. Nikolaus is back and kisses me good morning. Nikki James has her breakfast, a cup of

Vodka to start her day. Eve is down at her desk working on photographs while listening to Beyonce on her computer monitor.

11:00 a.m. Still feeling a bit groggy from the night before in the studio. I rather spend a quiet day in the comfort of my home with my makeshift family unit, but work is calling and I have to keep to a disciplined schedule. I had given the girls my word that I would be there today. So it's got to be done. And besides, I can spend the rest of the day home in once done, if I still was feeling this comfy cozy kinda way. All freshend up now . . . and it's time for work.

While down in the kitchen pouring me a cup of coffee, Nikki James is breaking from habit and begins to pour her a cup too. "I really need to slow down with the drinking. Right?" she asked me as if I never noticed.

"Yeah girl you got to get help," I say as she looked as if that's not what she was expecting me to say.

"Where you off to?" she asked as she scooted off the countertop that she seems to always mistaken for a seat. I tell her that I have a job to do, as she squeezed the carnation creamer out into her coffee. Nine sugars and a wallop of Vodka. I just look at her and shake my head. "I want to go," she says as if she was about 7 years old asking her mother to tag along to work for fun.

I tell her to come on and she grabs her booze and her bag and we head to the front door. As we walked down the driveway to get into the car, Nikki James seemed so elated to be going on a job with me. I assured her that this is just work and not fun as I needed to get back home in order to spend some quality time with Nik.

I told her that I had been running the streets all week

long and Nikolaus and I hadn't spent any quality time together in what seemed like forever. "My man needs some lovin'," I said as we were pulling out of the driveway.

All week long had been nothing but an escapade of exotic dancers from Club Onyx and reality girls from VH1. Everyone wanting a piece of me when all I wanted to do was be home up under Nikolaus. I was so happy that I was treading the path to exiting the pumping business quite well. I had acquired over $19, 990,000.00 saved up and was off to hit the 20 million mark by day's end, which was my goal to leave the business and invest in a legitimate future for Nikolaus and I.

It seemed that this last week of the business has truly tested my patience as I dealt with parties up in the Germantown section of the city, at a few parties hosted by Back Shots throughout the week, who was one of the top exotic pole dancers in the city. I really liked to hang out while doing the procedures of these clients, but they all seem to be weed-heads and I would always leave her place smelling like a smoker as so much of whatever she and her friends were smoking would stick in my clothes. Needless to say, I was kinda to the point now of getting over the type of girls that were beginning to now flood the market for my services.

However, then there were my girls like and of Rose Bud's caliber . . . those with class and really seeking something good out of life. "What would they do?" I thought to myself as I entered the entrance ramp of the highway out towards the Philadelphia International Airport. My times with Rose Bud and girls like her was always great and informative and productive. I benefitted from them just as well as they all did from me. I had made some great connections and had made a small fortune in our dealings as those types didn't mind paying top dollar for a job well done. Perhaps I could do it exclusively for them. Whatever the case, I now am far away from the threat of ever having to go back to the dreads of the "Family Business," thus, I must always remember of the blessing that the pumping business has been to me.

"Chill," I said to Nikki James as I looked over at her as I broke out of my thoughts, "that alcohol is going to kill you girl if you don't get a grip on it."

Nikki James had always drank. Even as a teenager, but never to this extent. She seemed to have a lot on her mind and wanted to zone out of reality through the travel size bottle of booze she kept as a staple in her bag. It seems that ever since that time a few years back at the turn of the millennium (year 2000), the time she went off to hang out in New York at that gay club with one of my old sex workers Alexus Ward, who left her to be drunkenly carried off by some Puerto Rican poppy after the club let out, she ain't been right since.

I remember her frantically calling me back home in Philadelphia when the alcohol wore off and she came to her senses and realized that this quack pot had dressed her in men's clothes while leaving her for dead wandering the streets of New York City, my poor Nikki James ain't been right since, As if she is hiding something so horrific that she has to cloak it with liquor. I sure hope she can let go whatever it is that hunts her. And damn that slutty bitch Alexus Ward. She should have been more of a friend to Nikki James and checked for her . . . if she was supposed to had been her friend at all.

Passing the Villanova College exit on the highway,

Nikki James breaks the silence that seemed to be so painful to her, considering my last statement to her about her drinking. "Girl, I really like that RUCKUS song you recorded last night. You should really cut a music video for it." I was still kinda in deep thought about what could it be that's got her so dependent on alcohol every day all day. But at any rate, Nikki James has always needed my assistance for emotional support and I wasn't about to let her down now . . . no matter how much I didn't understand what she was hiding deep down inside. We've been friends for what seems like forever and I'm sure she'll get to talking one of these days.

It seems though, that the moment she's ready to talk to me about whatever's troubling her—I mean really, really ready to open up—she shoves yet another cocktail down her throat. But that's how she is. Someday I'm sure she'll get around to telling me what it is that ails her.

"Yeah," I was thinking about doing a video for it too."

"Why?" I asked her. "You want to be in it?"

"Bitch, I thought you would never ask," Nikki James shouted out and started to gyrate in her seat while talking about selling it to the cameras.

"Girl, you're crazy," I said and couldn't help to forget all about her needing to stop drinking. Nikki James reminded me so much of the character Patsy from the British TV show, Absolutely Fabulous, and I was her Adeana many of our friends would always compare us.

We pulled into the Hampton Inn Hotel parking lot right next to Schefee's eggshell white Eddy Bauer Land

Rover. "Great," I'm thinking, "they're all here." I tell Nikki James that I don't know just how long I will be and that she should come up with me. We get out of the car, she grabs her purse and I grab my supplies and we, without a thought, head into the hotel entrance.

Walking through the lobby was like walking through the lobby of any of the many hotel lobbies I had visited around the world in my travels dealing in the silicone oil business of body sculpting. We board the elevator and got off on the fourth floor as left in my voicemail by Schefee, wondering what was taking me so long to get there. Off of the elevator is Schefee walking from her room towards me. "Hey Lil, I was just about to call you again."

I told her that traffic was bad as I went on to introduce her to Nikki James. They happily greeted each other and we all walked up to room 425.

CHAPTER 18

——————

MORE . . . MORE . . . MORE

"**O**MG!!! Hello Lillian. It's nice to see you again," Carmen said as she came over to hug me.

"Hello Theresa," I said as I looked over with a smile, still looking for the last of the threesome I met a few months ago. "Where is Betty?" I asked Carmen.

"Oh Betty's husband didn't let her come this time," Theresa answered back before I could say anymore. Noticing with one girl not attending, there was still a massive mountain of luggage bellowing out of their small closet. And that is when Carmen told me that they had flown into the country with three other friends, but they were off to see family in New York City, which explained all the luggage. I then proceeded to introduce Carmen and Theresa to Nikki James also as she sat down over in a corner for the duration of our visit together.

Excitement filled the room as I unloaded my supplies.

Carmen assisted me on setting up my worktable and then we began to talk about prices, products and so forth as I remember just how much Carmen wanted to see bulk in her last session, but seemed to be woefully dissatisfied on her last visit to me, because I was not willing to reopen her last session's wounds in order to give her more.

Originally Carmen had wanted $3,500 dollars worth of AdatoSil 5000 this time, because she had said the product didn't really take well from her last session. So she wanted to try something else more expensive. However, during her and her friend's entering the US and coming through US Customs off their flight in, she and her girlfriends all got flagged on suspicion for trafficking drugs into the country and were pulled off into an interrogation room by a Customs Agent for questioning as to just why they were back in the United States so soon after arriving and leaving just a few months back in November.

Carmen went on to tell me how they harassed her, accusing her of being sassy and difficult during their questioning. Thus, they confiscated some of her cash until she was to depart the USA. Therefore she could only buy a small quantity of product now, which seemed to upset her. She now only had eighteen hundred dollars to spend. Once we did the math, she then realized with the AdatoSil 5000 being so expensive, it would have barely been worth the trip over, being that she had already experienced a letdown on her expectations her last voyage over.

So with the facts as it stood, she decided to go with the Dow Corning brand I carried, which was a lower grade of silicone, but non-toxic and preferred by many of my clients on a budget, which allowed them to get more bang for their buck. I then went on to assure Carmen not to worry about obtaining her ideal bum any further. And that regardless of the rude American Custom Agent, I would do a fine job and he would not spoil her trip. With an expression of relief emblazed across her face, she went on to tell me more about their encounter with the Customs Agent and how he even went as far as to threaten to put her back on the plane to England if she should choose to not calm her sassy mouth down. She said she then humbled herself as she knew she needed to get to me, regardless of her pride being thwarted by the agent.

I once again assured Carmen that I would be very generous with the cheaper product, as it was very inexpensive for me to obtain. This seemed to make Carmen very elated and we began to prepare for the session.

I began marking them for their injections shortly after I had performed my sterility procedures with the help of them all. A bubble butt had become all the rage, so Theresa and Carmen had decided to try that shape in order to get a more dramatic effect.

Carmen went first this time, and Theresa was to go last. In all, each of their sessions were about forty-five minutes long. After all was completed, Carmen went into the bathroom to inspect her results. However, out of the bathroom Carmen had told me that she still did not see the results she was hoping a second trip over the Atlantic would bring.

Carmen looked over to Theresa and shouted in her thick, rich cockney British accent that she wanted "more . . . more . . . more" and that she had to have a really big bum. Being that Carmen now had no more money, she seemed more desperate than ever to convince me to front her an additional session in order to obtain the look she so ravenously wanted. I advised her that I had never gone back over my work so soon before healing. And that it wasn't about the money, but more about safety. She persisted more now than ever in asking me . . . no, begging me to give her the extra product I had on hand. It was a deep desperation coupled with the fact that I just felt plain bad about what she had went through with her disappointment of her last session back in November and the harassment that she then received just recently from customs agents as she was coming to see me again. I felt it to be somewhat my own obligation to help her reach her goal despite all obstacles. For now I could relate to such desperation as I was once in those very shoes Carmen was now trying to claw her way out of.

With this overwhelming emotion I was feeling, along with the driving feelings of obligation, I agreed to help Carmen in any way I could. I told her I would do an additional session for her free of charge. She was overjoyed at what I had just told her and immediately she hopped back on the bed for another round of silicone injections. As I began to set up more product for the next round, she then became very chatty and began to tell me more about just what happened with the customs agent and how the agent was so mean and arrogant to her. Also, she had gone deeper in depth about the word exchange that she and he had in his office of his suspicions of her and her travel companions trafficking drugs. She said it was that exchange that brought on his threat of denial entry into the USA, in which he gave her the choice to either shut up and answer their questions, or get back on the next flight smokin' to London. With that, she said she just had to shut up and take his arrogant tongue lashing in order to get back to Lillian's table for her ultimate goal of a bigger bum.

Looking back now in retrospect, with that choice of going home or staying for a session with me, I so wished that Carmen would have taken fates' offer of a last chance at life. The second session seemed to go just as smooth as the one just before. However, Carmen had been set on overseeing the whole thing. As I performed the procedure, she would contort her body in order that she could watch every drop that was being pumped into her as if the silicone oil would not reach its destination goal of pumping her up to her expectations, without her viewing it. As I went in with my final injection, her buttocks were much higher than it ever had looked before. I was elated to know that she would have had to be happy with these results, as her body was looking wonderfully comparable to all that she was wishing for.

All was looking great. However, Carmen asked for yet one more shot, as she could clearly see from her position that the syringe in which I was using to pump her contained enough for one more shot, and giving it to her I could see that she was finally satisfied. Her buttocks were high as they could possibly go. That ultimate Serena Williams bubble butt. Carmen was the happiest I'd know her to be during these injections. And she really and truly finally did seem satisfied. However, that last shot would prove to be the greatest mistake. Bonding our fates into one as Murderer & Victim forever in time.

During the end of the procedure, I noticed nothing alarming that would raise any alarms. Carmen was still very talkative, energetic, and elated to finally have the body she needed to conquer the world via the music video scene.

All she was longing for was right at her rears end and

man . . . I never witnessed a more happier client in all my work throughout the years. I was happy to have been able to make her happy. And that was a great feeling to feel.

I was amazed at the work myself, to be completely honest. It was a beautiful work of art. And I was happy to have another happy customer to spread the word of my great work if I should have a change of heart and further continue to do body sculpting in the future.

As I packed my bags to now head over to Schefee's room in order to withdraw some fluid from a boil she said she had felt the past few days, Carmen then told me that she wanted to apologize for being so aggressive with me in her attempts to sway me to giving her more product. She felt as though she might have been too forceful with me and was sorry if I was offended. However, she felt she just had to go back to London happy with her results in order to fulfill her dreams as a video vixen.

Happy with her results now, she told me that she had been pre-celebrating the night before with a few guys that they knew and invited up to their room for drinks. She nonchalantly then went on to explain that they were having a great time drinking some banned drink in the US called Four Loco. A drink that she had been blacking out from a few times just prior to my arrival, which then rose all sorts of alarms within me.

I asked her "What was Four Loco?" And that's when everyone in the room—Theresa, Nikki James and Schefee keyed in to the conversation, explaining to me that it was a notorious alcoholic beverage now banned in the USA for many deaths on college campuses across the nation.

Four Loco was a caffeinated alcoholic beverage that it seemed Nikki James was very well versed in, needless to say. As all in the room went on talking and joking about it, I was careful not to want to alarm others about my now looming worries. I had a very strong stance against any of my clients drinking, or taking any type of products that could possibly thin the blood during a procedure.

My Theory

See . . . many people think getting silicone injections are just something that is not too serious due to the fact that there is no major surgical work being done per se, As the cutting of the skin like actual surgery or any other thing deeply invasive, that would call for major anesthesia and sutures in order to close a wound.

Being that an injector only uses needles tends to send the misconception to others that it's a nonthreatening procedure. However, when I explain to my clients that they should not drink any alcoholic beverages or take anything like pain pills or diet pills or anything else for that matter that can and will alter the state of the thickness of the blood, it is so that upon getting these injections, one's blood can be as in much of its normal state as possible. When one has alcohol or intakes other blood altering substances in their system, the blood does not coagulate and clot normally as it would if alcohol or any other substance were <u>not</u> in the blood.

Thus, if the injector was to accidentally puncture a vein or artery while performing the injections, instead of the blood clotting and acting as a stopper to the puncture in the way as in a normal vein in order to heal and keep any foreign substance out of the vascular system . . . such as silicone.

Thus, if the blood is too thin, the puncture would not clot, thus allowing foreign substances to invade the bloodstream and circulate through the body, thus causing serious bodily harm or death.

Therefore, it is of the utmost important for anyone getting any type of work done, whether legitimate or not, to be sure to always follow directions of the provider. However, I would highly advise to always seek proper certified care providers, thus, never having to suffer the same mistakes as I and Carmen.

WARNING WARNING WARNING WARNING"

Everyone knew that I strictly forbid the taking of any type of painkillers, alcoholic drinks, diet pills, caffeinated drinks and so forth prior to my seeing them for injections. Moreover, I could definitely remember telling Carmen and the others back prior to their last visit in November of my pre-op directions of being careful with their diet and intake for safety reasons. Thus, I'm not understanding why would these girls party prior to my arrival.

But nevertheless, all seemed fine and Carmen and I talked about hooking up and hanging out in London on my summer trip to the UK later that year. We then exchanged personal info along with her Twitter handle as "Carmen London," and I took her info, although I usually never did when I worked with a person who served as in intermediary to bring me clientele like Schefee did. I never liked to feel as though I was stepping on someone's toes and taking them out of their position as broker, for I was a broker myself in my other business, and I strive to do good business.

After we exchanged info, Carmen asked me about how she could send me money in order to pay for that last session I had given her. I told her that it was for free. However, she insisted on sending me something for her gratitude. Thus, I gave her my Western Union account information as Nikki James and I said our goodbyes and headed out the door to Schefee's room up the hall.

As I was entering Schefee's room, Nikki James and I got to joking at how Carmen put us in the mindset of a black Amy Winehouse. We both really enjoyed Carmen and Theresa's company and looked forward to seeing them again.

Once inside Schefee's room, she was already getting undressed and in her robe, ready for me to do the extraction of her boil that she had developed on her left buttock. It was not much of a big deal, but once I pulled out the needle and syringe, Schefee began her drama-queen antics . . . as she's always . . . since the day we first started working together years back at the Microtel Hotel. She, with a passion, hated the sight of needles.

So for the next few minutes she would dance about the room in her stilettoes and robe, as I would have to calm her nerves about my taking my time with her and giving her an extra shot of lidocaine in order to sooth
the pain.

As my patience began to run thin, a knock came at the door. It was Carmen who had walked up the hall from her room in hopes that I would still be on site in order to help her reseal one of her seals that must have come loose due to her being on her feet and in the mirror inspecting her fresh work, although I had advised them to stay in bed for up to ten hours to recuperate.

The leakage of a loose suture was not unusual, as all that was needed was to reseal the injection site with a dab of crazy glue, which seals the skin along with the application of a cotton ball in order to create a bond with the chemical combination of the two in which to create a seal.

I told her to head back to her room and lie there on the bed and I would be right over to seal her back up. As she walked towards the door, she had begun to cough, which seemed very odd, as she had not been coughing prior to her coming into the room during our session, so I asked her was she feeling okay.

And she said she had a bit of a tickle in her throat and thought she needed a hot drink of tea in order to clear up some congestion that was forming in her chest. However, whatever the case, she was most concerned with the valuable product that was now leaking out of her buttocks and wanted it to be sealed more than anything. Otherwise, she said all was fine, as she left to go back to her room.

With haste, I concluded my visit in Schefee's room in order to get back over to tend to Carmen's leakage. Upon walking back into the room occupied by Carmen and Theresa, Carmen seemed fine but continued to have a bout with coughing.

As she laid on the bed, I leaned over to her and cleaned up her buttock area and redressed the injection site without incident, and asked her if she wanted someone to grab her some more tea. As I tended to Carmen, I began to wonder if she was having a reaction to her injections and the combination of the Four Loco she drank earlier.

I then told her that I thought we needed to call the emergency ambulance in order to have her buttocks drained for possible complications, and assured her she would be fine after, in order to have the procedure again at a later date.

She was not thinking anything of the sort, as she proceeded to convince me that all was fine. And perhaps she should just get something to eat. She told me that she would order them something from the Chinese food takeout, and all would be fine. She did not think what she was experiencing warranted enough for a trip to the hospital in order to drain all that she had struggled to get to obtain her massive bum.

She had just figured she felt the last wave of the alcohol in her system and was sure it was nothing to become alarmed about. By this time all alarms were ringing full volume in my gut, of just what the hell was in this banned drink and how in the world did Carmen and her friends get their hands on it, with them just arriving into the country. I asked her again if she felt bad enough that we should take her to the emergency room, or call 911, and again she told me that she would be fine once she ate.

By this time Schefee is now back in the room with us and I tell her to pour a hot cup of tea. She handed Carmen the cup of tea as I was feeling Carmen's chest and asking her yet again about making an emergency call, when I noticed that she and Schefee now had this underlining dialogue quietly going on with their eye and expressions. I quickly interject . . . "What's going on?" And that's when Schefee smiles and playfully told me that calling the emergency system would be the last thing Carmen would ever want to do, now that she's finally gotten the body she so desperately wanted. Schefee went on to say to me that Carmen has finally reached her desired size and beautiful figure, that she would never want to chance losing it for anything in the world, as she finally felt the best she'd ever had.

Although I knew just what the reason could be of Carmen not wanting to have to go to the emergency room to possibly have her newly formed buttock drained for safety reasons, my first priority was her safety and her maintaining good health. I then went on to explain very seriously to her right there in front of Schefee, Nikki James and Theresa that the most important thing right now at present was to insure that she was not suffering from complications with whatever might have been in that Four Loco and possibly triggering an adverse reaction to the silicone she had just received. I tried my best in order to stress to her that if she was having a reaction that her health should be considered first. That if there was any problem stemming from the combo, that that should be our first priority. That even if she should have to get the product drained out of her, she need not worry because she could always come back and get more done at a later date free of charge, as a make up session that I gave to all my clients if too much of their product was to leak out during their travels home after they waited the allotted time I advised for proper healing.

But Carmen once again assured me all would be fine with her, and she just needed to eat. Which she then proceeded to tell me about how she was getting more and more hungrier by the minute and wanted to call for the food delivery. There was nothing more that I could do, as I couldn't very well force her to do as I wanted. So I and Nikki James said our goodbyes and headed out the door. I said a final goodbye to Theresa and asked how was she feeling in which she replied that she felt just fine. "See you later Lillian," would be the last words Carmen would ever say to me.

Exiting the hotel lobby was just as noneventful as our arrival, as we walked through the lobby and through the double doors back to my car to pack in my supply bag and head back towards the highway. As I also remembered I had another client in the airport area waiting to see me before I headed back home. I saw this client also with the very same product I had used at the last appointment with Carmen and Theresa with no incident. Thus, I collected my cash from my client's husband and proceeded to take Nikki James home as she just remembered she had to study some lines she had for an audition Tuesday morning for a Mercedes Benz voiceover commercial she had been trying out for. By the time I got back home and relaxed, I wanted to phone Schefee in order to check on Carmen to see how she was feeling after she had eaten. Schefee answered the phone with the same calmness as always, as she told me that Carmen didn't feel any better. And as a matter of fact, she seemed to feel a little worse and that perhaps it might have been alcohol poisoning or something.

Wth! . . . I'm thinking. This poor child is just having the worse luck on this trip here to America this time around. She said also that she had called an ambulance and that they were going to take Carmen to the emergency room in order to run a few routine tests and she should be expecting her back in a short while.

I wanted to stay on the phone to ask Schefee more details of what all took place during the time that I had left the hotel and them finally deciding to call the emergency transports. But Schefee just shrugged it all off and assured me once again she was fine and probably just at worse was going to get her stomach pumped of all the Four Loco she'd consumed prior to my arrival at the hotel to do the session.

After that last conversation on the phone with Schefee, I might have called three or four times more, when Schefee told me that she received a text from Theresa stating that they would be headed back to the hotel shortly, once Carmen was done with a few more tests.

At that time it was about 10:00 p.m. and I was very tired, still from not getting a good night sleep the night before due to my Occult revival of a recording session with Nikki James laying vocal tracks for RUCKUS.

After falling to sleep by the telephone that evening, I awoke about 10:30 a.m. in the morning that next day, February 8th. Nikolaus was at work and about to get off and would be waiting for me to pick him up. Usually he would finish up at work about 7:00 a.m. at his BJ's stocking job. However, last night his boss had asked him to work an additional half shift. So I had a few extra hours to catch up on some much needed sleep. I didn't have to pick him up until 12:00 noon.

I didn't even get in the shower by this time yet because I wanted to phone Schefee to check in on how everything turned out at Carmen's visit to the ER last night. Without even a ring, it seemed that Schefee picked up the other end when I asked right away how was everything. In an "around the way hoot-chi- momma kind of sounding way" and much louder than I'd ever remember hearing her voice, she says, "What do you think?"

I say, "What's up girl? What's going on?"

And again Schefee says, in an even louder tone than the first time, "What do you think?" By this time I am in the middle of my bedroom on my very plush antique oriental rug, as I heard the next few words that brought me to my knees so hard to the ground that if it wasn't for that rug softening my fall, I too would have needed to go to the emergency room next. And that's when all the blood in my heart rushed straight to my head as Schefee again repeated the word I was praying I hadn't heard her say correctly the first time. R-I-P baby!

At that point my heart jolted and I'm in utter disbelief as Schefee makes sure yet again I heard her words and understood exactly what she was saying. CARMEN IS DEAD LILLIAN! In those next minutes I wanted so bad to think this was some demented joke that the girls were all playing on me right now. Because if it wasn't and this is all real, how will I ever go on to live with the fact that I and death stood side-by-side yesterday afternoon in the last moments of a deadly dance that would later claim Carmen's life.

The first words from my mouth was the hardest I ever composed. As my tongue felt so heavy and my mouth so dry, I was able to speak finally . . . "NO! Don't tell me that," I screamed through the phone as sweat was pouring down from my palms with such stress on my psyche like never before.

As my knees felt forever stuck and sinking fast in a pool of quicksand that my rug had materialized into upon hearing that news and the rest of the awful list of chain of events that had conspired throughout the night as I slumbered. I began to feel deeply desperate to grab something . . . anything . . . that would relieve me of my now pain, and guilt of having been the cause of poor Carmen's loss of life. Although I wasn't yet sure if it had been the injections because this type of thing had never happened, but the coincidence of the factors were too close to home.

"Lillian . . . Lillian!!! Pull it together," Schefee began to scream at me. "Have the police gotten to your house yet?" she asked me next, as if I was already aware of all that had happened.

"The police?" I yell back into the phone. "What do you mean the police?" as she began to tell me that the police had already been out to her mansion in Burgeon County, New Jersey in order to question her and seize any evidence they would need in order to prosecute the suspicious death case.

Her car, computers and many other electronics she began to list off that was taken from her home by the detective in the wee early hours of the morning, seeking answers to just what went on in that hotel room that led up to Carmen needing to go off to the hospital.

As the minutes went on and I began to realize all that was truly going on, and the severity of just what could happen to us, Schefee began to tell me of the story that she was going to tell the police, and needed me to go along with in order to clear us of any wrongdoing.

She goes on to say . . . That these were her cousins who flew in from London and were visiting her here in the U.S. to go on a few modeling runs with her, in hopes of landing a deal themselves by being discovered on the spot. She also went on to say that she would lie to the police and tell them that they must have wandered off and got some kind of buttock injections while out at the modeling run with her, as that was a norm in her field of work.

By this time, not only am I in a complete state of awe at the news of Carmen, I'm also amazed at just how well

Schefee is taking the sudden death of her cousin so "as-a-matter-of-factly." The fact that she had thought of this outrageously elaborate plan and was so unemotional at all throughout this mind blowing event that was building up all around her in the midst of what was now becoming a murder investigation.

As I'm wondering why in the world would we need to tell such lies, as it was truly an accident. Once I began to pull my emotions in check and zero back into the pure bullshit spewing out of Schefee's mouth, I'm thinking as I'm say, "Schefee what are you talking about? If Carmen is dead, there is a very serious situation we are now in, and some silly little lie about a model's run is just not going to cut it." She then tells me to pull it together again and that the police would soon be at my place for questioning.

By now I'm wondering "What the fuck are you talking about? The police coming to my home? How the hell do they know where I live?" I ask her as I already know that I never gave her my address out of caution of being home invaded due to the type of cash business I was in. She then goes on to tell me that she didn't give them any info. However, she assumed that if they found her out in Burgeon County, New Jersey, that they'd have no problem finding me, who lives within the city limits. By this time I'm thinking the very same thing about her ludicrous fabrication of a model's run story she wants me to correlate with.

As Schefee begins to go on about the whole thing, the things that she is saying out of her mouth are not adding up. Thus, something in my gut is now telling me that Carmen and Theresa are not at all family, like she led me to believe. In which, I later learn that Schefee did exactly what

I asked her not to do . . . get clients off the internet via blogs.

With the non-emotions that Schefee is exhibiting in the death of who's suppose to be her "cousin," coupled with the seedy way she's now trying to sweep the responsibility of just what happened under the rug, something just wasn't feeling right about the whole thing.

Meanwhile, I'm thinking . . . as my mind flashes of pictures throughout my house of all that I have in storage that could very much implicate me in not only the current situation, but other supplies that could very well be misconstrued by the police for illegal activities . . . i.e. my Biobeautylabs.com laboratory with all my skin lighting injectable and products. Not too sure if they were illegal in the USA or not, I began to panic, thinking of the many other charges that could stem from the now death of Carmen.

I have to get rid of it all! All the evidence must go! My mind is now running wild with the dark possibilities of anything in the house that could remotely seem like a bad idea to have around if the cops should actually find their way to my door. All of this before 11:45 a.m. in time enough to pick up Nikolaus from work and fix him a late breakfast . . . DAMN!

CHAPTER 19

GETTING RID OF THE EVIDENCE

As I rush in haste to the room in the house where I keep all my supplies . . . The stock closet of my dressing room. I began to wonder "where" . . . "Where" is everything? I can't seem to think right in the midst of my panicking. My nerves are moving my body as if in autopilot mode. I still can't seem to move fast enough. Adrenaline is fueling my legs and arm, but like a movie in slow motion, I can't seem to make any real assessment of just where the hell to begin. My mind seems to be locking up on me. Shit, I can't seem to think straight in all my emotions. This has to feel like what those people who are in a life or death situation talk about when they say they can't think straight in order to make sound and rash decisions. I feel stuck. Damn, I can't remember where anything is right now.

Oh yeah . . . in my pants rack behind the jeans on the last shelf level. I sling back the rack of jeans to reveal all my medical shit hiding behind it, out of sight from visitors. As I began to just totally demolish my once beautiful dressing room, I find it all staring back at me. Needles, lidocaine, silicon and all kinds of trouble that could surely sink my ship deeper if discovered.

Shit . . . I think to myself . . . The cops could be here any second. I want to scream. No, I think I want to cry. As I watch my dressing room become my enemy, harboring all that could take me down if the right detective should find their way here. Packs and packs of white powder L-Glutathione that I'm sure will be taken as cocaine at first sight. How oh how do I get myself into these damn situations. "Calm down Padge," I think to myself. "Just clear out all this shit and all would be fine once you get this all figured out." I want to just ball up in a corner and cry. I can't believe what is happening.

First things first. Get rid of the L-Glutathione that could easily be mistaken for coke, or some other illicit drug. I run down to my stockroom for BioBeautylabs. com, with all my skin lightening injectables that seem so wrong! I began to feel like the Angela Bassett character in the movie "Waiting to Exhale" as she rips apart her cheating husband's wardrobe room. It was the same visuals that were now taking place in mine, but on a much more serious level of motivation than a simply cheating spouse. We are talking about MURDER here, jail, trial and maybe even the electric chair. I'm thinking this is too much on my heart—help me God.

As I'm slipping and falling all throughout the house on my rampage to clear out anything that could send me to prison for the rest of my life, it seems that every single thing in my stockpile wants to fall off the shelves now into my lap. I can't believe this is happening . . . I think as my beautiful stock rooms become totaled in the search to find all the shit that links me to black market silicone injections.

As I get done with my now devastated home, I realize that I am not at all licensed to do business just yet with my import/export business either with illegal contraband that I had shipped to me from Asia . . . everything must go! I'm screaming to myself, "Just get it all out of here Padge! It's beauty products though." I try to rationalize with myself, but self preservation tells me that it all must go! I could get years for each bottle of this stuff too! "MY GOOD GOD" . . . Padge what the hell were you thinking to start such a racket as black market beauty?" I began to converse with myself in third party. "I don't know Padge . . . it all sounded great at the time . . . Well, whatever the case . . . There is no need to argue with yourself now."

There's a world of evidence that don't even have anything to do with illegal silicone injections, but would make you look just plain guilty! Get rid of it all without a moment to spare as Nikolaus will soon be calling me any minute to let me know that he's ready to be picked up from work.

Finally, I think I have it all, as I run out the house and up the driveway to get the car to load it up. I get in and start it, still confused in my mind as to where am I even going to take this shit and trash it. I pull the car down in front of the door and load up the trunk with all I have found. Bags and bags of stuff.

"Oh, hello Ms. Vicky," one of my neighbors Mrs. Wong says to me as I'm getting down to loading the last bags in my trunk.

"Oh, hello Mrs. Wong," I say, as I'm now perplexed to

have a witness to verify my activity to the cops if questioned.

"Nice day, huh?" she goes on to ask me in her let's make nice small talk kinda way.

"Yes mam Mrs. Wong, today is a great day," I say out loud while thinking to myself, I wish this bitch just go in the damn house and leave me to my business and find a damn dumpster in order to stash this shit. "Oh yes," I say. "Nikolaus is fine Mrs. Wong." BITCH GO AWAY. I want this lady gone!

"Sudi Ki."

Thank god she's leaving. Well Mrs. Wong can barely speak clear English. She would never be able to compose just what to tell a cop if he was to ask her, let alone translate what she might have just saw me doing.

I'm now in the car finally, as I bid Mrs. Wong goodbye. Just as I'm about to pull out of the driveway and make that jolt down Montgomery Avenue in order to dump the goods, an Ardmore police patrol car is cruising slowly by the grill of my car just barely out on the road looking for the right of way as he seems to be suspicious of me. I wonder does he know? As he cruises by the front of my Jag, does he know something, or is this just another case of some bigot ole white cop who can't take the sight of a young black person living in such a well to do neighborhood and driving such a high end car, most likely better than the one he got at home?

Well, I guess it is the latter, because he just cruises on by and up the road as I swing out of the drive onto the main road. Up Montgomery Avenue, I'm thinking to myself, "Where in the hell could I dump all this evidence?" Finally, it came to me. The dumpsters behind the Acme Supermarket, where Nikolaus and I met seven year back. Right in the rear of the LA Fitness center adjacent to the market.

Yes . . . and then I will jump right onto Route 22 up to Plymouth Meeting area so I could pick Nikolaus up right after. "Great Padge, perfect plan," I am thinking. I can do it all in a matter of 20 minutes.

So I thought as I'm slipping and sliding, falling in my stiletto thigh high boots on the ice patches at the front of the dumpster, it must have been a sight to see on the surveillance footage of the security cameras behind the Acme, as I dump bag after bag. I am falling all over the place to rid myself of the evidence that could send my ass to jail for not only the death of poor Carmen, but perhaps some hearty sentence for illegal import/export of beauty contraband from third world foreign countries. It was maddening to say the least.

After just 10 minutes of dumping at least 2.5 million in American dollars' worth of potential tax free cash in the damn dumpster, without a second glance, I jumped back into my car and headed up Route 22 to pick up Nikolaus.

I pulled into the BJ's parking lot just as any of the many other times I've come to pick Nikolaus up, after he ruined his car in a head on car collision, anxious to get to the Superfresh just a few months ago on one of his nights to cook dinner. That caused him to not only lose his car, but also losing his license for one too many moving violation points on his license.

"Hi babe." He jumps into the car and kisses me good afternoon and asks, what have I been up to all morning because he said it looked like I had been running a marathon before picking him up. "If only he knew," I mumbled under my breath as I pulled the keys out of the car's ignition as he proceeded to tell me about a great job prospect across the street from BJ's he got at Jone's Windowing and asked if we could stop by so he could follow-up on it before we headed home.

"Sure," I said, "but I got to ask you something on the way," as I spoke in a very somber tone. He looked over at me with no idea of what I was just about to tell him.

"Well, spill it out babe," he said, with much compassion as he then read the sad expression written on my face. And there sitting in the car in the parking lot of his job at BJ's wholesale products, I asked him . . . would he wait for me if I should have to go away to jail for a while due to something that had happened with my side business.

As the tears were falling from my face, my eyes still faintly blackened with yesterday's mascara on, due to a rough night the night before, he asked, "VIK, what the hell is going on?"

I told him that something terrible had happened Nikky baby. I could no longer control my emotions as he begins to hug me in order to assure me that nothing on earth could ever separate us at this now, our seven year mark of a wonderful love affair.

As I still can't seem to get the words to flow from my mouth, Nikolaus asked, "What the fuck is it Vik?" He goes on to tell me how much he loves me and how he just needs to know what is going on.

And there I said it . . . "One of the girls from London I saw yesterday for my body sculpting business must have had a bad reaction to the procedure or something, because she died."

Silence stilled the car as we just sat there in it, hugging and crying, unsure of what would become of such a beautiful thing we had been building. He again assured me that whatever I had to face ahead of this dreadful situation, come what may, that I would not have to face it alone. That he would be there not only for me, but with me, by my side every step of the way. He kissed me on my forehead and we exchanged seats, as he felt it was a chance worth taking for him to drive without his license because now I was too distraught to drive us anywhere.

Taking the wheel of the car, as I sat quietly in deep thought, he pulled us out of the BJ's parking lot and into the next, Jone's Windows factory.

By the time we had gotten home, Eve was up in the

kitchen as Nik went upstairs to take his shower before he went off to bed. I told Eve to take a drive with me around the back roads of Ardmore where the beautiful mansions stood nestled in the hills on the sprawling acres of snow covered grounds. Homes that I had vowed to own one just like in a short while after I had secured enough money with laundering my small fortune through my new internet business BioBeautylabs.com. A business which I had planned to take me to the next level of success by way of a multimillion dollar thriving internet based skin care line company.

It seemed that all my dreams would now be going up in smoke, to soon be buried with Carmen London. As I pulled over at the last house on that stretch of road, I turned to Eve to tell her that something bad had happened to one of my silicone business clients. It was one of the girls from London. "What happened?" She looked at me as she sat on the edge of her seat, not ready for the next words I would be telling her.

"SHE'S DEAD." There was a quick silence for a moment as Eve processed what I had just told her. And then in a bar-raid of questions she broke the silence.

"What are you talking about Padge?" she asked me with a half in shocked tone to her usually strong and hearty voice.

"She's dead Eve," I said to her for a second time, as I began to try to make sense of it all, as she and I never heard of anyone ever dying from injections before.

"She's dead," Eve repeated in an unbelievable and dazed look. "How?" she then asked, as I sat there with her, wondering what the hell could have happened. I then told her that the only thing I could really grasp that was different in the process yesterday in my performing the injections, as opposed to the many other thousands and thousands of time I had performed them throughout the years, was that she had been drinking. Drinking some banned liquor in the country called Four Loco. As we sat in the car, now in complete silence, Eve asked me what was I going to do, which seems to be the million dollar question of the day. As I sat there wondering . . . what does one do when they have just found out that they may have been the hand to take an innocent person's life?

After all my crazy shenanigans, my deeper silence of responsibility stepped in and I felt that after all it was a mistake that no one could have possibly foreseen. I felt I not only wanted, but needed to go to the police and own up to my mistake, but that would probably mean going off to jail right off the bat. I don't know . . . everything was feeling confusing and I was so out of my skin at that time.

I next dropped Eve back off at the house, as I was now going to head over to my parent's home in order to talk with them and pray. Oh yeah . . . and to drop off all the cash I had been saving in all my stiletto and Red bottom shoe boxes in the closet of my dressing room that I managed to grab in the mayhem of stripping down my dressing room riding it of all evidence.

To add more fuel to my now frantic nerves of what all was going on, now I was carrying almost 10 million in cash throughout the city on a rant of hysteria of also trying to get rid of the fruits of my crime. I figured if I was just calm and cool . . . I thought to myself, I wouldn't raise any alarms to anyone who might want to rob me or kill me for the small fortune I was now driving through the hood of west Philadelphia, on my way to momma and poppa's house with.

Finally, without incident, I arrived there with a parking spot that could be no more perfect parking than the spot right in front of their door. As I walked up the steps to the front door, mommy must have seen me through the glass window of the door as she had the blinds drawn open for the early afternoon sunlight to pour into the living room.

Because she seemed to open the door before I could even reach for the doorbell, unaware of the hectic morning I was already having. She welcomed me in and asked if I wanted to sit down to have lunch as she and poppa were just about to sit down to my favorite grits and liver meal. Mommy always makes the best liver and grits, smothered in onions I've ever tasted, but not today mom.

I sat quietly for a moment on the couch, unlike I usually would come in and be bouncing off the walls on first arrival. Poppa stared at me inquisitively, wondering what was on my mind and why the hell I was gripping for dear life to all those shoe boxes I had just sitting there on my lap.

My mother, loving my shoe collections, and Louboutin Red Bottoms being her favorite, was just staring at them, drooling as if I was about to give her them as a gift. As she mentioned something about a new purse she had, that she thought would look great with a nice pair of Red Bottoms and wished she and I wore the same size so she could borrow my shoes sometimes.

With as little emotions as possible, as I was now on the cusp of breaking down, I asked mom to take the boxes up to her dressing room and hold them for a few days and that's when poppa asked, what was the matter Padge and I proceeded to tell him all about this new business that I had been involved in now for the last few years, and just how wonderful things were, and then of the situation with Carmen, as mom's face went blank . . . and a hot plate of grits and liver hit the floor.

Poppa then looked at me with horror in his eyes and asked, "Was this the girl out by the airport?" It baffled me that he would know this as he said, "Dear Jesus God, it's you that they're looking for." And that's when he and mommy went on to tell me that it was all over the radio and TV news networks everywhere. He said that he had been watching CNN when the story first broke, and he and mom was just about to tune in to it on the TV in the kitchen as they ate their lunch, for any news updates. By this time it was everywhere . . . NBC News, CNN, ABC, CBS, Fox News and more . . . even all across the radio stations and even on KYW News radio, which poppa always kept on in his den for his sports news updates every ten minutes. Right at that moment as mommy was talking, poppa really seemed to grasp the magnitude of just where this was all heading for me and on what scale things were about to weigh on our family as a whole. Right then and there he and mommy grabbed my hand and sighed as we began to all pray to God to guide us all through the tsunami that was now headed straight at us.

CHAPTER 20

MAKING ORDER OUT OF CHAOS

After a few minutes of prayer and my parents assuring me that all would work out fine, and how the Lord loved me, I told them that I needed to take care of a few matters at the house preparing for whatever was to come next. Poppa was very nervous for me as it all showed on his tearful-eyed face and I could tell that he didn't want me to go anywhere, but to stay in their protection. But I figured if the cops were going to come and get me, it was going to have to be on my terms and at my own home.

So I told mom to keep my "shoe boxes" safe, and I would be sending a few more over shortly. Little be known to her, she would be holding a fortune from my illicit activities that she'd have yet to make in all her life working as a maid down at her beloved job, the Latham Hotel down there in Center City with all them rich white folk whose wealth was that of my aims to reach by any means necessary.

But not this way I thought. I am nobody's murderer as they were now labeling me this infamous buttock injection killer on the loose in KYW News radio brief updates on the quarter hour which I had now playing on the radio in my car as I scurried back home. I felt overwhelmed. OMG! "Nikki James," I thought while driving up not too far from the city limits. I need to call Nikki James and let her know all that's been happening. God . . . I hope she's back from her auditions.

I picked up my phone as I pulled over in the cut of, 63rd Street and City Avenue, before I was just about to hit Lancaster Avenue out towards my house.

"Hello, Nikki James?"

"Yeah biotch, I was just about to call you," she said. "Can you please come back and get me? I want to celebrate with you about me getting the gig."

I could tell by her trivial tone of speaking that she had no idea she had been the eye witness to a homicide only hours ago.

I told her to brace herself as I gave her the news of Carmen's sudden death and all that I had known about it possibly being linked to me and the silicone injections I had just given her. Listening to my awed tone, and knowing I could not have the mindset to travel all the way out to the northeast of Philadelphia to pick her up, she was floored to say the least, and told me to head home and she would be on the next train out to my place.

Immediately I cut her off and told her to not come because she was there too, and I didn't want her to get into any trouble because of me. With my then little knowledge of the law, I didn't want her to go down as an accomplice to murder. But Nikki James would have none of that, as she told me, "I am your friend to the end bitch, and if you go down, we go down together." As she had been my friend now for more than half her life, I knew there was no talking her out of it. So be it. She then said, "I love you bitch." Stay right there and I'll call you from the Ardmore train station.

I headed home in a huge haze of memory at this point. I can remember crawling into bed with Nikolaus like some sort of scared puppy dog, as Eve just worked on a few new air brushing jobs she had just gotten while she wondered just when it would be that the cops found out who and where I was.

I can also remember laying there with Nikolaus wondering just how much longer I would have the comfort of feeling his warm skin against mine in our bed before this nightmare would unfold to the next level. Laying there for a moment, I began to realize that Nikolaus must have put on my favorite compact disc by Nina Simone before falling off to sleep. As I listened to it play softly in the background, I thought how ironic it was as I sat there listening in my room to Nina sing to her lover Porgy, and about he not letting them come and take her away from him. It was as if the tune was speaking the words my heart was feeling so deeply, but dared not express into words. For if it was the words that I said from my lips just two nights before, becoming my reality and living out loud now, who knows what will become if I sang along to these words Nina's singing now. But I just can't help to . . . it's what I'm feeling . . . "Oh please, oh please my Nikki . . .please don't let them come and take me away from you either," I thought in an overly dramatic, but befitting sentiment.

So many times before, I'd listen to this very song

playing and I must say how it always lent a visual to me of some authoritative figure coming and hauling poor Nina Simone off to some place of captivity as she begged her lover Porgy to not let it be so. I never saw the play Porgy and Bess in which the song was written for. But I would imagine it to be of some dramatic occurrence similar to that of what I and Nikolaus were experiencing at this moment.

It seems that I had finally landed such a great guy. With a great life, upwardly bound, we seemed to be heading towards pure bliss. To lose it all now would just be another facet of an already life spiraling down and out of control just as quick as it was built, due to my hand involved in the death of another. The music now playing had me sadder than ever by now. All I wanted to do was to make it all just go away. Oh how, I wish this could have been some dream that I could wake up out of and find it all not to be true. But it was. All of it was true. I was now on the edge of losing, not only all that I had built in life from the time I had left my parent's home those many years ago in defiance, but now I was to lose the greatest love I'd ever known. Which may seem to sound so trivial to others, considering that I was also at the precipice of losing the most precious thing of all . . . my freedom and liberty.

I drifted off to sleep in Nikolaus' arms as he held me staring off into space, probably wondering the same thing that I was . . . how much longer would we have before everything that we knew would vanish like a streak of lightening, our home in which we grew to love so much in these past years.

I woke up not too long later to a loud ringing on my cellphone and house phone simultaneously. As Nikolaus grabs the house phone, I answer my cellular. "Nikki James is at the Ardmore train station mom," I yelled across the bed into the other phone that Nikolaus was holding out to me in an 'I've got everything under control type of manly manner.'

"Nikolaus tell her I'm fine and I'll call her back. I'm gonna go down to the train station up the road to get Nikki James and I will call her right back."

As I jumped into my car, I called my mom as I headed down Montgomery Avenue towards the Suburban Square train station, but I couldn't see Nikki James anywhere. Shortly thereafter, I decided to head back toward my house. At the top of the block I see her with a big Louie Vuitton overnight bag rushing frantically towards the other side as she was attempting to walk the long road the rest of the way to the house.

"Nikki James!!!" I shouted.

"Geees," she screams while dropping the bag and throwing her arms in the air in frustration, but relief to finally see me. She jumps into the car and proceeds to dig through her purse for her flask. "Girl, this shit is all over the news everywhere, like you some damn serial killer or something," she says as I pull off. "What are you going to do?"

"I don't know," I say as she goes to put her flask back into her purse after taking a huge gulp in order to calm her nerves. "No, wait," I tell her before she sticks it away. "Give me a swig too girl. My nerves are shot too."

"Oh my dear lord Padge, what are you going to do?" she asked me again as if the swig of whatever we're drinking has just given me new insight.

We went back home to my house and we all tried our best to act as normal as possible while the strangest quietness seeped through the house that was usually full of such life and vigor. As Nikki James settled in, I went upstairs to my bedroom to talk to Nikolaus as Eve came up into the kitchen where Nikki James was trying to now fry up some chicken in her failed attempt to act like it was just another one of her normal getaway trips up to my house in the country away from the city.

Finally she called me down into the kitchen in order to give me her thoughts, now that her booze had settled into her system. It was a very rare occasion when it would be she that was the one advising me, instead of the other way around which was the cornerstone of our mother/daughter relationship. And that's when she said to me, "Girl, it don't make no sense in just waiting here like a sitting duck just for them to find you. We need to go to some neutral ground to think things over and come up with a plan of action."

Thus, we all agreed and I figured a hotel up the road would be a good place to check into. It was the Radisson, which was a very, very busy spot, easy to get lost in the shuffle. So I thought, but Eve was against it straight from the door, sighting that the way the news broadcast were running all over the nation by now, that if . . . or . . . once they knew just who it was that they were looking for, I would be recognized easily. So without a moment to spare we all ran through the house collecting anything we thought we would need out on the road, as we were all use to that type of lifestyle from our days in the "Family Business." We all jumped into the car in haste as we headed up to my niece Jessica's apartment in Upper Darby, Pennsylvania.

Jessica had already heard the news by this time, but never put one and two together to think that the girl out by the airport had anything to do with me, until that is the moment she laid eyes on all four of us at her door with looks like we ate the canary bird.

"Oh my fucking god. It's you they're looking for." "Jessica, stop the swearing," I yelled back at her as

we all forced by her in a rush to get any updates, as we could hear the news playing on blast from the door even before she had answered it. All of us bombarded into her small apartment in order to work out a game plan as quick as possible, and that's when we saw it on Fox 29 news . . . they were doing an all out manhunt for this infamous black market silicon butt injection killer. I wanted to cry again as I stood there watching the TV wondering if they had known yet. However, I could not allow myself to now lose my cool as I've always been the emotionally strongest and leader amongst us all, and I was no way about to buckle under the pressure now, with myself soon to be public enemy number one.

That night went on quickly as everyone crashed on Jessica's large sectional sofa and living room carpet. I slept in Jessica's bed with her and her baby son, my nephew Semaj, like the many other times when they would come over to my house for the weekend and sleep over in my bed like one big old pajama party with pizza. In order to not scare Semaj, Jess and I just let him believe that I was just visiting over their home to have a pizza party that night. We ate pizza and Philly cheese steaks and all fell off to sleep with the TV still playing in order to hear any updates if it was to show any new developments overnight.

The next morning or rather the next afternoon, we were all planning our next plans to leave Jessica's place. Momma and poppa called me to let me know that they wanted to have a family powwow with one of my sisters that was coming over to Jessica's place with them. My sister Nicole took off from work when she heard that the city's police department was on an all out manhunt on the news for someone that had killed a girl out by the airport doing illegal butt injections. By this time she had put one and one together and figured it might have been me since she had dropped by my home and no one was there, which seemed very strange. Especially being that she was the only one in my family who I had previously shared the knowledge of my side business of doing injections.

"Knew it was you," she said as she rushed in the door to hug me with her eyes bloodshot from crying after hearing the firsthand news from our parents on the way over to Jessica's place. Just then we had all gathered into the living as the news flashed across the TV screen on the developments of the black market silicone butt injection killer on the loose in Philadelphia. "We will be right back after these commercial messages."

As we all waited those five minutes, which seemed like an eternity, the broadcast was now back on the air. With a clipboard in his hand, and my house out in Ardmore serving as the screen's background just behind the news broadcaster . . . I knew that the mystery was over and they now knew just who they were looking for, as he then went on to tell the world my government name. "Padge Victoria Windslowe, better known as the recording artist The Black Madam is now a person of interest in this bizarre killing of the woman named Carmen London who flew to the US from the UK for black market silicone injections that led to her death." We all stood there in gag nation for a moment, knowing that it was now just a matter of time before my life would forever change.

The Philadelphia police department had met up with the Ardmore township police and at that very moment, were performing a full on raid of my home. The day was now turning for the worse, and I just wanted it all to just go away, but it was way too big now. For the authorities now had a face to go with the case and the news had one for their stories and headlines as the case then took on a life of its own.

Black Madam pictures and music videos were everywhere now. All over the news, all over the radio and even on the many cable channels broadcasting my name and pictures all across the planet. I truly felt as if I was some evil villain in some new Bat Man movie . . . like poison ivy. "The Black Madam on the LAM!" the reports all announced. All I could think now was who was LAM? And how was I on him? My mind was shot out in distress. Reports were coming in everywhere, as everyone's cellphones all began to ring as the news of me took flight. I was no longer a simple girl trying to be a star from my posh neighborhood of Ardmore, Pennsylvania . . . I was now INFAMOUS.

As we all looked at the next footage on the screen, I could see poor Nikolaus being hauled into the police station at 57th and Pine Street for questioning. I had warned him to not go back home, and to just come back to Jessica's place in order to meet up with us after he got off from working overnight, but he wanted to check on the house, and happened to be there just moments before the detective came in to it in order to

serve him with the search warrant to raid our home.

I sat back in a daze, wondering what was to be next as the normal TV channel programming resumed to the

Oprah Winfrey show with a special performance by Jennifer Hudson performing her new single, "Where You AT." That moment too would now be forever etched into my head as I thought in the midst of it all that was going on . . . where in the world was Nikolaus, as I called and called him without an answer to his cellphone. Were the police keeping him? Were they going to let him go after questioning? Was he still at the 57th Street police district? Or did they perhaps book him and take him to central booking as an accomplice?

Meeting Nikolaus
Our Back Story

Of all I've been through . . . I can sincerely say that God sent me no better love to endure it all with me than when he brought Nikolaus into my life.

It was the hot summer of 2004 in June on a beautiful afternoon at home with my mother, Eve and our good friend Jazmine who was visiting for the season in the home that I had made for me and my mother and baby brother Daron in the Wynnefield Heights section of Philadelphia shortly after daddy had died. At that time I had put all my risque business on hold, as I stayed home to tend to my mother who was deep in mourning over our loss. For daddy was the only man she had ever known as they were together since they were both fifteen years old back in the sixties. Eve and Jazmine were getting tired of the "Family Business" on the road and I invited them to stay with us for awhile, as our home was huge.

This one particular afternoon we were all hanging out on the deck with the nicest summer breeze blowing in from the north. It seemed the perfect beach-like day when Jazmine suggested that we should just chill outside eating some crabs to enjoy the sentiment of summer. I had had a few hours to kill before I had to be at BMR recording studio downtown Philly, in order to cut the vocals to my new songs . . . "ROCK" and "Lucifer's Rising."

Thus, I was feeling just what Jazmine was feeling and volunteered to drive to get us all some steamed and seasoned seafood with ice cold Pepsi Cola to wash it all down. As I was leaving the garage, mom stopped me and asked if I could grab some French bread also and she would make us all some of her great Black- Italian pasta to compliment our seafood extravaganza. As I was in the market just walking away from placing my order of about 10 pounds of Dongeones crabs, seasoned and seamed in butter and old bay, I searched for the baking aisle in order to find the bread mom wanted.

I remember being in this market on several occasions with my aunt Lela-May when I was a kid, but it seemed that everything was now revamped and all different. I must have looked lost and confused when a very young, tall and extremely handsome guy walked up to me, smiling with looks of a male model off of a soap opera, asking me did I need any help. I told him that I was looking for the bread aisle, when he practically took me by the hand in order to personally lead me to the right aisle. There was a ton of choices and this customer service helper had no problem with staying right there to help me make my selection. He seemed to be very helpful and attentive as he was into his job as it was evident that he took pride in it and was very serious about his business.

After I had grabbed all that I needed and was about to thank him for his help as I had to get back to the seafood department to pick up my order, he stopped me by grabbing my hand once again and looked me straight into my eyes as he told me his full name and age of only 18 years old and some bit about him knowing exactly what he was doing, and could he please have my phone number so we could hang out sometime. I immediately clutched pearls, as I was standing there sixteen years his senior at 34 years old.

However, despite my age, I must have truly looked about ten to twelve years younger than I was, as two elderly women shopping in the same aisle stood there edging him on and saying just how much of a lovely couple we would make.

Thus, I figured what the hell . . . he's 18 years old, at least . . . he was legal. Figuring I had nothing to lose, as I had just gotten out of a seven year relationship with a slut of a man-whore Jessy Newell. Thus I thought I deserved to treat myself to a diversion of some young fun. I gave him my number and by the time I got home just up the street from the market, Nikolaus had called my cellphone about twenty times, as I thought to be sure I had given him the right number. But he said it was just to be sure I got home safely . . . and yet he would continue to call me all afternoon as if he was stalking me.

My phone had rang so much in the course of us all eating our crabs and pasta out on the deck, that we could barely enjoy our meal as everyone wondered just who the hell was blowing up my phone like that. Eve immediately assumed that something had to be mentally wrong with Nik . . . as why in the world would he figure that it was okay to call someone he had just met as if he was some sort of deranged stalker or something.

It was really quite weird just how persistent Nikolaus was being as even I started to think that maybe he was a little off. I mean I know my effect on men is devastating . . . but wow . . . he'd been calling me from the moment I gave him my phone number. Finally Eve suggested that perhaps I should answer the phone and tell him—thank you but no thank you—as I always have this weird way of attracting the strangest kind of men . . . at supermarkets . . . and drug stores . . . and coffee shops as if I had a sign on my head stating that I take in the deranged strays of society. Eve told me that the last thing I needed was some crazy guy lurking around the house with mom in such a depressed mood.

I figured it was some good advice she was giving me and finally I answered the phone on about the 30 th ring and suggested that we meet on the parking lot of the Acme as it would soon be time for me to head down to the city to record, and I figured I could just give him the polite courtesy of letting his feelings down easy, as I could clearly see that despite how devastatingly handsome he was . . . I must had been his first potential of getting his first shot.

As I pulled into the parking lot, there he was standing there so pathetically adorable with his dated member's only jacket and Kango hat that cocked to the side as if he was about 40 years old. He had the most pitiful puppy dog eyes I had ever seen, as he looked so happy to see me again. It was as if getting my number might had been his greatest accomplishment, as it was evident that he was a very sheltered kid. As hard as I would try in those few moments I had to let him down, I just couldn't tell him never to call me again. He had then asked me where was I headed to. And I told him I was off to the recording studio in Center City and that I was currently working on an album and that's when he mentioned that he played the violin. I mean I was in a situation that I just had to have a heart. Thus, when he asked me if he could come along with me, I couldn't refuse. Now, by a rule I live by, I never really like to bring friends into the studio with me to work, as I love the exclusivity of closed sessions. I'm a taskmaster when I'm in my producing zone of being Black Madam that I can tend to be very rude and short as it's always all about the recording process.

But Nikolaus was cool. He played the background scene as I, Franz and Taj worked on creating magic. He even volunteered to get our things to eat and anything else we might have needed but were too engrossed in work to stop and get. It was really nice having Nikolaus around. However, it wasn't what I would call a relationship for a very long while.

It would take him to move off to college out in Kutztown, Pennsylvania and come home on spring break before he would truly catch my eye of the great catch I had in him. As he would mature so much in those few months that we were apart. It was on that spring break that we had loads of crazy fun-filled sex at the most sleaziest cheap motels on dates and times together that would solidify us as the union that we are today.

Nik is a wonderful man and I couldn't have asked for any better. I get very sad when I think of such a good guy going through such a crazy situation just because he chose me to fall in love with, but he takes it all. The outing of my past, of once being born male, and the fact that I was a transsexual spread across the front pages of the press, as he found out about my being transsexual as the scandal hit after already being with me for then seven years. And still he's there. Thank you God for that man.

Thus, with now my man who was innocent of any wrongdoing down there on the line, it was now the time for me to act, and act now. Mommy and poppa were in the kitchen with the others, calling around in order to secure my legal counsel when I saw more footage of Nikolaus on the television, walking with a black hoodie covering up, being released from 57th Street police district, fighting off all the news cameras that were everywhere, trying to get a statement from him. It seemed that all that I had just prophesized just a few nights ago in the recording studio with Nikki James while recording my new track RUCKUS, was all coming true to fruition. This was truly life imitating art on a grand scale to the fullest.

As I sat and talked with mom and pops in the kitchen of Jessica's apartment, we all decided on just what attorney we would go to in order that I do the right thing and surrender myself into the authorities asap. We figured someone local from my hometown of Ardmore and called a few of the biggest ads we saw in the yellow pages phone book. Although, I didn't know it then, it would turn out later to be a bad choice . . . as the team we picked would try to juice me for all that I had, utilizing my fear as their golden ticket.

But I had seen someone in the ads with a background as a prior District Attorney himself and jumped at the chance in order to land representation with a good track record. After speaking with him on the phone, my parents and I went right down to his office. I walked into Mr. Guld's office in Ardmore with black skin tights and a Coco Chanel black and silver dress, the same black stiletto 5 inch heel boots in which I previously skid all over the ice back when I was ridding myself of all that evidence. I must have looked a pretty sight as I walked into his waiting room, dragging the floor with my very long goth looking black couture woolen chinchilla fur coat that I had just got for my past birthday from Nikolaus . . . and my black on silver studded GUCCI purse and sunglasses, although the sun was down and it was far past dusk.

"Hello Mr. Guld," were the first words I said to my new attorney, as I looked then to introduce him to my parents. I then went on to explain to him that I was The Infamous Black Madam that was all over the news at that moment.

PART III

CHAPTER 21

THE BLACK MADAM ON THE LAM

Once securing representation I immediately felt a weight fall off of my shoulders, as I was no more in the dark about my rights and the many other legal options that Mr. Guld had advised me on and also for the fact that for once in my life I felt like I had someone for a change to lean on and guide me.

First things first. Mr. Guld advised me that, as of now I should go home and get a few good nights of rest over the coming weekend, as he would now notify the Philadelphia police and detectives on my case along with the District Attorney's office of my representation. And that I would not be coming in for questioning without their official furnish of a warrant. Thus, I took my new attorney's legal advice and headed out to Delaware to my sister Sherrie's home in the gated community of Sullivan's Court located in Bear.

By the time Jessica and I pulled up to her mother Sherrie's home, it might have been about 12:45 a.m. because all the lights were out and I could plainly see that everyone had been off to their own rooms for the night. When she opened the screen door to her mother's house, I stood back to look at this huge estate looking home of my younger sister's, for just her and her two youngest children now, with her older children, Jessica and my nephew Jonathan out of the house and living on their own, I thought, "Why in the heck does Sherrie need such a huge home for the three of them living there?" And just then I remembered . . . That's my sister who was also a Sagittarius like me— needed to live lovely at all cost.

Sherrie opened the door after hearing Jessica ring for more than two minutes in a frenzy, immediately with a joyful greeting as if it was just a family social call. But once catching herself, as she thought, "Why in the world am I at her door and so late in the evening". . . being that I'd never been out to her home since she moved to Bear, Delaware, let alone come to visit her at such an ungodly hour at that . . .

She immediately registered that something was wrong, and her happy to see me face switched to "Oh my God what's happened?" Right there at the door I asked her did she see the news or hear about the girl who died out by the Philly Airport by silicone injections.

And frazzled in her night robe she responded, "Yes, but what does any of that got to do with you and Jess out here so late?"

And there I told my sister Sherrie, at the front door of her home in which I'd never been before, that I was the murderer the police were looking for as I walked in to sit down for a very long night of explaining it all to yet another.

That night I went on to explain it all to my sister as she fixed me something to eat for dinner in her very enormous chef's gourmet kitchen as if she was living on one of the sets of the Atlanta Housewives or something. Feeling just so bad and upset for me and all that I had gone through without her even knowing, just made her cry as she couldn't stop from hugging and kissing me on my forehead and cheeks . . . as we sat there and cried together after Jessica left in order to head back home where Eve and Nikki James were still waiting to hear what had happened at the meeting with the attorney earlier that day. My sister Sherrie then stepped into big sister mode in order to protect her big sister from harm by demanding me to stay with her and away from the city of Philadelphia for as long as was needed. I stayed with my sister Sherrie for two and a half months with Nikolaus and Eve eventually coming to join me.

My sister Sherrie was indeed the good sister as she cooked for me, drew hot baths in her Jacuzzi styled jet stream tub for me, and even moving out of her master bedroom suite so that Nikolaus and I could feel more at home together in it with privacy. It would be her house there in Bear, Delaware where I and Nikolaus would begin to pick up some of the pieces to our life together as Nikolaus would commute back and forth to work as I stayed harbored from the law by my loving sister.

It would be months and months and months as I and my family awaited the coroner's report and autopsy that had not come in yet. Without this much needed report as to confirm the causation of Carmen's death, the Philadelphia

District Attorney's office could not pursue charges against me. Thus, they could not move forward with their case against The Black Madam.

It would be many more months to pass the expected two and a half months for the reports to come in. Day by day, week by week and month by month I would call my legal team in order to see if the report had surfaced and any new words of a possible arrest warrant pending, but none would.

However, what he did suggest was that I come back into the city of Philadelphia and stay with my parents. As he explained that when it did in fact come in, and the DA would come with charges, I could at least have a Philly home address in order to be granted house arrest, as I was fighting my case in the court of law. My family's home would serve as leverage in order that I come across looking like a non-flight risk.

Phrases like address leverage, pre-trial house arrest, bail and being a flight risk would soon become words of my vocabulary as each time I would call any one of my three attorneys that would make up my legal team. Christopher Mannix, Douglas Guld and Sean Collen, Esq., would be the team that would at first shield me like only a woman with money could get. With a strategic plan, they had kept me safe from prosecution for the next year to come.

Eventually, I did get around to doing as they had advised me. As Nikolaus and I packed up to depart from my sister's house, it was so bittersweet as she wanted only to keep me with her safe as long as possible, but knowing that this was something that could possibly help my case if I should ever be charged for Carmen's death. She happily said her goodbyes as Nik and I packed our car to head back to the city where not too long ago I was villain of the century.

As I was to move in with my parents, I must explain that regardless of my age, my mother and stepfather were still very old fashioned and would not approve of Nik and I shacking up together right under their noses out of wedlock. In my own house they would overlook it, as it was my sin and my sin only, but they felt if they were to house our unwedded bliss . . . they would be responsible also for my sins of pre-marital fornication. Although sex was the furthest thing from Nikolaus and my mind . . . we just wanted to be together through the storm at all cost.

So . . . as I set up house as my parents' home, I also set up house for Nikolaus, just a few minutes up the street at another one of my sisters' home with her family. Nicole, at that time had been my closest of all three of my sisters, as we shared a bedroom as young siblings through high school. Thus, she knew my most deepest and darkest secrets and I hers. So it was not too far of a stretch for me to ask her and arrange for Nikolaus to reside there with her and her family— husband Barack, my two nieces, Venicia and D'Nae along with my nephew David.

Although Nikolaus and I were yet to be married and I felt it inappropriate to ask my parents for Nik to stay with me there, my sister Nicole was anything but religious, being that her and her husband Barack lived together for about 10 years before I had paid for their wedding to make their union sanctified in the eyes of the Lord and my momma and poppa. Thus, I had no problem spending most of my days to come, over at her house in the bedroom that my sister had assigned to Nikolaus.

However, as the nights got to be too lonely in the guest

room of my parent's home, I opted to spend most of the nights over at my sister's house with Nikolaus. Through all that I was going through, it was his love and the love I felt so deeply for him which kept me strong. It was the weirdest feeling for Nikolaus and I . . . this having to depend on others for our shelter and well being.

For all my adult life I fended for myself and made a way out of no way. I felt that I had always been the one in my family as the eldest sibling and child, that it was my obligation to take care of everyone. But the time had now come for the shoes to be reversed and let my family take care of me for once, which was all great in the beginning.

However, welcomes wear down and people, even family, start to act funny when they feel that it has become an inconvenience to bare the load of another's weight, whether it be a sister or not. Things got to be too much as my sister Nicole and her family relocated from the house in which she lived when I and Nikolaus first arrived to stay with her, to a new home she had just purchased in the midst of my legal woes. It was a much smaller house, located in Upper Darby, Pennsylvania. It would be this smaller home of hers in which the true bonds of our sisterly love would be tested as Nikolaus and I began to feel as though we had worn out our welcome. Despite all the many times that I had performed the very same sisterly duties, I was now depending on Nicole to do the same for me and mine. She became a monster.

Thus, to avoid making matters any worse, Nikolaus and I moved on in an attempt to get back on our own.

We stayed one night with Nikolaus' mother and her "best friend" Ms. Sharon. Ironically just up the block from the police station at 57th and Pine where the police had taken Nikolaus the day they had raided our home back in February earlier that year, being the very precinct that investigated Carmen's death.

Well, one night was more than enough as we were now untrusting of living with anyone else. As we then moved out the next afternoon to the Crosslands Motel, not too far from Center City Philadelphia just over the Benjamin Franklin Bridge in Maple Shade, New Jersey, and commuted each day back to Philly in order to get Nikolaus back and forth to his two jobs in the Plymouth meeting area out on the city limits. By this time too, I had found a small job to occupy my lonely hours throughout the day without Nikolaus. During the day I was working as a personal care giver to a wealthy woman who lived alone in a condo off Presidential Avenue just outside the city. With such a desperate feeling of wanting to prove to myself that I was indeed a good person and not the killer bitch the news had labeled me, the job served a great purpose in the healing of my broken heart of the pain of being labeled a murderess.

It was indeed an awkward time in our lives, but this is where I really grew by leaps and bounds in trusting Nikolaus, and he did also with me on an even deeper level. Life had seemed to give our union its toughest blow and our love was still standing stronger than ever. The nights all bled into days, as the days did the same. Nikolaus and I became more of a working machine, as we worked day and night in order to sustain our emotional sanity of feeling useless as we waited for the coroner's report to surface. But still it never did. With most of my savings tied up or seized by the police, the rest being inaccessible and hidden way in my family's home. Nikolaus and I lived under the radar as if we were just ordinary folk in order to keep a low profile.

It was the most common we had ever lived in our relationship as free spirited jet setters around the globe at the whim of my desires. The simple life actually felt nice though . . .

However, living out of a motel like a vagabond gypsy couple in love, was all brought into bright focus on morning, that led up to our next path on this journey in needing to begin to live a more sensibly structured life, despite living on the road like rock stars.

It was a Friday morning when Nikolaus forgot to set the alarm clock the night before, and we woke up much later than the usual allotted time in order to get him all the way up to his job in Plymouth Meeting. We being so in a rush . . . we got showered and dressed and headed out the door . . . drove all the way up the 4 mile stretch of road to the pay toll of the Ben Franklin Bridge only to realize that we were one dollar short of the correct toll. I knew I put the four dollars on the side desk back at the motel the night before. But somewhere in all the madness and rushing around after waking up late, it somehow got lost by the time we got out the door and into the car and to the bridge. Now, besides losing more precious time on top of waking up late, we were now gonna have to waste fuel also for the trip back to the motel in order to search for the lost dollar. I had closed all my bank accounts, did away with all my credit cards, and stashed my lump sum at my family's home in cash for legal feels if needed, unavailable to us in our attempt in trying to lay low and live on a budget, that things were truly becoming challenging.

Who would ever think that living like common folk could get this rough. There, just as I suspected, on the floor by the bedside night table. It must have blown off the table when I woke up to grab the clock to see what time it was. It was now time to rethink our location for living on the LAM.

Needless to say, Nik and I figured it was now time for us to do the next logical thing and relocate back to the Philadelphia area closer to his jobs, so that nothing like this or worse ever happens again. We then made the transfer from the Crosslands Motel in Maple Shade, New Jersey to their Extended Stay sister location in Plymouth Meeting, Pennsylvania. It turned out to be a great decision to say the least. It was like having a piece of our carefree life back again. We could now sleep in later with just a 5 minute travel time up Plymouth Road from our new location to Nik's morning job, instead of the 90 minute it use to take from the Crosslands. We both were in a much happier state of mind as the layout to our Extended Stay suite came equipped with a full size kitchen, and also a full size bathroom with a bathtub, unlike the stand up shower at our previous place.

The simple life was beginning to look and feel alright, as I thought to myself, "We could do this." With countless hours I'd spend at my latest discovery, The Dollar General store, I learned to decorate on a dollar budget, as I decked out our new temporary makeshift apartment, with all the great things I would find for just under a dollar. Every daily call I became accustomed to making each day to my legal team in order to find out any updates . . . turned up negative . . . to where as they were all beginning to think that I might have dodged a bullet, despite my being plastered all across the world's press as a murderer.

I was happy again with life's possibilities and hope for new beginnings, beginning to open up to me again. Which then the memories hit me all at once again, as I truly began to suspect my witchcraft designed studio I made back home at our previous house in Ardmore, must have been truly the source to all the ruckus that was unleashed into my life.

If my memory is correct in thinking back . . . when Eve and I finally sat down to talk over the death of Carmen at my sister Sherrie's house, and about all that had taken place right after Nikki James and my adventure that night into the abyss of the unknown territory of occult black magic and the dark arts realm of my recording studio, we came to the strong conclusion that this whole thing was spoken into existence by the words that I had so carelessly spoke in that bewitched isolation booth in my studio. As we then began to do all the math, searching the moon phases of the calendar for that month of February when Carmen died, we realized the night we recorded RUCKUS was on the night of the full moon which is known in esoteric studies of real magic to be the driving source of destruction utilizing powerful black magic sorcery.

As we both came into the light of what we both truly felt happened that night in the studio, she and I devised a perfect plan to undo any remnant of the spell that was still lingering around, thus leaving me free of fear of prosecution for Carmen's death.

With the dark spell that must have been cast over my life by my recording of RUCKUS, we decided that like in the movie Jumanji, which playing an exotic board game unleashed major turmoil in the player's life, with the only way to get life back to normal was to complete the game to the end. Thus, I was to go back into the studio before tearing it down, in order to re-record RUCKUS without all of the dark and demonic lyrics. I was to end the recording on a good and positive note of my not being prosecuted for the terrible death of Carmen London.

Thus, the plan was on that last night in my old home in Ardmore, under the cloak of night on the New moon, not knowing still if my home was being watched by the police to see if I would ever return there. Before Nikolaus, Eve or I were to do all the packing throughout the night, I was to record a new version to the song, before packing our possessions up and putting everything in storage and leaving to live on the LAM.

With the sudden change of fate with the police on my trail suddenly curtailed, we couldn't help but wonder if the mystery of the occult all to be true. Could it all just be yet another coincidence that after re-recording RUCKUS with a positive ending for me, have changed the hands of fate in order to halt the police and the Philadelphia DA's office from pursuing charges for one of the most publicized murder hunts the city has ever seen?

I think not. For it was all real. For as we were done with all the packing and loading our trucks to forever leave the place we had all called home, I remember inscribing the occult symbols for warding off evil and those who wish me harm on the exit, atop each doorway of the old house before forever exiting each room, after saying a prayer to the Lord to leave all that I had unleashed, to be forever banished to that location.

It would be a whole year later when I would meet up with the vigorous detective Katherine Gordon, and she confessing to me that she and the DA had long given up on the murder case of Carmen London, which would convince me that our plan really did work. However, she and I would have new

I don't know, but it all sounds too coincidental for me.
As I know there is indeed a secret realm in which has
attracted me all of my life. It's a place still undiscovered by
mankind . . . operating behind the scenes in other
dimensions waiting for a curious human to reach out and
over their veil of protection to welcome them into our
world for power . . . riches . . . and the God knowledge that
is not of our understanding.

"I don't know,". . . just thinking out loud again. . . which
also gets me to remembering yet another lil tidbit to this
whole wicked puzzle to my life and its occult ties. My being
adamantly in pursuit of success in the well guarded world
of the commercial music business, and how the secret sects
of the Illuminati rules it with an iron fist. With their secret
rituals of sex, perversion and the ties that bind them all to
loyalty and discretion through the barbarism of their blood
sacrifices of other humans as a requirement for induction
into their cult, I cannot help but to also wonder if it is those
that I have summoned to me by the call of my occult laced
music video that had great success as I was awarded one of
the new artists whose music video was to be featured on
FUSE MUSIC TV and other Viacom music outlets just a few

months before the death of Carmen. I really can't discount anything as I know that all is possible in the secret realm of the dark arts.

And with that thought in mind . . . let's traverse yet again back in my past, during the time when I came back to Philadelphia, awaiting the coroner's autopsy report . . . as I was always scouring the internet on the daily looking for anything or any new updates on my pending arrest. Every now and then one of the Philadelphia Daily News writers, Stephany Farr, would seem to get a hard on about me and my case and would spark up new flames in order to try to reignite the once blazing inferno that had sent my life into a living hell due to Carmen dying. And there it would be . . . the Black Madam still on the LAM . . . she would write her pieces, which use to drive me mad, as that truly was not the case. To have people thinking that I was being a coward and not taking responsibility for my mistakes was just not what my parents had brought me up to be.

CHAPTER 22

SEARCHING FOR THE LIGHT IN DARK PLACES

But any how . . . on one of my searches through the internet, I had come across this link that someone had discreetly sent me via the server I must had been visible to. It seemed to be just a harmless link which, me being my naturally curious self had no qualms about clicking into. At first I never paid any mind to its content that somehow downloaded to my laptop, feeding my computer daily updates of some meetings that were taking place weekly in the city.

A few days later I would even begin to receive anonymous e-mails into my inbox labeled Ordo Templi Orientis, or something like that, which turned out to be some small meeting group that was looking to invite me down to one of their meets with the hopes of recruiting me as one of the elders had seen and loved my music video.

Phenomena, which was a very "Eyes wide shut" type of concept of secret societies and its whole New

World Order conceptual idea, which led those powers that be in that mystical community enthralled with the possibility that I could be some reincarnation of one of their founders from ages long ago by the detailed secreted layout of just how my music video looked.

Needles to say, curiosity once again took a deep hold of me by way of wanting to seek out someone perhaps more versed in the dark arts than my own self just fiddling away at what the darkness whispered into my ear. It was answers that I was in search for, and anything that I could find to help me understand just how my words could have possibly killed someone through magic. So . . . yes, I did . . . I e-mailed the person back who reached out to me, in order that I attend their next meeting.

It would be a few days after I had long forgotten about my contact, but there it was sitting like a beautifully decorated Pandora's Box . . . in my e-mail. I received what seemed to be very warm and welcoming invitation from the coordinator of this secret meeting group that seemed to have an air of excitement. Feeling a little silly about it all, I then mentioned the invite to my niece Jessica who would be down for anything that would help her aunt stay out of prison. However, the mere thought of some secret meet group scared the shit out of her and thus, she wasn't willing to accompany me. It would be a good thing however, being that if it had been some crazy killers looking to eat me . . . at least Jessica would still be alive to tell the authorities just where to begin their search for my half-eaten body . . . hmm, I wondered what parts would be left over . . . JTOL . . .

It now was the day of the clandestine meeting with the OTO. Still Jessica had not changed her mind in regards to attending the meet with me. But curiosity had me by the grip of answers that could possibly free me, so I was on my way.

With my car keys in hand and the confirmed RSVP emailed back to me with the address to where I was to meet those that could possibly once and for all help me close the dreaded chapter of my life with the death of Carmen and the possible hope of really finding out just what the hell I did that brought my words true, I jumped in my car.

It took me a few rounds around the block in order to find exactly where I was to meet my coordinator. However, a few tries around and I got to finally see this mystical who was part on an order that had the whole world either afraid of them, or ready and willing to sell their souls for success and riches in life.

There was nothing at all too different from this person to the next . . . just that he seemed to be impeccably dressed in a black Tom Ford suit with a pair of the nicest men's shoes I'd ever seen. As he took me up into the building owned by the mystic group, I could practically taste the permeation of his Armani fragrances cologne in my mouth. He was so intoxicating, that I would have suffocated had the elevator taken a moment longer to reach our destination floor atop the city skyline overlooking the city from a height I don't think I'd ever been before. I could actually see the curvature of the earth as I looked on, trying hard not to seem impressed. Oh, but how I was so impressed. Next time you are in a skyscraper building and you get on the elevator, look for the 13th floor. You will notice that there is none. Must think because it's a bad luck number, but this day I learned the truth of the matter. It's because secret groups such as this one that is sanctioned by the Illuminati believe in the power of 13. Thus, they save the power only for themselves by placing the thirteenth floor at the very top of their buildings in order to be closer to their master who is the rule and Prince of the air. Hence, that is why the music industry is so important to the Illuminati. For the air holds the airways, and music and sound travels via those waves in the air in order to control, possess, and conquer those they seek to initiate or destroy.

Utilizing a secret greeting—everyone who joined the meet used the occult code numbers of 93—which if you were to write it down on paper and turn upside down, it would spell out 36 . . . hence 666.

As I watched the room begin to fill up with many of Philadelphia's society wealth, I knew that I had been welcomed into the real deal. "Oh shit" . . .

After walking through what seemed to the ordinary eye as a lot of high end offices decked out in the finest of all seventeenth century furnishings and ancient paintings and biblical etching in gilded frames, plush red velvet looking carpeting, with the now strong scent of frankincense and mere burning in the near distance, one of many men who were dressed identical to the coordinator greeted me and directed us beyond a heavy black curtain that uncurled the next room which looked like something out of one of the most beautiful gothic cathedrals I have ever seen.

And now I know just why some of the world's most majestic skyscrapers pyramid rooftops look so damn beautiful from the outside looking in. Because they are the high churches of the Illuminati and it can't help but to be beautiful from the outside looking in. For with in those tops of the buildings, will literally kill a person with power and awe of its beauty and dark forces within it. If I did want to run for the doors now . . . like the hypnotic deadly dance of a cobra enchanting its prey . . . I was stuck.

Although now I cannot remember his name, I do remember my coordinator having a very sinister, but beautiful way about him. As if he owned the world and it was his secret. As things were being prepared for the next step into this secret world, I remember my talking to this man who was in love with the art of music. I mean he knew about everything from Beethoven to Bach, from Mozart to Hanover, from the Rolling Stones to Blondie . . . Jay Z to Cold Play. The more and more musicians I named the more he could keep me enthralled with the many personal stories and accounts he would tell me.

To my body it felt like we might had spent five days standing there as he literally exhausted me with his undying knowledge of all things music. Finally, as he was finished mind fucking me, he began to compliment me on the music works that I had done . . . ROCK . . . PHENOMENA . . . COME ON IN MY KITCHEN . . . VOODOO GIRL . . . HYPNOTIC and one of his very favorite he said . . . LUCIFER's RISING. I was yet again amazed as to what depth he had knowledge of my little old indie recordings. But he knew it all . . . the tempos and pitches of each . . . down to even the keys and how many breaths I had breathed on the tracks. I was amazed to have captivated a fan like that of what he seemed. But something underlying was telling me that there was a whole lot more beneath the surface of his accolades than what he was willing to express to me right then and there.

As I was later invited to meet a few of his associates, as he would call them, I couldn't help but feel like I was somehow transported back in time by the beautiful old tapestries and golden silver room that was so heavenly adorned by a beautiful ornate chair which looked as if there would soon be a royal coordination or something.

As we all walked further, we were all asked to take off our shoes and socks as we entered into yet another room that was even more beautiful than the last. There we were asked to do the unthinkable . . .

In that room we would all get totally undressed bare and to the skin with not a drop on but the skin that we were all born in. It was there that many very small blond-haired, what seemed like children . . . but I knew better . . . were there to wash and bathe us. It was all so surreal as these little naked beings all washed the participants and redressed us all in black cloaks with hoods. It was erotic to say the least, as the men in the room began to get erections as they would watch us women with embarrassment. It was exciting and scary at the same time as the adrenaline kept me on high as to what would come next.

In the next few minutes we would also be visited by yet another set of very small framed child-like beings. One was male and one female, as it was easy to tell because they too were naked. These two seemed to be more in control of things . . . more than the others who just came to wash us. As the duo pulled back the curtains to an altar of a red-headed woman sitting on it naked, with her legs cocked open, it was crazy to see. We all wondered why she had been sitting there in a daze as her vagina dripped her menstrual into a golden chalice that was positioned right under a gold enclave of the altar with grooves which allowed her bleedings to bleed through a network of channeled carvings into the altar, plated in gold in which her mistral traveled in order to drop into the cup. Odd, weird and some really eerie shit, but there was no getting out of it now, as I acted as if all was normal while cursing myself on the inside.

Once the candles were lit, the small human beings walked through the center of the line, up to where we had been directed to form, all facing each other as in a soul train line. For that was the true meaning of a "SOUL TRAIN." The small little people walked all the way through our line, straight up to a freestanding door that seemed to be just simply standing in mid-air at the end of our SOUL TRAIN line, without any logical support structure. And there they knocked on the door six times, in six successions of six. At that time I didn't think things could get any freakier than that of the red-headed woman dripping her monthly cycle into a cup, but just then this door opened that literally led to nowhere. As an extremely abnormally tall naked man with red hair also, dressed in a ancient Roman-like crown seemed to walk through out of thin air . . . and I was done.

As he walked through the doorway leading to nowhere . . . from nowhere, he walked right past me as something that I would say felt like the magnetic pull of magnets coming in contact with each other that seemed to grip at my soul. Passing all in attendance, I could clearly see that I was not the only one affected by this man's presence, as everyone looked like the life force from their bodies were being tugged on as he passed by all, walking up to the red-headed woman sitting on the altar.

He then grabbed the chalice, along with a golden plate containing cubed squares of some caramel-like burning substance. We then were all asked to join in the feast of a Black Mass. I didn't know what the hell to do. I was freaked out and scared, but I did not want to upset these people . . . or things . . . or whatever . . . and possibly become the next little pieces of diced up squares served at the next meet. Thus, I ate and drank and joined in to whatever the ceremony was all about.

At this time I was not quite sure what was to happen next. I had drank a strange woman's period blood, and probably eaten a little square piece of a burnt person. As then a smell of electricity burning filled the room. I got dizzy and very disoriented to the point of not being able to barely keep on my feet. Not trying to seem out of place—thus, not making it home alive—I wasn't quite sure what the hell happened next, but between the smoke, the cubes, the fire and the blood taking hold of my senses, all I could remember was all the little people helping us all back into our cloaks that somehow we had lost during the process of being out of it. The 2nd step to Illuminati initiation was the Black

Mass . . . in which I had just survived. Which then led

me to wonder what the hell had been the first step . . . "The blood sacrifice of Carmen?" . . . a voice said to me in a whisper.

The whole experience is something that still haunts me today and scared the shit out of me, as I fear the sect seeking me out for the final sacrament. To even ponder the possibilities of what could have possibly happened to me that day up in that satanic temple in the sky with the Minister of Music himself . . . I can't help but feel every now and then, like I lost something so precious to me that day. If I committed to something that I can never get out of . . . or worst. And what kind of smoke and mirror trick it was that would allow a man of flesh and blood to defy logic and mostly the laws of physics in order to show up out of thin air . . . or was he a man at all . . . just thinking out loud.

As the meeting came closer to a conclusion, the man who had invited me walked over to speak with me about whether or not I had enjoyed the mass. I told him I thought it was like no mass I had ever been to, considering I was Catholic.

He then went on to ask me about what was my motivation in coming to a meet like theirs, in what he jokingly said could have been an abduction or some sort. He then handed me a card with a symbol of stars, a sun and a lion and snake on it, and asked me to write what I most desired on it and return it to him before I left. In writing on it, all I could think of was nothing else but to rid myself of the bad luck of Carmen's death.

"And so mote it be". . . as it was done. That is until I was tricked into servicing another girl in a sting operation a whole year later. Against my better judgement, I had gone against my own mind to see this (what was thought to be a friend), which we'll discuss at a later date. I know this all sounds woefully unreal to believe. There are so many facets leading up to that day Carmen lost her life, that seems like something out of some supernatural horror movie. I don't believe in coincidence, and to back that fact up, even one of the world's greatest minds of history, Carl Gustav Jung, stood firmly behind the theory of there not being any coincidences, but synchronicity of cause and effect. After that day up in the air, I went to get an HIV test and everything in between, for my mind betrays me . . . as I cannot remember just what took place at my secret meet with the Illuminati's OTO sect. And to think that I dared contemplate bringing my niece to such shenanigans . . . "Please forgive me dear Lord for that day." As that was before I became saved and was lost, seeking for the light in the darkness. I wanted to rid myself of whatever forces that were unleashed into my life in my search of the ultimate power.

LAST THOUGHTS

So as the months went on and still no word from the coroner's office on the autopsy report of just what killed Carmen London . . . Nikolaus and I worked our way back to some point of normalcy in our life. My meet with the Secret sect of the Illuminati's OTO order based in Philadelphia had seemed to pay off. As there was no hint of an arrest over my head anymore.

The vast fortune that I had used to secure my legal team seemed to had not been needed at all. Nikolaus and I along with Eve finally found a beautiful new home in which to call our own again and began to build our roots back. In the posh green landscape of the Chesterbrook section of the rich mainline town of Tredyffrin township, out on the main skirts of Philadelphia in Devon, Pennsylvania, it seemed that my prayers had been answered. I was not going to have to face the legal storm to fight for my freedom in the trial of the decade.

But, it would be just as Nikolaus, Eve and I were just beginning to let down our guard in feeling safe in our new home, I received a call from an old client of mine . . . Tiffany, who I felt was a friend. She was so happy to hear that all had seemed to work out fine for me as the drama in my life seemed to die down without an arrest. She also told me that she was hanging out with yet another client of mine, Back Shots, who wanted desperately to talk with me as she also had been so worried for me through my troubled times. I told her to go ahead and let me speak to Back Shots . . . And it would be this conversation that would pull me back into the game once again . . .

To Be Continued ...

notorious

Black Madam
Book II

A Reality Reading Memoir By Padge Victoria
Windslowe

Copyright 2017

NOTORIOUS
BLACK MADAM
BOOK II

Finally . . . after about 11 and a half months of the passing of all the drama and scandal as my name, face, and past gender identity having been sprawled across the front pages of the world's media and news . . . London . . . Philadelphia . . . Africa . . . India . . . France . . . Italy and God only knows where else.

Nikolaus and I, along with Eve, Nikki James and my family as a whole, finally reached some peace of mind. As Nikolaus and I, along with Eve got to move into our new beautiful four-story townhouse in Wayne, Pennsylvania with great anticipation of finally being able to have a new start, 403 Cannon Court was our home in the uppity mainline section of Chesterbrook.

It was a beautiful house with the first floor level as a gym and office set up in order to help me lose the dreaded whopping 75 pounds of stress weight that I had put on while dealing with the ongoing stress of Carmen's death. The second level of the house was a sunken sun-drenched living room and dining area with a huge patio overlooking the mountainous terrain of the very scenic Valley Forge Park, with a master's chef kitchen, powder room and a grand foyer entrance.

The third level of our new home had a beautiful master bedroom comparable to our old house back in Ardmore, with yet another private patio balcony overlooking the very same view as the one down below in the living room area. However, unlike our prior home, Nikolaus and I had the luxury to have our own private bath in our master bedroom suite which was great, being that Nikolaus never liked to put any clothes on in the middle of the night when he would fall out of bed to walk over to use the toilet. I also had the fortune to get another room big enough for my wardrobe and dressing room just a few steps out of our bedroom, into the next. It was just as nice as my last, with all my beautiful worldly fashions just waiting for me to lose all of the weight I had gained. And yet there was still more . . . In my dressing room there laid a secret flight of backstairs that led up into the fourth floor of our new glamorous home. This would be the space that my best friend and assistant Eve Harlowe would occupy. There she could have quite the upgrade than she had prior, in the old house in which she would make my BioBeautyLabs.com laboratory and stockroom her work and living quarters. For in our new home, Eve now had her very own private quarters for her to work hard in her new thriving internet modeling airbrushing business, which had grown through my time of trouble to her getting jobs from some of the leading fashion magazines you read today. To say the least this house was the perfect solution to all that we had all gone through with unstableness that an international scandal could cause.

As it all seemed just right at home, and we were beginning to feel life was back to normal, I was doing a lot of decorating the house to my specifications. I had just put on the finishing touches and details of all the archway curtains throughout the house when I remembered that Back Shots had phoned me earlier in order to schedule a 7:00 p.m. session with a dancer I had previously serviced a week back whose injections hadn't taken. She went on to explain to me that the girl that I had seen, complained that she hadn't seen any results and that a lot of her product oozed out during her travels back home after the session. Thus, I was going to honor my free make-up session for such damages, as I always promised.

I agreed on the time with Back Shots, and told her that I would bring some of my personal product that was sure to stick and get the job done to her satisfaction. The product would be the Dow Corning DC2X which always was much more resilient in the body than the higher grade of product due to its natural origins and original usage. "Then it's all set." I told Back Shots that I would meet up with them at 7:00 p.m. sharp as I then hung up the call.

For the rest of the day Eve and I ran around town shopping for a new bed and linens for her bedroom/ office. We later ended our day at Five Guys hamburger restaurant that Eve was so excited about me trying. Where I vowed to this being the last of our splurges . . . as we were to commit to now losing all the weight we both had gained out on the LAM. My troubles seemed far away from us, and now it was time that I got back into video vixen shape for my next project, as I would emerge as the comeback girl-Black Madam. Although I had had very high hopes of losing the weight and getting back on the ball with my music and all, I couldn't help but remember earlier that day—just before I had got my day started—I had felt a bit down after walking past the full length mirror in the hall, connecting the master suite from my dressing room. There, in that mirror I saw the fat naked beast I had become after all that I had just gone through. I was a pure mess on the outside which insidiously reflected the catastrophe I had been all those months on the inside, waiting to see what would become of my future after Carmen died.

Ten months of pure madness and stress had turned my once beautiful girlish figure into what looked back to me from that mirror, to be the perfect mate only for a male rhinoceros.

I remember sitting at my laptop computer earlier that morning before Eve asked me out to go shopping. There, on the computer at my dressing room desk, I watched the footage of the Phenomena music video I had just filmed before any of my troubles, as I prepared the files to send out to the distribution company in order to get the video in rotation on the networks and venues. As I watched on in sadness as I looked nothing like the woman I once was, just short of a year ago. It felt to be almost impossible to reach for my incredible weight loss goal in time for the video promotional tour my Wrath Entertainment Production company was planning. Besides, what I had just gone through in the press, losing these pounds seemed like it would be the hardest thing I had to do.

And that's when that ol' Black Magic Monster came

tugging at my skirt strings again. I was so upset and angry, so mad and so fat that I thought only something divine could bring me back to pre- scandal state. As I sat there at my table in the wee hours of the early morning while Eve was still asleep and Nik was still out at work, I contemplated it . . .

It all occurred to me that God was not doing his best to help me at all in my quest for World Domination in music. In fact, it seemed to me that he must have been dead set against it. And that is when the diabolical notion came to my mind of old blues player Robert Johnson and the stories of him selling his soul to the devil for success in music as the greatest guitarist to ever live.

"Am I crazy or what? No Padge," a voice in my head answered back. "Just hungry for your true destiny," it added. The feelings taunted me . . . urged me . . . beckoning me like never before. Come on . . . the voices said to me as my ears rang of voices in stereo, playing a symphonic, seduction, sequence of a summoning from the darkness that took over me.

"Come on," it said. "What have you got to lose . . . but a soul." I thought to myself how good it would feel to be back on my road to success. For in that moment it felt worth it . . . to gain the world at my feet . . . for the world was here and now . . . and what good is a soul if one can't enjoy the pleasures of it. Without another thought, I drew the curtains and drapes closed back in my bedroom while listening to be sure the coast was clear. And there I did it. I lit a few candles that were on my vanity set, pricked my right hand index finger till it bled, as I began to chant the incantations that were whispered in my ear. The rush was awesome and the fear was overrode with what some might call greed. I couldn't believe it. After so many years of denying it . . . there I was on schedule like clock work, selling my soul to the highest bidder. If it was a God to get it first, then I would know that he was real and all I would ever need. But, if it was Satan who wanted it more, then success would only be waiting for me just a few heartbeats away, once I sealed the deal. There, I did it . . . as my bloody finger was all the proof. Let us see just which way the pendulum shall swing.

As I finished up my meeting with providence, I was now a lady in waiting for her destiny. I opened the draperies and cleaned up the blood and candle wax. The paper in which I committed my soul was sealed in a blood bond with my own life's currency . . . the spell was all completed.

"Padge, Padge."

"Oh boy," I thought. It's Eve and she's up, calling me from the bottom of the stairs about to cook breakfast.

"Yeah Eve," I yelled through my closed bedroom door as I put everything back into place in hopes that she'd not come in and smell that undeniable scent of mysticism in the air. "Good morning Eve," I said, entering the kitchen as she was placing some bacon in the frying pan. "What's up?"

"Bitch, you ain't hear me calling you the last ten minutes?" she answered back in a 'where-the-hell' were you kinda tone of voice. "It was time to eat a good breakfast," she said, as I had promised to devote the whole day to her in order to shop for her new bed and furnishings for her new living quarters.

After clearing up breakfast and we both getting ready for the day's adventure, I grabbed my purse and jacket as we both headed out the front door. Nikolaus was still at work working another shift and wouldn't be home until 3:00 p.m. Eve and I ended our day of shopping, and here we now are at Five Guys. Although I knew it was now time to pull up the waist strings with my diet, shopping all day had me so famished. Thus, she and I packed the car with our things we'd bought shopping, and walked to the joint for what was reported by Eve to be the best burger she ever tasted.

On our way back home we stopped at Nikolaus' job to pick him up. He looked so exhausted, but said that he still had to work later for his regular shift although he had just pulled a double for his boss as a favor. We arrived home and unloaded the car as Nik went straight up to bed. Time was moving swiftly as the six o'clock hour was upon us and I had just remembered about my meet in just an hour with Back Shots and her friend Strawberry. My business phone kept ringing all throughout the day as Eve and I shopped, but it was on vibrate, so I never heard it through all the hustle and bustle. "Could it be Back Shots trying to reach me to cancel their appointment," I thought to myself. But as I checked the call log, I saw that it wasn't her. It was Toya trying desperately to reach me. Wondering what could possibly be the rush as she knows I would always get right back to her the moment I had time. As I called her back, the call goes straight to voicemail. "Hum," I thought. "It must not be too important if she shut her phone off. I quietly headed out of the bedroom while Nik was asleep, and headed to Eve's room to let her know that I was now headed out to an appointment, and would pick something up from the supermarket for dinner on my way back home in a few hours.

I was now off to Philadelphia for my date with fate.

It took me about 45 minutes in my drive from the mainline into Philly. I didn't have much on my mind as I cleared it listening to some soft jazz music on the car radio, as I got into the artistic zone of perfectionism, which had always been my ritual before seeing any of my injection clientele. It was something that soothed and relaxed me in order to take away the daily stress of the day.

I began to get very excited thinking about the task that was ahead of me, as the adrenaline began to pump through my now heated veins. Body sculpting had always been a great pleasure to me. As I truly enjoyed the great pleasure of the power that engulfed me after seeing a woman finally get the desired body image that she felt nature had forgotten in her. It was indeed that number one driving factor in the service I provided, as I could fully relate to that feeling of my clients because I once felt exactly the same way many years back during my transition.

Many in the mainstream from the outside looking in would assume that such injections were superficially a want and not a necessity, but there is truly a great magical transformation, of the mind, body and spirit when ones outer appearance matches what one feels they should be on the inside.

I can remember one time in particular while working on a mysterious woman who would always come from the west coast in order to see me. She would be dressed from head to toe in religious Muslim garment. For the life of me I just could never understand just why she would travel so far to see me for services to enlarge her buttocks if she was only going to cover herself up in all her religious clothing. She would come and spend thousands of dollars far beyond what I would charge for the services she received, just for my discretion she would say. At first I thought she meant it by her being Muslim, thus not wanting anyone to know of her worldly desire of a bigger behind. As I could clearly see beyond her vial that she was a beautiful olive skinned complexioned exotic woman with a voice that struck a huge chord in my bones of familiarity. However, I could never figure out just where I had heard her voice before. I figured she might have been some oil tycoon's wife or mistress from Dubai or Saudi Arabia or something. For it was clear to me that she would travel far to meet me for her sessions. She never would bring any luggage, which indicated to me that she traveled to Philadelphia for one thing and one thing only . . . and that one thing was to see me in order to get her fix of the candy.

She would speak briefly about her private life of having many siblings in which she was extremely close with. However, none of them knew of her meets with me . . . SMH . . . for that matter not even I truly knew the identity of my mystery client as she never would get fully disrobed in front of me. Always keeping her headdress on even during her sessions. All I could ever see was her bottom half in which she only undressed from the waist down. Money was no limit to the woman, and she became one of my most lucrative cash cows. She loved the privacy I gave her and she had no problem letting me know that she would pay anything to keep it between just she and I . . . as she would always jokingly say to me, "This Candy aint for EVERYONE!!!" stating that even as close as she was to her own sisters, that not even they, she would be willing to share her secret with. Even moreover she was extremely particularly interested in all the work I did on Rose Bud. With a driving desire she seemed to want to stay ahead of the curve of whatever Rose Bud was doing, and wanted to always one up her.

Finally, on about the sixth session this mysterious woman was just about to the end of her completed work, and excused herself from the room and went into the bathroom. There she would critique her work and admire the results we had accomplished. It must had been about ten minutes she had been in there this day as I was beginning to wonder if she was alright in there. I peeked into the crack of the door as I saw my mysterious client fully undressed for the first time. She was drop dead gorgeous from head to fucking toe. A brunette with amazing eyes, beautiful bust, with full lips. As she realized that I was there watching her adore the work I had performed, startled, she immediately softly closed the door and excused herself again. When she came back out of the bathroom she was fully garbed again and presented me with $25,000 as a bonus for the great job I had done, but mostly for my discretion with anything that I might have seen in my observation of her out of costume, which I now came to realize her religious attire was, and not was she at all a Muslim sister of the faith.

However, what she really was . . . was a very discreet Hollywood reality show star on E Networks in a show with her family. And she was now seeking to up her star quality by making her ass bigger and better looking than anyone else on air. And that was my second intro to yet another of rap star Mr. Craze's love interest. It was after that visit that I then realized that I must truly be on to something here. Where as this woman could have gone to any of the top Hollywood surgeons, but would rather dress up in a costume just to come and see lil' ol' me for my illicit black market procedure.

That day I was truly honored and felt to be the holder of many secrets to many of the power players in the entertainment world. Ms. Dubai would not be the only one, as many, many, many more celebrities and/or their significant others would trail that dirty dark road to Philly just so they could be blessed by The Madam.

It would later get back to me as I was being dubbed the MICHELANGELO of Black Market Body Sculpting in the industry and seemed to be on every "Lil Girl's" wish list . . . from Atlanta . . . to New York . . . to LONDON and TOKYO . . . from Paris, France to the French district of Canada's Montreal . . . Eastern Europe . . . to the United Kingdom . . . and all up and down my Homelands of America . . . all my lil' girls were calling for The Madam.

However, after Carmen's death, those glory days of the business was now over as the fact lay . . . I'm not sure if it was my hand or not that was the cause of her death—and with that being the case—I can no longer take pleasure or pride in something that could harm another to the point of mortality.

As I pulled into the picture perfect parking spot just right in front of Back Shot's front door, I was ready to simply help an old client out who said she had a problem with her last injection session.

As I shut the car down, looking in the rearview mirror, I could see a strange looking burgundy old Cadillac with dark tinted windows, not really thinking much of it as it looked like a dope boy's ride. I shrugged it off as I proceeded to get out of the driver's seat and go to my trunk for my supplies. The feeling of that same car being an undercover cop car crossed my mind. But it really did look too obvious to be one. As I then dismissed the thought into just being post traumatic stress disorder from all that I had been through that previous year . . . besides . . . I thought why would law enforcement want me . . . just out seeing a friend on a more personal note, as they had plenty of time to come and get me all those months I waited for them. Why would the police want me tonight with just the small amount of personal shit on me, when there had been plenty of times I drove around with up to a quarter of a million dollars worth of product on me?

I thought no more of it as I grabbed my bag out of the trunk and headed up the steps to Back Shot's place and rung the doorbell. Once in the house, the first thing that I noticed was just how calm everything was, as I was use to her place being more like a three-ring circus, with a little bit of everything going on during my visits . . . tattooing's, piercings, stripper stage clothes being made on the spot, rehearsal on the pole in the middle of her floor as Back Shots was the city's go to person for girls learning how to pole dance. "Quiet as kept" . . . there was even low key drug sales going on right there as I pretended to not notice. It was all none of my own business, just as long as the girls I was there to service partook in none of the madness before my working on them.

However, none of this was going on that night, or at least from where I could see. The house was of a serene nature as Back Shots welcomed me in to wait for the exotic dancer Strawberry. As we waited, she would be on and off her cellphone with some friends in Atlanta,

Georgia dancing that night. I could hear in her tone that she was upset with them for leaving without her. She finally hung up the phone, and we began to chat some about the free session for Strawberry and just what could have possibly happened that her session didn't take. About 20 minutes into the wait, Back Shots and I began to wonder where was Strawberry, because she had never been late before. Back Shots then went on to call her to see just what was the hold up. When she answered she said that she was late because she was trying to grab some Percocet's to ease the pain of the needles she would be getting. However, that struck me very weird as I never like anyone to take anything before their sessions, but I shrugged it off as nothing.

Just a few minutes later there came a knock at the door . . . nothing alarming . . . just a simple knock. Back Shots looked out the window and told the knocker, "No thank you," and stated to me that it was some Jehovah's Witness people at the door as she walked back over to me.

Again they knocked and Back Shots went back to the window, frustrated at the persistent Clergymen and their stubbornness to not want to take no for an answer. When then her face went blank as she realized that they were not stubborn old clergymen at all. It was Lieutenant John Walker of South West detectives and Detective Katherine Gordon and a host of what seemed to be the whole damn police district waiting to come in.

As Back Shots began to panic as the knocks grew harder and then on to strong kicks on the door as they were now trying to force their way in, she screamed out to everyone in the house, unknown to me, that the cops were at the door. She then, in a frantic rush, ran up the stairs to the second floor as I was left at the dining room table to greet whoever was kicking their way into the house. Then for a brief moment I thought to myself, "OMG! What if this is some sort of home invasion and I just happened to be at the wrong place at the wrong time, thus being caught up in the crossfire of whatever Back Shots and her crew had going on." I know . . . I'm so damn delusional . . . right? . . . lol . . . My thinking that I was in the middle of some drug war about to play out right in Back Shots' living room as the kicks at the door grew stronger and stronger. Damn, I thought to myself, I could die tonight . . . but it was actually the police . . . and I was never so relieved and happy to see them. I felt elated that it was really the police and that I would live to some day tell this story. In my heart of hearts I had known that I really tempted God earlier that morning with putting my soul on the block . . . and figured he was mad enough at me to let me go down in some senseless crossfire of a drug transaction gone bad, but my heart was truly relieved to welcome in the police as they began to descend on us all in the house of illicit behaviors.

YES!!! . . . I was not about to get all shot up on this home invasion in my mind. I mean I never even got a chance to get to the supermarket that night in order to pick up something for Eve to cook us for dinner— Nick needed the car in order to get back to work in just a bit—and we had just moved into a really nice neighborhood. "Oh my God, I don't wanna die now," I thought. Within a few moments the house was full of the boys in blue, with Detective Katherine at the helm. My nerves were now calm as a cucumber, only to soon come into the cold realization that no . . . today would not be the day I died, but the day that yet the birth of another chapter in the now ongoing saga of The Villainess, Black Madam.

"Shut up and stay there Ms. Madam," the cute, tall officer said as he handcuffed me to the dining room chair I was sitting in, as he proceeded to clear the rest of the way for the others. Guns all drawn, the rest of his posse filed in. One by one they all came in to get their view of just who was this woman that had them all boballing their heads around like Keystone Capers of a comedic satire almost a year ago in their investigation that yielded up zero.

They searched throughout the house and to my amazement there were at least eight other people upstairs having a drug pow wow that I happened to be so in the dark on. I really thought that Back Shots and I were alone in the house that night. Bloodshot red eyes . . . our new guest from upstairs looked stoned enough for the rest of us all that weren't. The detectives all rounded them up as they all sat on the couch looking like they were about to be hauled off to the city jail. But Detective Gordon assured them that today had been their lucky day, as they were here tonight for just the star of the black market underworld of illegal butt injections. They all looked over at me as if to say that they were thanking their God it was me and not them that the police were so interested in.

It would be hours there on the couch as the police did whatever it is that policemen do while holding their prize catch of the day for all the world to see.

It was getting very hot inside the house as I was not allowed to move from the seat in which I had been assigned to for the duration.

As I sat there at the order of the police, I stayed put. With all that was going on, all I could think of was how so ill prepared I was for such an event as the Black Madam's debut to the world. I wasn't looking my best at all as I had just planned to see Strawberry and head to the supermarket to pick up dinner afterwards.

As she walked in, she had an air of defiance as I could practically hear her say to one of her cronies, "Let's see just who this Black Madam is in the flesh." Victory seemed to ooze out of her pretentious arrogance, as her cockiness gestured . . . "I have the law on my side," in an over the top dramatic way.

"Hello Ms. Katherine." I introduced myself.

"It's Detective Gordon to you," she said back as she ordered me to shut my mouth. My back was killing me as I hurt myself falling in me heels just a few days ago with the wealthy woman I was caregiving to when I jumped to her aid as her own legs were giving out in her kitchen, as she was headed straight down fast to her marble floor which landed myself in the emergency room with a slipped disc in my back.

As I asked her if it would be okay if I took off my back support band, she warned me, "Not another word." Detective Kate Gordon seemed to be elated in her triumph to have finally captured the woman that had alluded her for a whole year. Like I said . . . it would be a few hours in the house as the police secured the whole city block and surrounding areas. The Germantown area of Philadelphia was on lockdown for what seemed to be the whole night as I was now extremely uncomfortable sitting there in that damn one spot, as if being scolded like a child as Back Shots seemed to be having a whole nervous breakdown, with her toddler daughter's bright yellow Big Bird hat on as she waited to see just who she could get in order to come and get her child before we were both hauled down to the police station.

While capturing a few precious moments of privacy as the cops flustered in and out of the house, which I would very soon come to find that the whole police district was in cahoots with the world's media outlets and news broadcasters in a frazzled media windstorm in order for the world to finally catch a glimpse of The Black Madam being capture. "Back Shots," I said in a whisper as I could clearly see she was scared as hell, "if they ask you about the silicone and supplies, just tell them it must have been my personal stuff and you know nothing about it," I said in a menial attempt to trying to save her from all that I was about to go through. "Tell them that I came by only to get some stage clothes made tonight and that you needed to measure me or something."

Back Shots seemed confused and agitated but seemed to be onboard. My idea was to free her of any responsibility of having to do anything with my illegal business and all I had ahead of me legally. For she was truly an innocent party with a child to provide for and another on the way, as we had just found out that she was pregnant. Therefore, she wasn't even receiving anymore injections herself.

It was indeed a semi sad, but comedic moment as I and the Philadelphia police watched a distraught Back Shots wandering about with this Sesame Street, gigantic bright yellow Big Bird hat bobbling atop her head like some sort of crackhead coming off of a fix. The twitching and quick movement of her head from right to left . . . as the weight of the bird on top of the hat would sway one way as she went the other.

Finally, the detectives yelled into the door that they were ready, as if to announce a curtain call. As I was escorted to the door of the house that had been my trap, I was overwrought at the sight of the once quiet street that I had first arrived to a few hours ago. It was now a disco of flashing lights as the whole planet was now watching The Black Madam via every media outlet streaming and broadcasting live . . . CNN, CBS, NBC, ABC, BET, LONDON SUN, BBC, FOX NEWS, HLN, GOOD MORNING AMERICA, TV ONE . . . and that was just the camera. It must have been every freelance reporter on Rupert Murdoch's payroll. And the many more radio and podcasters on deck. Satellites blazing and even what looked to be a few remote controlled drones were all there to capture the moment for the viewing public. I had then looked over to the officer that was escorting me and asked him if I could cover my head with my coat, but he said, "No ma'am. This is your world premier." And we slowly moved forward through the sea of blitzing clicks of the camera. And there I was . . . so ill dressed for the moment . . . as the first question came in . . . "BLACK MADAM . . . are you guilty?"

"Speak to my attorneys," I said as I was swiftly escorted to a waiting black SUV. Thus being the beginning of one of the most Notorious high profiled cases Philadelphia had ever seen.

I first was transported to the arresting police district at 57th and Pine . . . South West Detectives where everything seemed to then calm down as I felt so vulnerably human, and not the sociopath nonremorseful killer the press were making me out to be.

Detective Gordon and her partner asked me if I'd like them to order me some takeout for dinner.

"NO," I told them as my mind wondered what all I would be having to go through in this next journey I had ahead of me as I could hear poor Back Shots being brought

in screaming and crying that she's being framed . . . SMH .
. . poor thang . . . I wondered about bail, and would it be
granted? I then told the cute detective partner of Detective
Gordon that I had changed my mind. I will take a ginger
ale soda and a Greek salad to eat.

Meanwhile as Detective Gordon went to place the
order for my dinner as it would be a very long night ahead
of us all her partner came back into the room and sat down
to talk with me off the record. The interrogation room was
gloomy and gray with very hard furnishings that screamed
cheap and old, but not in an antique kind of way old . . . but
"a this is from the seventies and gots to go in the rubbish
fast . . . kind of way." He was very good at calming my
nerves as he was tall and handsome with a very big gun as
I could see it sticking off the side where his pocket was. And
for the life of me I was never ready to hear just what he had
to ask me next . . .

It seems that he and his girlfriend had become huge
fans of my music and videos that were being blasted
around the world in last years media blast of the case when
Carmen first died. He wanted to phone his girlfriend and
where as we could virtually have a threesome right there in
the interrogation room via his cellphone. Well, not a
threesome in the sense of some cheap sex in the guise of
policeman and his prisoner and the policeman's girl, but in
the way of my singing my song "Come On In My Kitchen"
live for he and she. As I took the phone and said my hellos
to his lovely lady who then went on to apologize for my
being arrested by her beau, as she conceded to knowing
that this must have been a tough moment for me, but

wanted to know if I would sing for them right then and there.

I decline to say the least. For once in my life I just wasn't in the mood for a show. Finally, they got the picture that it just wasn't going to happen and she said her goodbyes as the detective disconnected the call. Detective Gordon re-entered the room with dinner.

After being shown off at the 57th Street police district, I was then transported down to Eighth and Race to be booked and processed. I hated the Round House as it's called by all because of its round shape outer appearance. One of the first friendly faces I had seen while there was an old childhood schoolmate of mine from back at my grammar school . . . Stephen Girard. It was Tonya Thorton. I had already known she had worked for the Philadelphia police department due to my prior run-ins with the cops in the past of the "Family Business." However, never on this grand magnitude. She also acknowledged just how different this time was as I could clearly read the genuine concern in her face.

I could now hear all the news footage hitting the air, as my story played on all the TV channels and on high volume throughout the cell block. I just sat sunken down in my holding cell as the coldness of the nights' air blew straight in to assault my body only covered in a thin leather jacket. Finally, it was time for me to go in to see the Magistrate for my preliminary arraignment via video screen a few doors down from my cell.

At first my bail was set for a small sum of only $750,000, until my brilliant attorney Christopher Mannix put up an argument of excessiveness. Once arguing the details of my arrest and non-flight risk possibility, the Magistrate's memory was now jolted to remember just who I had been . . . I was not just a simple girl, Padge Victoria Windslowe sitting in front of him. I was the NOTORIOUS BLACK MADAM from the press and media. Bail set at $10,000,000 . . . (10 million) All I could then think was . . . "My Black Ass is going to JAIL!!"

NOTORIOUS

Book II

COMING SOON . . .

This Memoir is written in memory of CLAUDIA SEYE ADEROTIMI, within who's fate has been bonded with mine due to the circumstances laid out in this book. With all that has transpired since that day in room 425 at the Hampton Inn on February 7th, 2011, my only comfort is that I know you know my intent was pure and without malevolence. However, still I can only endeavor to beseech your forgiveness from the depths of my heart and soul till my own dying day . . . I am so sorry.

This Memoir is also written in memory of the many women who've lost their lives, along with the many more families who's lost loved ones in our current culture's senseless pursuits of beauty via BLACK MARKET means and methods. In order to educate the world of how dangerous this idea of depositing free flowing silicone into the human body for enhancement and modification, we need help. Join me in my quest to initiate my campaign to bring awareness with the STP CAMPAIGN to Stop the Pump, along with the Black Madam's Black Ribbon Walk for Inner Beauty, in order to bring awareness on the many self-esteem issues of not only silicone injections, but also issues such as Bulimia, Anorexia, Obesity and more. J oin the Movement Today by contacting me at SURESHOT BOOKS & PUBLISHING.

STOP THE PUMP

TO THE ADEROTIMI FAMILY, I give my utmost and humblest condolence and apologies to. But most of all I send my heart out to Claudia's Mother . . . to you Ms. Eunis, I would like you to know that all I wanted to do was to help Claudia reach her goals as someone once helped me. So many times, I've wanted to speak to you personally on these matters in order to give you the true factors that led up to the death of Claudia, but could not, due to protocols of the American Courts and Justice System. I wanted you to know the truth, and not all the speculated assumptions of the Philadelphia's District Attorney's office, who painted such a heinous scenario in order to win their case. Not caring, nor considering the more fire they would add to your already pain of loss, I feel they left you to hurt more, by allowing you to believe that malice was involved when it wasn't.

However, despite all they've added to the fuel of your hurt, I would like you to know THAT I TAKE FULL RESPONSIBILITY FOR MY ACTIONS that caused the death of Claudia, and thus, I give you my heartfelt apologies for your loss. Regardless of my attempts to help, I know I have harmed you FOREVER, and for that I am terribly sorry. I would only hope that these pages of my memories leading up to and beyond the death of Claudia find their way into your hands in order to bring you solace in the pictures it paints of a strong and vigorous Claudia in full pursuit of her dreams in her last day on Earth. If ever you wish to speak to me, I would welcome your presence with humble gratitude in order to set the records straight by answering any questions you have and finally, I would hope that you accept my donations from sales of my ASSsets products for as long as they're on the market as a

token of my sincerest apologies to you and the rest of the
Aderotimi Family of London England.

STOP THE PUMP

To all who've not been mentioned on the acknowledgements of this book who've thought they should have been but weren't. Thus, I Say, I have weathered through the greatest fall I would ever know in life, and I did it all without you! When I looked for you, you were not there. When I called out to you in need from my imprisonment, you ignore my pleas. The hard part is over now, for I have found my place where it is that I belong. And that is a place without you depleting my energy, my love, my spirit, and my resources. I am aware now of the falsehood of friendship and kinship I once was blinded into believing we had. For GOD has a great way of spring cleaning one's life up and I am grateful for my load is now lightened. I owe you nothing! Thus, please do not ask . . . Request . . . nor find me in my new life where only those who rode this storm out with me belong. I mean you know I have no ill will, I just don't have the time for you, just as you had no time for me when I needed you most. With the anticipated success that will surely come once I am home on my grind . . . doing all that it is I do as MADAM, please remember that it is not money or success that has changed me, it was the lack of your care, love, compassion, and humanity for me when I needed you most, that did it. I'm good now, and you better know it hunny! Have a great life! Cause I plan to. BLACK MADAM WORLD DOMINATION IS BACK!

Hear the music that inspired it all!
Song Titles

ROCK
INFAMOUS
VOODOO GIRL
HYPNOTIZE
LUCIFER'S RISING
REASONS
PHILLY ALL-STARS
RING THE ALARM
RUCKUS
BED OF ROSES
ABDUCTION

- **RIDE**
- **RODEO GIRL**
- **DAM MADAM**
- **THIS THING WE DO**
- **THE HEIST**
- **COME ON IN MY KITCHEN**
- **I AM**

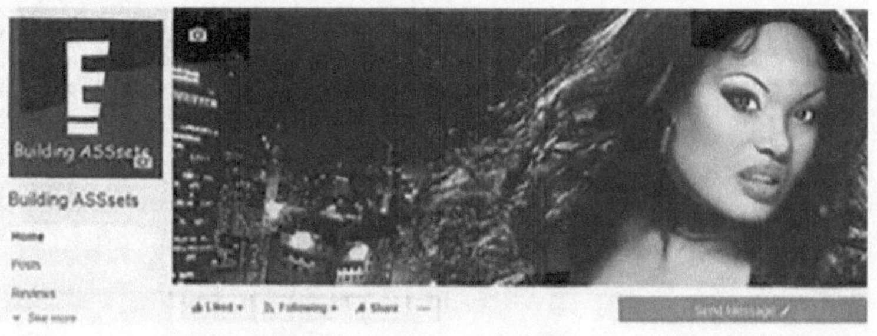

Building ASSsets

THE BLACK MADAM REALITY SHOW PITCH TO
    NETWORKS

"Building ASSsets" ... The BLACK MADAM Reality TV Show Pitch to E! NETWORKS is a documentary series based on the release of Notoriously, Infamous imprisioned Transgender Recording Artist... The BLACK MADAM, Who's serving jail time for the Internation Scandal of Black Market Silicone Buttock Injection Services to the Stars.

"Building ASSsets" Reality Show will display a woman who's bent on turning her bad & notoriously salacious situations around for the good, as she works against all odds to Brand the synonymy of her name forever being linked with Black Market Silicone Buttock Injections Gone wrong.

Watch on, as an intimate camera lens follows Madam's day to day life as she's released back into the free world to establish her Brand with the new invention of her product "ASSsets™" ...

{The safe non-surgical female butt enhancement undergarment}, in which she plans to taketo market in order to give women options.

Thus, With a new book on the market entitled INFAMOUS; her product line "ASSsets"; along with her STP (Stop The Pump) awareness Campaign, {a platform she intends to use as a vehicle to save lives by spreading the word of the deadly danger of Silicone butt injections}, a Madam's work is never done! Climb aboard the ride of a lifetime, as Madam invites you the viewer into her TRANSWORLD EXPRESS.

TO SEE FULL PITCH BOOK GO TO...
www.BuildingASSsets.com

JOIN THE MOVEMENT!

Help make The MADAM's vision of her new Reality Show "Building ASSsets" a reality by joinging her team.

Get in on the Ground Floor of this exciting venture by your contribution to help finance this project when you visit The Black Madam Project with the GoFundMe link at www.madamnation.com

Discussion and book group questions on reading -INFAMOUS .

Enjoy the 200 questions that the author poses to the reader and what it is that you the reader took from the book.

For an in depth one on one communication with the author on these questions posed, Feel free to answer the questions that you feel most in common with, and send your response to the author for a possible answer back to you.

Feel free to communicate these questions on line with your friend...

Thank you for your reading the Reality Reading Series Memoir- INFAMOUS by BLACK MADAM. To join further discus ions of the reading of INFAMOUS please join one of the blogs or forums that discuss her readings. If you can not find just the right fit for you on an already established BLACK MADAM BLDG OR FORUM, please feel more than free to start your own? For more on The Black Madam go to www. madamnation.com or find her on Facebook.

Don't forget to follow Black Madam on Twitter @
FREEBLACKMADAM

INFAMOUS READING GROUP GUIDE

Welcome to the Black Madam' s INFAMOUS reading group guide to many questions that could and should be brought up in your reading group in the discussion of her first installment of the BLACK MADAM Trilogy.

1. What were your thoughts on the open letter to The Madam's Old lover, The Dr. John Mancuso?

2. Did you feel that.it was reckless that she expose him in the way that she did in the letter although they once shared a deep feelings for each other?

3. Do you feel that The Madam should have included the family of the doctor in her open letter to him for all the world to read?

4. Can you the reader relate to the pain The Madam must had felt to have the doctor turn State's Evidence on her to save is self and reputation?

5. Do you think that The Madam and the doctor will ever make up in the future once this scandal is a far memory in the past?

6. Do you think that the doctor really did supply The Madam with her tools and knowledge of the trade of Silicone Injections?

7.   Did anyone notice the clever way that The Madam put the doctor's miss deeds out to air, although she was claiming to keep all of his secrets?

8.   Do you believe that the doctor should pay the price of all his legal, professional and personal misdeeds in the end?

9.   Do you believe in the super natural?

10.   Can you relate with The Madam when she correlate the movie DEVIL to her evil plot to blackmail the doctor?

11.   Do you really think that the Devil used this movie night date with The Madam and her boyfriend Nikolaus, in order to send Madam a message?

12.   Have any one in this group viewed the Black Madam Music Video Phenomena, in which she was filming during the time frame of the happenings in this book?

13.   If not, search Black Madam music video PHENOMENA on the web...ie... www. youtube.com

14.   Do you agree with Madam in the strategic manner in which she repaid -the executive cif the sound st.age for trying to go back on his word, and cheat her by adding extra fees- to what she already paid for during the Production of PHENOMENA?

15.   Do you believe that some one could actually cast a spell or place a hex on some one?

16. Do you understand the concept of Life Imitating Art and how Madam refers to it in chapter one?

17. During your reading of the first chapter, did you notice the significance between the scene in the elevator of the movie Devil, and how it correlated to real life actuality of Madam and the doctor?

18. Did you think it was a sign to The Madam, how the director Shyamalan's name and work kept showing up in Madam's first chapter unintentionally?

19. Do you believe that the Illuminati rules the music industry?

20. Have you listened to the BLACK MADAM's controversial recording ROCK? If not search the web for it on www.youtube.com or www. soundlcoud.com under Black Madam.

21. Do you believe that some dark spirit actually gave the name Black Madam to her during her residence at 666 Panama Street in Society Hill Philadelphia back in. 1995?

22. Do you believe that the Ouija board is a real tool used to connect to other worlds and spiritual realms beyond our own?

23. Have you ever used the Ouija board? and if so, what happened?

24. Have you ever heard the rumors of Rapper Ms. Wonderful having Black Market Buttock injections?

25. Do you think that Madam should have joined forces with Scheffee in order to see Scheffee's family for buttock enhancing?

26. What do you believe Mad am was trying to tell the reader in her brief but powerful signification of what Boss Money could be doing behind Beyonce's back with his personal assistant from Deff Jam Records?

27. What do you think Jim Jones' woman will think, after reading that Scheefee was having an affair with her man behind the scenes?

28. Do you know the West Indies terminology for VooDoo?

29. Do you the reader believe there were any ill workings for The Madam to use her street name Lillian for her street dealings?

30. Do you think that The Madam should have given Carmon- London the extra session her first time she came to America, but was disappointed at her first results of her buttock injections?

31. Do you think Carmon London's desperation to seek out a bigger butt is a reflection of society's pressure to look perfect?

32. Do you think that society in general places too high a standard on women to fit the stereo typical profile of what it is to be beautiful?

33. Why do you the reader think it is, that Madam could not get Carmon London off of her mind during the overnight shoot of the PHENOMENA music video?

34. Do you think that deep down inside, it could have possibly been a spiritual connection that Madam felt, which was a predestined bond that Carmon London and Black Madam would later have as Victim and Murderess?

35. What do you think of the conversation that Madam first had with her mother about getting a sex change for her 21st birthday?

36. What did you think of Madam's Mother, after she announced her desires to become a woman? Was it just nerves, or do you truly feel that Madam's mother was indifferent to her child sharing what she felt was great news to her mother?

37. Did you the reader feel for Madam as she tried to explain her plight to her father up in her parent's bed room on the announcement of her wanting to get a sex change?

38. Who can understand the father's disappointment in hearing that his only son wanted to get a sex change and become a woman?

39. Do you know of any one in your family or circle of friends that might be hiding their true identity as a transgender female or male?

40. Do you the reader feel that it was courageous for Madam to stand her ground. with her father and declare, come what may, that she would become a woman?

41. Do you think it was a contradiction of Madam's father whith bringing his children up to stand for what they believe in, but once Madam did, he condemned her and disowned her?

42. Do you think it was Madam father's fear of the stereo typical Drag Queen ideal that was the cause of his not accepting her as his daughter?

43. Do you understand the difference in the titles of Transgender and Transvestite vs. Dragqueen and Transsexual?

44. Do you understand the difference from a Transgender and a Homosexual?

45. Do you believe that it is nature that determines who will become transgender, or do you believe it is a choice?

46. What do you think of the fact that Madam's father was willing to accept her as a Homosexual man, but not a Transgender daughter? Can you relate to that decision of her father?

47. Did you think it was Noble or Foolish of Madam deciding not to take a welfare hand out while she was struggling to make it out there on her own?

48. What do you think of Madam's cleverness to start a racket in fake prescriptions for selling female hormones in order to make ends meet?

49. What do you think about the fact that Madam didn't want to be close to her Homosexual cousin Milton on her mother's side of the family before her announcing her getting a sex change to the world, thinking that others would know her "T" before she was ready to tell it?

50. What are your thoughts of Lionell's down low behavior behind his girlfriend Angel's back?

51. Do you think by Madam using her penis to penetrate Lionell was a sign that her father was right about her being a Homosexual man like her cousin Milton from her mother's side of the family, by her masculine action of sodomizing Lionell?

52. Have any of you ever suspected a male companion of yours to possibly be on the "DL"? If so please share.

53. Was any one surprised to read how easy it was for Lionell to flip back into a Thug the next morning after he was so Dick hungry just hours before?

54. Who saw the connection between the title of this chapter "Hot Cakes And Sausage"...with what transpired between Madam and Lionell? Explain ...

55. Do you understand why going out with Eve the next night for a girls night out was so important to Madam, after all the shenanigans of Lionell wanting her to be his "TOP MODEL" the night before?

56. Who immediately caught on to what Eve w s insinuating of Madam being Lionell's "TOP MODEL?"

57. Who caught on to the connection between Eve's Friend Angelique, Lionell's girlfriend from the and suburbs name Angel?

58. Like Angel, have any of you ever had or knew a friend who had a boyfriend who was bisexual, but they were to in denial to accept it?

59. What do you the reader take from the statement that Madam gave Angel about taking Lionell home to examine the merchandise to see it was true that she had been there?

60. Do you think it was a normal assumption of the nosy Ms. Catherine to assume that Banngy Boy Music Productions, was really Banging boy productions, as sex for sale provided by the Madam in her early years?

61.	What are your thoughts of the budding friendship between Madam and her new friend Nikki James?

62.	What do you think of the land lord Mr. Katz calling Madam to accuse her of illicit behavior in his tenement?

63.	Did you feel it was a normal assumption of Mr. Katz to believe Madam was running a whore house in his apartment building?

64.	Could anyone relate to the pressures that Madam was now feeling to find a new residence in order to get away from the threats of her current land lord?)

65.	What are your thoughts of the Madam's decision to actually partake in the illicit activities that she was so wrongly being accused of?

66.	Did you feel the pain that Madam must have felt in the betrayal of her cousin Milton in his scurrying her and Nikki James off with one piece of chicken wing each, as he cooked a beautiful dinner for his new piece of ass?

67.	Could you the reader empathize with Madam's feelings of despair in having to eat her pride and call home to her parent's for help?

68.	Were you cheering for Madam when you read the insert about the many phone messages left in Madam's telephone voice bank?

69. Did you immediately understand the gravity of just what- her many phone messages meant to the future of Madam and Nikki James?

70. What are your thoughts of Madam stepping up to the plate in order to turn a trick to save their independence in their new life as young Trans Women?

71. With all that you've read, what would you have done if you were in Madam's shoes?

72. What do you imagine the humiliation that Madam must have felt in her long walk to the Four Seasons Hotel in order to have sex for cash to preserve her new way of life? What feeling did you feel as you read those passages?

73. Were you happy for young Madam in the fact that ... she didn't have to really degrade herself with the Client Michael in their meet, due to the fact that he ejaculated prematurely?

74. Do you think that the hands of fate have been walking with Madam, thus it was already deemed that she wouldn't have to sell herself for a dollar from the start? Thus she just had to show the Universe that she was willing to go out on a limb in trusting for what she believed in?

75. How did you feel when Madam and Nikki James walked out of the Four Seasons Hotel with a bright new destiny ahead of them and they would not have to give up on their dreams to become women, thus getting their sex changes?

76. What did you the reader think of the desire Madam began to feel about her- illicit activity later on in life, and now wanting to exit out of the adult sex industry due to what happened between two of her sex workers and her advertiser Ms. Diana's husband?

77. Do you think it was Madam's conscience that convicted her of her illicit work with the escort business and her father's death that weighed heavy on her heart to want out?

78. Could you relate to Madam's need to want to protect the innocence of her beau Nikolaus in regards to her life as a madame?

79. Could you feel the frustrations of Madam as she and Nikolaus drove to his flower shop job that Saturday morning, with Madam not wanting to ruin such a beautiful moment with the call of a pervert wanting to suck a tranny's penis?

80. Do you think that it was G o d's divine hand involved, when "ANGEL" called Madam as she drove home from dropping Nikolaus off, with tears of frustration in her heart of wanting out of the "Family Business?"

81. Do you think it was a good idea for ANGEL to advise Madam to get -back into the Silicone Pumping Business in order to get out of the "Family Business?"

82. What are your thoughts of young Madam's and John's (Dr. Mancuso) first meet and Madam's ambitions from the start t make the doctor her husband?

83. Do you really ■ believe that John actually loved young Madam?

84. Do you really believe young Madam really loved John eventually, or was she just out to marry well?

85. Do you think that John should have told Madam that he was already a married man?

86. Do you think that young Madam should have been wise enough to realize that John was a trick, and not anyone to fall in love with?

87. What were your feelings for Madam's dreams of marriage to Dr. John Mancuso going up in smoke as a his revelation of being a married man ensued?

88. If you were Dr. John Mancuso's wife Pamela, what would you have done? Fight for him, or let the cheater go?

89. Could you the reader empathize with Madam's hurt and broken heart, of still wanting to fight for the doctor's affection?

90. Do you think Madam was being a true bitch with how she sabotaged the doctor and his wife's marriage, when she was fighting for his love?

91.   With a few years past after Madam had chosen to let the doctor go, do you think it was wise of. her to entertain his notions of rehatchment a few years later when she walked in on him in her Rittenhouse Square Escort business that morning with Alexas Ward?

92.   Do you think it was greedy of Madam to accept the doctor's gifts of expensive cars, property, trips and hundreds of thousands of dollars, in his attempts to win her heart over again?

93.   Do you the reader notice in the life of Madam, that every time she seems to be at the precipice of the end of her ropes, how God manage to give her a new life line?

94.   What are your views on Madam's expansion in her Black Market Beauty trade with her "Secrets of the Orient" tours to Asia, Her Biobeautylabs.com, and all the connections she was forging worldwide with the many physicians she was meeting?

95.   Do you believe that Madam really did embed Black Magic in her new home recording studio as she explain in Chapter 13?

96.   What are your views in the diagram that she laid out to the readers on the usage of the powerful sacred geometry?

97.   Did you understand the rationale of the Madam and her reasoning for studying the Occult during

those tail end days of her exit out of the "Family Business"?

98. Did you understand what Madam meant by the expression... a powder keg of black magic via sacred geometry in the end of chapter 13?

99. Has anyone in this reading group ever viewed Black Madam's Music Video "Come on in my kitchen" ... in which she has become a prisoner of the Devil's affection?

100. If not, search it on the web under. Black Madam Music Video, "Come on in my kitchen" on www.youtube.com or where ever else it's being shown.

101. Do any of you think Madam should have still reached out to rapper Ms. Wonderful despite her and Rosebud's quarrel?

102. What do you the reader think of Black Madam and Rosebud's strategy in regards to get Mr. Craze to sign Black Madam in giving Rosebud another means to hang on to her light in the Entertainment Business without having to be subjected to Mr. Craze's Diva antics?

103. How many of you saw the episode of "Keeping up with the Kardashians" with Mr. Craze and Ms. Dubai hanging out in New York City while he was still dating Rosebud and knew it was only a matter of time before Rosebud was out, and Ms. Dubai was in?

104. What do you think of Rosebud's comparison of sex with Mr. Craze and an ape? Or do you think she was just used to the delicate lovemaking of her lesbian sex she was used to sharing with her old boygirl flame back home in Philly?

105. Do you think it was a good look for Madam to advise Rosebud to leave Mr. Craze after his abuse at the airport?

106. During the Murder Trial of The Black Madam for the accidental death of Carmon London, The jury pool weighed their Guilty verdict heavy on the fact that Mad am used the expression of her being a "Practicing Physician's Assistant," in regards to her working for her doctor friend in Thailand with their "Secrets of the Orient" excursions. However, looking at the expression/title Physician's Assistant one could take the wording two ways. One with it being a title for a doctor's assistant in a medical procedure, and the second as a laymen person who worked for a- doctor as Madam did in Assisting him to get more patients. With these two definitions of Madam working as a practicing physician's assistant, which one do you think she meant, and do you think the jury got the verdict right?

107. Do you think that Madam called this fate of murder to herself with the recording of the song Ruckus that night in the recording studio with Nikki James?

108. Do you believe- that it is more than a coincident that Madam use the words "MURDER WAS THE CASE THAT THEY GAVE ME, NOW MADAM's HALF CRAZY ... THEIR COMING FOR THAT ASS INJECTION LADY?"... a day before she would meet Carmon London for services who the next day would die of complications, thus Madam's own words she spoke in her recording Ruckus came to fruition?

109. Caught up in a frenzy of emotions during the recording of Ruckus, do you believe that some other un-worldly being was guiding Madam to some destiny of art imitating life, or life imitating art?

110. As Eve came into the recording studio ranting and raging about Madam's toying with the Dark Arts, don't you think it wise that Madam should have taken heed?

111. Look up the phrase in the bible that speaks of the power of the tongue, Where as God tells that life and death lay in the power of the tongue... and Text this phrase to all that you know... God created the universe by the method you have just put into motion by the words of your mouth. Thus, Man is created in his image, Therefore man releases his faith in words. WORDS ARE THE MOST POWERFUL THINGS IN THE UNIVERSE

112. With Madam awaking on February 7th, just hours after recording -the tune Ruckus, She felt tired and

had to convince herself to keep her commitment with her clients flying in from the UK, Do you think she should have postponed her fateful meeting with Carmon London and friend, or do you think that their destiny was set and there was nothing- either Madam or Carmon London could do to avoid the events that were soon to ensue?

113. Do you think that it was fate that was warning Madam with her now getting over her Black Market illicit Silicone Injection Business that danger was on its way?

114. What do you the reader suspect that Nikki James is trying to run from in her habitual drinking habits?

115. As you read about the confrontation between Carmon London and the US Customs agent, and he giving her the choice to get back on the next flight to LONDON due to her sassy attitude, Do you see the divine hand of God in the mist ... giving Carmon a second chance at life?

116. Do you think Carmon London should have took Madam's advice on taking it slow with the building of her new buttocks?

117. Do you empathize with the overwhelming emotions Madam was feeling in wanting to help Carmon London reach her goals?

118. What do you think the number one driving factor was that allowed Madam to do a second session free of charge for Carmon London?

119. Do you think once Carmon London finally got the buttocks she so desperately desired, she was truly happy?

120. After reading the entries of the BANNED alcoholic/caffeinated beverage FOUR LOKO, do you think Carmon London's consumption of it just hours before her injections played a part in her death?

121. Why do you believe that Carmon London didn't want to go to the hospital in order to get her buttock drained when Madam had advised her to do so?

122. Do you feel that Madam was showing genuine care and concern for Carmon London by trying to convince her to call an ambulance?

123. Would you the reader say it was negligence on Madam's part by leaving the hotel, since Carmon London continued to deny her request to seek medical help or call emergency 911?

124. Do you think the middle man Scheffee played just as much a part in Carmon London's Death, thus she should have been persecuted too?

125. Do you the reader feel as though Madam did a good job in her description of just what it was that she was feeling upon learning of Carmon London's death via Schffee? explain ...

126. With the nonchalant attitude that Scheffee showed towards the sudden death of Carmon London, do you think they were really cousins as Scheffee led Madam to believe in the beginning?

127. Do you think Madam should have gone with the lie Scheffee wanted to tell the authorities of Carmon London and her friend wondering off to get buttock injections at a model's run?

128. After rea ding the chapters on Scheefee , an d the knowledge of knowing that Madam advised Scheffee of only wanting to service Scheefee's family and friends, do you think Scheefee might had been dishonest by going against Madams wishes and better judgement, and despite Madam's advising her the contrary, Scheffee still went online to recruit strangers that were willing to pay her for their connection to The Madam under the guise of Family and friends?

129. Do you think that Madam did the right thing by getting rid of two and a half million dollars in her Biobeautylabs.com products in order to curtail any other charges that might stem from Madam's Black Market Beauty Import exports business?

130. Please explain your thoughts as Madam ran through her home in order to clear out any evidence it held.

131. Do you think Mrs. Wong noticed anything odd about Madam's behavior as she greeted Madam while Madam packed her car with all the evidence?

132. Do you think the Ardomre Township police patrol man was suspicious of Madam, or do you think Madam was just being paranoid?

133. What are your thoughts of Madam dumping all the evidence in the dumpster, but still thinking of her beau Nikolaus who needed to be picked up from work? Do you think she was delusional to the fact that she still wanted to play the perfect Suzy Home Maker Wifey?

134. As you the reader read the transaction between- Madam and her beau Nikolaus, explain your perception of the relationship they shared? Explain the gravity of it?

135. Do you think Nikolaus meant it when he said he would stand by Madam?

136. Do you think- that their relationship will weather the storm of what is all headed at Madam by way of legali ties?

137. With Eve now in the know of Carmon London's death, do you think she's thinking "I told you so" in regards to two night's before with the sadistic recording session that took place between Madam and Nikki James recording RUCKUS?

138. Do you think it was wise for Madam to drive through the streets of the hood of Philadelphia with over 10 Million dollars cash in her car, in which she planned to take to her parents' home for safe keeping?

139. What did you the reader feel between the intimate conversation that Madam had with her Mother and Step Father of the looming possibilities of being a murderer?

140. What do you think went through Madam's mind when her dad told her about the news broadcast of the girl out by the airport dying of silicone injections?

141. Do you think Madam was right in not wanting Nikki James to come out to her house, in fear that Nikki James would get into trouble as a coconspirator, since she witnessed the events that led to Carmon London's death?

142. Do you think that Nikki James showed that she was indeed a true friend when she told Madam that- she was coming any way?

143. Did you get the connection Madam was making between the Nina Simone Song "I love you Porgy" and that of what her and Nikolaus were feeling at that moment?

144. Did you think it was a good idea that Nikki James advised Madam and the household to leave the house to find neutral ground in which to think of a master plan?

145. Express your feelings of what could have possibly have been going through Madam's head as- she stood and watched her home on the News serving as the backdrop of the ongoing investigation of The Philadelphia Infamous Buttock Silicone Injection Killer?

146. Could you the reader relate to the fear that Madam must have felt in knowing that Nikolaus was now in custody down at the police district at 57th and Pine street for the mess she created?

147. Do you think that Madam was robbing the cradle when she gave into Nikolaus' advances when they first met at the ACME -supermarket back in 2004?

148. Do you the reader think Nikolaus was a little too overzealous of his feeling for the Madam upon their first encounter?

149. Do you think that Nikolaus' expression that "He knew exactly what he was doing"... was his way of letting Madam know that he was aware that she was Transgender when they first met in the ACME Supermarket?

150. Could you empathize with Madam not wanting to hurt Nikolaus' feeling in the parking lot of the ACME Super market where she intended to let him down easy?

151. Express the emotion that you felt when the two sisters... Madam and Sherry talked through out the night of the death of Carmon London, and explain your feelings of their sisterly bond, as Sherry opened up her home to welcome in Madam and those of her household?

152. Explain what the message is when one uses the expression ... "Am I My Sister's Keeper?"

153. Elaborate on Madam's words when she says that Sherrie was indeed the good sister?

154. Do you think it was ■ courageous of Madam's Sister Sherrie to harbor her in her home in Delaware as the police sought out Madam?

155. If you were in Sherry's place, what would you have done?

156. Do you think it's a thing of the past, the idea th at Madam didn't want to ask her parents if Nikolaus could stay with her at their home, or do you think it was the respectful thing to do, by honoring her parents Christian values?

157. What are your feelings on Madam's sister Nicole's reasoning for not standing by Madam during this dark storm of Madam's life, regardless of the fact that Madam had always been there for her and her children?

158. Did you find the awkward dark humor Madam tried to convey over to you the reader with the

episode in chapter 21, where she and Nikolaus lost a dollar in their haste to get out the door to work after waking up late, thus, having to get turned away at the toll bridge crossing because they were one dollar short?

159. Explain some of the visuals that were painted in your mind of Madam's struggles from High Society living to now having to decorate their living quarters on a dime at the Dollar Store General? Did it paint pictures of the old TV show with Zsa Zsa Gabor in GREEN ACRES of a High Society Rich Woman moving off to the country for love?

160. Did the relationship between Madam and Nikki James put you in the mindset of Patsy and Adeana, characters of the British TV Comedy Absolutely Fabulous?

161. What did you think of Madam's comparing her bewitched studio isolation chamber to that of the movie Jumanji, where Robin Williams got lost in a game of misfortune of unbelievable consequences, and had to complete the game before bringing life back to the norm?

162. Do you think Madam recording the song RUCKUS with a more positive lyric before dissembling the ISO both in order to leave her prior home in Ardmore helped in her keeping the Philadelphia District Attorney's Office off of her tail for the murder of Carmon London?

163. Do you believe in the possibilities of other realms and dimensions of reality, like a parallel universe that perhaps Madam unknowingly tapped into in order to alter her own living reality to that of the words she recited the night before which brought death to her door step?

164. Do you think Madam was right to go with the advice of her legal team and not surrender in until an arrest warrant was served?

165. Do you think such Illuminate groups truly exist like that of which Madam talks about in chapter 22, The Ordo Templi Orientis, The OTO?

166. What are your feelings about all that she described in chapter 22 of the meeting with the Illuminati's OTO sect?

167. Do you think it was foolish of Madam to venture out alone to a meeting of such?

168. Do you understand Madam's motive for wanting to find out just what it was that she did that could have possibly killed Carmon London with words?

169. Do you blame Madam's niece Jessie for not wanting to accompany Madam to her secret meet with th e Illuminati's OTO?

170. What are your thoughts on the secret code that Madam mentions in the chapter for entry into the Illuminati's meeting? 93... which when turned upside down is 36... thus the Satanic number of 666

171. What do you think of Madam partaking in the drinking of the red headed woman's menstrual blood funneled into-the golden chalice?

172. What would you have done in that situation, knowing that there was no way out once in?

173. What do you think of the Minister of Music who orchestrated this meet to meet up with the Black Madam?

174. Do you think Madam's Occult laced music videos really attracted the powerful eyes of the Illuminati?

175. Why do you think that this coordinator of this meet knew so much about the intimate knowings of some of the world's greatest recording acts like JAY Z, COLDPLAY, all the classical works, and even the music of an indie Artist from the underground like BLACK MADAM?

176. Why do you think this Coordinator was attracted to Black Madam's music in the first place?

177. Why is it that you think he loved her song Lucifer's Rising?

178. If any of you have never listened to the BLACK MADAM recording of Lucifer's Rising, search it on the web on youtube.com or soundcloud. com and explain what your sentiments of it?

179. What are your thoughts on the knowledge Madam gave the reader on the true reasoning that most high-rise office buildings don't have a 13th floor?

180. Do you believe that these secretive groups could be hiding some secreted knowledge of power from mankind, only using it to harness power for themselves?

181. What is it that you the reader thinks took place in the Black Mass once Madam and the other initiates fell unconscious?

182. What are your theories on the being that seemed to manifest out of the clear blue, as Madam and the others were in disbelief that he actually walked from nowhere through the free suspended door into the room?

183. What do you think the childlike beings that Madam spoke of really were?

184. Have you ever heard of Carl Gustoph Jung? Do you believe in his theories of synchronicity, and there being no coincidence in life?

185. What do you think the card that the coordinator at the meet gave to Madam symbolized . . with the Snake, the Stars, a Lion and the Sun? do you believe it was some sort of payment for what ever happened when Madam and the others feel unconscious and naked?

186. What do- you think Madam means when she says that "Her mind betrays her"?

187. Do you think it a coincident still that there was no more pursuit of the Black Madam for Murder after Madam took these superstitious actions as most would call them?

188. What is your feeling on SUPERSTITIONS?

189. During the end of the reading, were you happy to hear that Madam, Nikolaus and Eve were able to relocate and reestablish roots after such a world wind of darkness?

190. Besides Madam, who was your favorite supporting character in the reading of INFAMOUS?

191. Are you anxious for the next instalment of the trilogy franchise of the Black Madam Brand?

192. For the Next 24 hours, Tweet #BALCKMADAMNOTORIOUS in order to connect with others sharing your interest in the BLACK MADAM

193. What do you think the expression #CHICKENWING means? ANSWER: A cheap ass person

194. What do you think the expression- #HOT CAKES &

195. SAUSAGES means? ANSWER: a term for a guy on the DL

196. What do you think the expression #BUTCH QUEEN means? ANSWER? a Homosexual that to the naked eye seems to be straight.

197. What do you think the expression #CUNT TUNA means? ANSWER? the epitome of looking feminine.

198. What do the expression #TOP MODEL means? ANSWER: a pre-op transsexual woman that has no problem penetrating a man.

199. What do you think the expression #FREAK BULL means? ANSWER: a straight guy that will have sex with anything as long as it's got a warm spot.

200. What do you think the expression # GREEK means? ANSWER: having anal sex.

201. What does Madam mean when she refers to the dreadful "FAMILY BUSINESS"? ANSWER: Her Escort Service.

202. Did you truly enjoy the reading of INFAMOUS?

RESOURCES

SureShot Books Publishing LLC, Books, Magazines & Newspapers to ALL Correctional Institutions.

RO. Box 924 Nyack, New York 10960 www. sureshotbooks.com 888 608-0868

The Black Madam TIP Project (Transgenders In Prison) Building Equality & Better Living Conditions For America's Transgender Incarcerated Community. Write to SureShot Books Publishing LLC to Join. RO. Box 924, Nyack, New York 10960 Attn: T.I.C.

BLACK & PINK NATIONAL OFFICE: A Trans Community Advocacy, News Letter for incarcerated Transgenders. Pen Pal service, 614 Columbia Road, Dorchester, MA. 02125 www.blackandpink.org

Queer Detainee Empowerment Project (QDEP) Hotline: 347-645-9339, Mailing: Java Street, #237 Brooklyn, New York, 11222 info@qdep.org. An alternative to detention program (ATD), that works with Trans genders detainees and their families currently in detention centers and those that are recently released from immigrant detention centers, seeking status in the United States.

T.I.P. JOURNAL-gender Identity Center of Colorado Inc. 1151 S. Huron St. Denver, CO 8022Newsletter for Transgender prisoners. Write for details.

TRANSMISSION PRISON BOOKS, P.O.BOX 1874, Asheville, NC. 28802, Offers free books and resources to Transgenders in prison.

LGBT Books to Prisoners, C/O Rainbow Bookstore, 426 W. Film an Street, Madison, WI 53703, Sends free books to Trans genders in prison.

Association for research & Enlightenment, C/O Prison Outreach, 215 67th St. Virginia Beach, VA 23451. Meditation & Reincarnation. Visit: LGBTinprisons.com

Prison Legal News/ Human Rights Defense Center, P.O. Box 1151, Lake Worth, FL 33460

Trans living International Magazine. P.O. Box 3, Basildon, Essex, SS13 3WA United Kingdom

Prison Watch Project, American Friends Service, 1501 Cherry Street, Philadelphia, Pennsylvania 19102

Prison Activist Resource Center, P.O. Box 70447, Oakland CA. 94612.

Inmate Services, Photo Processing, P.O. Box 500127 Atlanta Georgia 31150 phone: 470-375-5872

Prisons Foundation. P.O. Box 58043 Washington DC 20037 www.prisonfoundation.org.

TIP/Trans health Information Project, Philadelphia, Naiymah Sanchez, 267-457-391-2149 W Susquehanna Avenue, Philadelphia, Pennsylvania 19122

Pennsylvania Prison Society, Emily Cashell: 245 north Broad Street, Suite # 300, Philadelphia, Pennsylvania 19107-1518 Phone: 215-564-6005

HFO, INMATE SOCIAL MEDIA & REAL LIFE/ WORLD MANAGEMENT, Help from Outside, Julie Capel 206-486-6042, 2620 Bellevue Way, NE #200 Bellevue, WA 98004

RR Branam Company/ Inmate services: 1515 W. Wisconsin Ave., Suite 1, Appleton, Wisconsin 54914

Prison Activist Resource Center, P.O. Box 70447, Oakland, CA 94612

DCS Prison Calls, 1969 S. Alafaya Trail #405, Orlando, FL. 32828. Pay less for collect calls

Critical Resistance, 1904 Franklin Street, Suite 504, Oakland, CA. 94612 International Movement to end prison industry.

Voice Freedom Calls, Eric Juvet, 2620 Bellevue Way NE Bellevue, WA 98004 VoiceFreedomCalls.com Access Your Own Voice Mail in Jail!

Dennis Solbin's SafeStreetArts.org / Poetry & Arts of Prisoners

PRISON PEN PAL RESOURCES:

Inmate Mingle: P.O. Box 23207 Columbia SC 29224
Info@inmatemingle.com

FEMALE PEN PAL ADS: P.O. Box 319, Rehoboth, MA 02769

INMATE SCRIBES & Personal Assistants Service: P.O.BOX 818 Appleton, WI, 54912

Elite Paralegal Services: PO. Box 1717, Appleton, WI. 54912

TRANSGENDER CHILDREN SUPPORT, All my

Trans children of the World, It's a new age for you all! BLOSSOM BABY! Contact TRANSNATION

SOCIETY EMBASSY FOR SUPPORT for Parents of trans children Coming Soon. Subscribe to TRANSLIVING INTERNATIONAL MAGAZINE for all updates.

To the American Humanist Association, A Very Special Thank You to My HUMANIST Family & Legal Team . . . David Niose, Monica Miller and Charles Pierson of the Appignani Humanist Legal Center for their Help and Protection of MY FRfeE THINKING Right's while incarcerated, along with their help against the much Trans Hate that thrives in our American Correctional Facilities. #FR6E YOUR MINDS

American Humanist Association Pen Pal Program, 1821 Jefferson Pl., NW, Washington DC. 20036 Contact: Sincere Kirabo or current Social Justice Coordinator.

NOTE FROM MADAM! If you are in prison, or have family and friends who are serving time, please utilize this personal resource list of mine, in which I utilized during my incarceration for networking and making moves even from within jail. Sometimes our family and friends can get very busy in doing life. Use this list to make power moves and do for yourself, while showing the world how long your arms still are, even in a prison cell.